LILY

PREQUEL TO THE REGULATORS

Carolina Mac

To: My daughter, JL Madore, who encouraged me to write my first book.

CHAPTER ONE

Will today be the day Matthew kills me?

MY hand trembled as I fumbled in my purse for the key to the side door, my bags of groceries resting on the doorstep. A speck of dirt caught my eye as I bent to retrieve the bags and I made a mental note to remove it before Matthew arrived home from work. How much time did I have—I checked my watch—three forty-five.

While unloading the bags on the kitchen counter, I inhaled and tried to concentrate on dinner. My thoughts kept coming back to Matthew. The past few weeks, everything seemed to set him off. At least everything *I* did. Marriage had not turned out the way I had pictured it, all hearts and flowers and happily ever after. More and more I wondered if this was as good as it was going to get.

The vacuum hose was neatly coiled and hung in its' place, my cleaning caddy tucked out of sight. Spotless. Just the way Matthew demanded it. This morning I even went the extra mile and cleaned up all of his expensive toys in the garage. The windows shone bright, Matthew's tools hung on the racks in order of size and color. The floor was swept and hosed down. Scanning the main floor, I inhaled deep. The air smelled fresh with a faint hint of pine.

I double checked everything one more time—no chance he could find fault with anything.

Each and every day began the same way. I turned off the alarm at six a.m., took a quick shower, dressed and went downstairs to the kitchen. Once the coffee maker was started, I set the table for breakfast, brought in the morning paper from the front step, placed it on the right hand side of Matthew's placemat, and waited for my husband to make his appearance.

Matthew was a creature of habit. Monday through Friday he came down dressed for the office in one of his custom made suits, sat down at the end of the table and drank his coffee while he checked his emails on his phone. While he sipped his juice and immersed himself in the financial section of the Globe and Mail, I served his scrambled eggs, toast and sausage.

Last week, I thought I would break the monotony and make him French toast. Big mistake. Matthew rewarded me with a backhand to my right eye. Thank God for quality foundation and concealer. Safer to stick to the routine.

My husband rarely glanced at me in the morning and he seldom spoke. I knew better than to strike up a conversation while he was engrossed in the news of the day. I busied myself with kitchen chores until he was done eating and sent him off. Eating breakfast alone after he was gone was a gift. I read the paper and drank my coffee without the worry of offending Matthew with my ineptitudes.

After cleaning up my dishes, I ran a critical finger

over the top edge of the only picture I had been allowed to add to the family portraits on the mantel. Three years ago, today. I realized now that I was more in love with the idea of being married and having a home, than I was enamored with the man himself. Passing a cloth over all the smiling faces of Mathew's life my chest ached.

On my birth registration, my mother was listed as Grace Brownell, a seventeen year old, unwed mother, and my father was listed as 'unknown'. I'd thought of delving into my past to get a sense of who I was, but Matthew vetoed the idea saying I might not like what I found out. He insisted I drop it, but the curiosity still nagged at me. I might not like the truth, but it was human nature to want to know the details.

Mathew's father was a respected banker and his mother never worked outside the home, devoting herself to spoiling her only child. He wanted me to be just like her. I never met the woman. She passed away the year before we started dating and he inherited the family home - a quaint Victorian on Hawthorne Lane with lots of charm, bursting at the seams with antiques. When Matthew first suggested we make our home in the old place, I couldn't wait to see what I could do with it. A lot of my redecorating ideas were vetoed, but I was allowed to choose paint colors and freshen up some of the rooms.

It amazed me how deceptive photos could be. The Mathew I saw captured in moments with his parents was not the man I met at the door each night. He was handsome, sophisticated and fifteen years my senior. During our brief courtship he was loving and attentive, showing no outward signs of the person he would become. Had I been a fool to rush into marriage with a person I barely knew, or had I been too young at twenty-two to make a sensible decision? The real question was . . . *How am I going to get out of this mess?*

Grabbing the five pound bag of seed from the pantry, I headed out to the backyard to refill the feeders. The yard was cloistered by a high board and batten fence dripping with wisteria. Mature maples provided shade and seclusion. Gardening had been my mother-in-law's passion, and the perennial beds she established were crowded with Hosta, primrose, ferns and bleeding hearts.

Almost hidden in the back corner sat a dilapidated wooden bench where I loved to read in my spare time. The flower bed behind the bench was overgrown with lily of the valley and the delicate fragrance floating from that spot was my aroma therapy. Now that spring had announced her arrival, the garden was my sanctuary.

I checked my watch again—plenty of time. Matthew left work in the city center at five p.m. sharp. He stopped on his way home at 'Chuck's Place', his favorite bar, for two or three vodkas with his co-workers. He used to stop for only one drink, but this past year his drinking had increased markedly. I dared to mention once that drinking and driving was dangerous. Matthew countered with 'not minding your own business could be dangerous, as well.'

His philosophy was 'drink as much as you want, drive slow and you won't have an accident'. I doubted the wisdom in that but learned the hard way not to argue. He habitually arrived on our doorstep precisely at six-forty-five expecting his dinner to be ready the moment he entered the house, and I did my level best to comply.

THE hum of the Mercedes' diesel engine filtered into the kitchen just as the oven timer beeped for the crème Brule. The side door slammed, and Matthew blazed in, color rising in his face.

"What the hell were you thinking, *you idiot*? You left the garage door open."

I inhaled sharply. My hands trembled as I raced through my memory of the day. How could I have forgotten?

"Anybody could have taken my golf clubs, or my tools. I told you never to leave it open. Why can't you do what I tell you? Are you stupid, bitch?"

"I'm sorry, Matthew. I must have forgotten. I was carrying in bags of groceries. It won't happen again."

"You're damn right it won't." Matthew's briefcase swung at my head. I reeled backwards, screaming, as white pain exploded behind my eyes. Warm blood gushed into my eye and ran down my cheek. Tears mixed with the blood as I clasped my face and stumbled to the powder room.

With the door locked behind me, I sat down on the toilet lid with a guest towel pressed against my bleeding temple. I hung my head between my knees waiting for the dizziness and nausea to pass.

What now? Please, God. Lay a plan on me.

Bang! Bang!

Mathew's fist pounded the solid wood door. I jumped and felt a shockwave race from my neck to my waist.

"Come out of there, you good for nothing slut. You'll

be sorry if I have to break this door down. I'll give you three seconds to get out here."

"I'm not coming out, Matthew. Not until you promise you won't hurt me," I sobbed, my head throbbing.

When his footsteps faded, I took a deep breath but remained wary. It must have been over an hour before my trembling stopped and I inched towards the door. I listened and heard nothing but the television. Silently I turned the lock, opened the door a crack and peeked out.

Matthew was sprawled on the Queen Anne sofa in the living room, one leg dangling onto the hardwood floor. He was breathing heavily through his mouth, an empty glass tipped on the carpet. The hockey game was blaring on the flat screen.

Please let him be passed out.

I crept into the hallway and tip-toed up the stairs to the bedroom. Locking the door of the ensuite I drew a hot bath. While the water was running, I rummaged under the vanity for the first aid kit. After sponging the encrusted blood off my face, I taped a bandage over the gash above my right eye. The wound was deep and stinging, and probably needing stitches, but I made do— avoiding yet another trip to the Emergency room.

I sucked in my breath when I looked in the mirror. My long dark hair had been cut short at Matthew's insistence and without a trace of makeup, I looked haggard and Goth.

Where were the bright colors I used to love? Matthew thought I looked more attractive in darker clothes, but I silently disagreed. The woman looking back at me wasn't beautiful. She was thin and pale and could easily be ten years older.

I'm not even a person anymore. I'm just Matthew's wife.

I faulted myself in part for this. For the last few months, Matthew had been drinking more and his temper had been flaring. He phoned me three and four times a day from work to make sure I was at home. Several times he mentioned selling my Jeep when he was in one of his rages—to keep me at home where I belonged. Hoping he was just going through a bad time, I waited for things to calm down. Matthew was always extra nice after he'd been cross with me. Usually he bought me a gift or the odd time, took me out for dinner. That was just the way it was, and I'd grown afraid to criticize him in case it set him off again.

After a long bath, I crawled gratefully into bed and fell into a restless sleep. Matthew came upstairs and slipped into bed beside me just before midnight. Holding my breath, I lay perfectly still and pretended to be asleep until the breathy chuff of his snoring began.

Happy   *Anniversary.*

CHAPTER TWO

STICKING to the normal routine, I made Matthew's breakfast as if nothing had happened. No words were exchanged, and no mention was made of the violence from the previous evening. He just ate and went off to work. The least I had expected was an apology or the hint of one, but nothing—not a word. Laundry and cleaning filled my day.

When I heard the car pull into the garage at six forty-five, a shiver ran up the back of my neck. My hands shook and silverware hit the kitchen tile with a clatter. As I bent to retrieve the cutlery a weight pressed in on my chest like a tightening vice. My breath came in short gasps.

What's the matter with me?

I cringed when Matthew breezed into the kitchen and gave me a quick peck on the cheek. I couldn't believe the change in his mood.

"Get ready, honey. We're going out."

"I made dinner, Matthew. It's all ready."

"Come on, Portia. You'll have fun. This is my boss's retirement party. Everyone from work is going. And it's an open bar." He grinned at me.

That should make for a night of fun and frolic.

A couple of tears slid down my cheeks as I put the food into containers and stowed them in the refrigerator. "Can you give me a few minutes to change my clothes?'

"Sure. I'll have a drink while I'm waiting for you.

You should have one too, honey, it will put you in a party mood."

From halfway up the stairs, I called down, "I'll have one when I get to the party."

I had just slipped off my blue jeans and I was rifling through the closet without much enthusiasm, when Matthew barged into the bedroom and pushed me towards the bed.

"I think we have time for a quickie before we go."

"I thought you wanted me to hurry up and get ready."

"This won't take long."

I'm sure it won't.

Matthew took off his suit pants and jacket and yanked off my underwear. He pushed me backwards with force onto the bed and shoved his hand between my thighs. The booze on his breath repelled me as he leaned down and stuck his tongue in my mouth.

"You're being rough, Matthew. You're hurting me." I turned my head away, my cheek still hurting from last night.

"Then lay still and stop annoying me."

I tried to wriggle out from under him. When his hand rose above my head, I closed my eyes. *"Ow! Don't!"* Blood trickled slowly down my temple, the gash over my eye opened up.

He laughed. *"Don't?* You're bought and paid for, bitch. You'd do well to remember that."

"Let me up," I yelled. "I don't want to have sex with you like this. Get off me." I shoved him hard, and his body didn't budge and inch. He outweighed me by seventy-five pounds.

Matthew laughed and pinned my arms down on the bed over my head. I squirmed and struggled but I couldn't make him let go. My wrists were burning from the twisting. He thrust his erection inside of me and grinned. Hate surged through my body filling me with a fire I'd never known. He would pay for this.

When he was finished with me he stumbled into the bathroom.

I lay on the bed with my eyes closed, shutting out the last twenty minutes. Tears flowed as I pulled the duvet over my head. Hurt and revulsion mingled in equal parts. I wanted to vomit.

Please, God, let me die.

Matthew blasted out of the bathroom and noticed I hadn't moved off the bed. "Why aren't you getting ready?"

"I'm not going."

"Oh, yes you are." He grabbed my arm above the elbow, dragged me off the bed and bounced me onto the floor like a rag doll. "Get dressed."

It was like watching a black and white movie and I was cast as the helpless victim. My head ached and my eyes were out of focus. Black and purple bruises were appearing on my arm and hurling would be next on the agenda. I staggered to the shower and turned the hot water on full blast.

"Hurry up. I want to leave in five minutes."

Fuck you, asshole.

Even the scalding water of the shower couldn't wash his filth off me. I toweled my hair dry, all the while trying to envision what I should do next. I threw a black cocktail dress over my head, covered my face with concealer and blush. There was nothing to be done about my arm, so I grabbed a shawl and ventured downstairs.

Matthew was waiting for me in the living room nursing another drink. "It's about time. I don't know why I bother with you, Portia. Let's go."

I said nothing. I followed Matthew out to the car and eased my battered body into the passenger seat. I could not bring myself to speak to him. Not now. Not ever. My mind was focused on one thing and one thing only.

How to end this nightmare.

MATTHEW hadn't told me where the party was, but I recognized the house as we pulled into the driveway. Bob Winterstein lived at this address with his wife, Marcy. We had gone out a few times as a foursome and I liked her. They had relocated to a new neighborhood at the west end of the city where the properties were large and the home designs unique. Their house was a Federal reproduction complete with portico, shutters and all the trimmings. Very charming.

At the door we were greeted by Marcy, smiling, and Bob with drink in hand.

"You guys are late." Bob said, slurring his words. He exhibited the perpetual red face and bulbous nose of an alcoholic. His massive neck hung out over his shirt collar and his eyes bugged out like he was being strangled. Shaggy hair, graying at the temples stood up in a cowlick completing his unkempt carefree look. "Come on in. You'll have to catch up to the rest of us."

Matthew displayed his million dollar smile and led

me through the door.

"The girls are hanging out in the kitchen," Marcy said. "Can I take your wrap?"

I tightened my grip and tried to muster a smile. "No thanks, I'll keep it."

Marcy nodded and headed for the kitchen and I followed along behind her. She looked like a little firecracker in her hot pink dress topped with her head of spiky blonde hair.

"We're drinking margaritas." Marcy handed me a frosty glass filled with lime green liquid, and politely pretended not to notice my UFC survivor look.

I did my best to smile a thank you and found a seat on one of the kitchen bar stools. The granite island was loaded with pretzels, nuts, fruit and vegetable trays, gourmet dips and hot hors d'oeuvres. Marcy knew how to throw a party.

From where I was sitting, I could see my reflection in a large beveled mirror on the other side of the room. The gash over my eye was puffed out like an Easter egg wearing Cover Girl. My eyes were circles of red and my arm was wrapped in a shawl like a bag lady.

I forced my lungs to draw breath.

The girls in the kitchen laughed and chatted non-stop. They were exchanging stories about their kids, their jobs and their social lives. I had none of the above, so I just listened and tried to nod and smile at the appropriate intervals. After finishing my margarita, I excused myself and looked for the powder room. My makeup needed repair and I needed a moment alone to work on my composure.

After a few minutes of deep breathing, I headed back to the party. On my return trip to the kitchen, I noticed the study door standing open. The end wall was smattered with the mounted heads of dead animals recalling happier times. Below the heads were multiple glassed-in gun cabinets. Bob was a hunter.

Not once during the evening did Matthew check on me. Not that I wanted him to—the farther away the better. He spent the entire time drinking and joking with his friends. It was a relief, of sorts, knowing I was temporarily safe from his brutality, protected by a crowd of strangers.

When the party wound down, Matthew was so drunk I had to drive home. Marcy had taken the car keys out of his hand and given them to me over Matthew's loud protests. He staggered towards the car shouting obscenities for all the neighbors to hear. Bob helped him into the passenger seat and closed the door.

"I could have driven, bitch. You did that to embarrass me."

"Marcy thought it would be safer if I drove."

"Safer? With you driving? Bullshit!"

With that, Matthew slumped down into the passenger seat and passed out, making the drive home pleasantly silent. As I pulled into the garage, he raised his head for a moment, gave me the stare of death and bashed his head into the window as he went down for the count. I laughed to myself as I got out of the car. Matthew could spend the night in the garage—it served him right.

CHAPTER THREE

WHEN I awoke alone in the king-sized bed, I chuckled at the thought of Matthew waking up in the car. He would not see the humor in it. This might be a tough day.

I smiled as I donned my ripped Levi's and pulled my black Springsteen concert shirt over my head. These clothes were my favorites and were reserved for my private time in the garden.

I started the coffee maker and grabbed a yogurt from the fridge. I couldn't go into the garage to get my pruning shears and gloves, so I scooped up some gardening magazines from a shelf in the kitchen and took them out to the patio table while I waited for the coffee. The morning sun was already warming the garden and my spirits as well.

This morning what I needed most was a plan. A plan to leave Matthew.

Matthew stuck his head out the window, and I nearly jumped out of my skin.

"Portia. Breakfast."

I closed my magazine and hurried into the kitchen to cook his usual. "Won't be a minute."

"Why did you leave me in the car, you stupid slut? You're getting worse every day. I'm going to have to teach you a lesson."

Washing my hands under running water in the sink, I didn't hear it coming. When his fist caught my upper arm, I heard the bone crack. Screaming in pain I staggered for the downstairs bathroom. I turned the lock on the door just as he caught up to me.

"That's it, Matthew," I sobbed, "I'm leaving you. I can't live like this one more day."

"Try it, bitch," Matthew snarled through the door. "Leave me and I'll hunt you down and kill you. I'll find you no matter where you run."

My hands shook as I peered into the medicine cabinet. I found some extra strength pain killers left from the time I sprained my ankle tripping on the garden hose—that's what I told the doctor in Emergency but Matthew had actually pushed me down the stairs. I swallowed four with a gulp of water, clutching my arm and crying while I sat on the toilet lid to think.

I remained frozen in time until I heard him stumbling up the stairs. I unlocked the bathroom door and tiptoed into the kitchen. With a trembling hand, I picked up my purse and closed my fingers over my car keys to keep them from jingling. Slipping out the side door I headed to the garage.

It was awkward and painful getting into the car and turning the key to start it, but using my left arm, I drove to the hospital. My shoulder throbbed when I turned corners. I wanted to scream but going alone was better than the alternative.

After X-rays were taken, the doctor on call came into my treatment cubicle. He was tall, dark and cute enough to be a Chippendale in his off hours. His name tag read, Dr. Alexander.

"You have a fractured humerus. How did this happen?" He asked with a frown.

"I fell off a stool in the kitchen and hit my arm on the counter on the way down." I hadn't lied too much in my life up to this point, but practice made perfect.

"Uh huh," he mumbled. "I'm going to put the bone back in place and then immobilize your arm. Can you flex your wrist for me and try to extend your fingers."

I winced with the pain of it but tried to comply.

"This is going to hurt." He focused on the X-ray above my head and maneuvered the bone back into place.

I held my breath. Ringing filled my ears and blackness crept near.

"Breathe for me, Mrs. Talbot. In. Out. Come on, now, the worst is over. Now we'll brace the fracture and give you a sling for support."

"Thanks," I whispered as I exhaled.

Doctor Alexander gave me a knowing glance as he put my arm into the sling. "I noticed on your chart that you're no stranger to this Emergency room, Mrs. Talbot. Here's a prescription for the pain, and here's a number to call if you need to report anything or speak to anyone. Don't think you're doing yourself any favors by not doing so. Once the violence accelerates, you're in real danger, my dear."

I nodded.

"Make an appointment with your family doctor and have another X-ray in four weeks."

I forced a half smile and said, "I will. Thank you. I'll be fine."

But would I? I had nowhere to go. I had to go home. What about Matthew?

After the lengthy wait in emergency and a stop at the pharmacy, I arrived home around five in the afternoon. The kitchen resembled a bomb site. The counter was littered with empty liquor bottles, dirty glasses and spilled orange juice. I blew out a big breath of relief when Matthew wasn't anywhere to be found on the main floor. I wasn't in any shape to check the bedroom.

I struggled for several minutes with the child proof cap on my prescription bottle, finally managing to extract two of the pills and swallow them. Pulling a blanket down from the closet shelf with my left hand, I lay on the living room sofa, closed my eyes and let the pills put me temporarily out of my misery.

When I woke, the room was dark. It took me a moment to realize where I was. How long had I been sleeping? I listened. No sound from upstairs.

He must have tied a good one on today.

I retrieved a flashlight from under the sink and started skimming through my gardening magazines looking for an article I'd seen earlier this morning. At the time it had seemed unimportant. Now I needed to find it. My life depended on it.

CHAPTER FOUR

DAWN was breaking and a faint gray shaft of light was peeking through the living room curtains when a sound from upstairs startled me. Matthew was stirring. The pain in my shoulder had kept me from sleeping soundly. I had dozed off and on throughout the night, but my broken body was crying out for solid sleep. Matthew would be livid realizing that I hadn't come up to bed. Something I had never dared before.

"Where the hell are you, bitch? He called from upstairs. "You can't hide from me."

I made my way into the kitchen without answering. I started the coffee maker, took another round of pain killers, and rummaged in the pantry for the pancake batter.

Matthew's mother had always made him pancakes and bacon on Sunday morning.

And the last thing I wanted to do was break with tradition.

I set the table with his mother's Sunday best dishes and took the family silverware out of the velvet lined case. Sometimes I created a lavish table setting when trying to make up to him for something unforgivable I had done. It had always cheered him in the past.

In the center of his mother's antique runner I placed a small vase of Lilly of the Valley picked from my backyard garden. The small bouquet filled the air in the dining room with a heavenly scent.

"Breakfast is ready, Matthew," I called up the stairs. The smell of bacon had no doubt reached him on the upper level, but he didn't answer. I loaded the table with butter, syrup, blueberries and orange juice.

It wasn't too long before there was stumbling on the stairs. "Shit—I don't have time to eat. I'm late for my tee time. Why didn't you call me? You're worse than useless, Portia . . . worse than useless." His voice trailed off as he stomped into the garage.

"I did call you, Matthew. You must have been in the bathroom." I said to no one in particular as he backed out the driveway. I exhaled and put my plan on hold for another day.

After clearing up everything from the breakfast that never happened, I sat down with a coffee and tried to keep my emotions in check so that I could think. Crying was not going to solve my problem, although that's all I wanted to do the last few weeks. I jumped when the phone rang.

"Did Matthew go golfing?" Marcy was whispering.

"Yes, he left a while ago. What's up?"

"We need to talk. Can I pop by tomorrow morning for an hour?"

"Sure, I could use the company," I said. "You can come over now, if it's urgent."

"Can't get away right now," she whispered and hung up.

My hands were shaking as I put the roast in the oven for dinner. I didn't know if Matthew was coming in time for the evening meal, but if the food wasn't ready it would be my funeral.

Possibly literally.

Around six he blasted through the door and gave me a peck on the cheek. "What's for dinner, baby?" He slurred.

"Roast beef," I said, "how was golf?"

"Won fifty bucks from Bob—that prick couldn't sink a putt if his life depended on it." He snickered.

"Good for you," I tried to sound pleased.

I served dinner and cleaned up afterward. Matthew made himself a drink and adjourned to the living room to watch CNN. When he was soundly sleeping on the sofa, I tiptoed up to bed.

CHAPTER FIVE

MARCY arrived at ten. Though the morning temperature had skyrocketed into the eighties, she was sweating it out in jeans and a long sleeved turtleneck. As I ushered her in, she handed me the casserole she had brought and pulled up the collar of her sweater, hiding a patch of bluish purple on her neck. Portions of her face were covered with a thick coating of liquid makeup, but I pretended not to notice.

"I made you some comfort food for later," she said as she sat down at the dining room table. I thanked her, carried the casserole into the kitchen and fixed a tray with fresh coffee and warm muffins.

"Oh, that smells heavenly. I didn't have time for breakfast," she said.

We munched on our muffins and chatted about the weather, the sale at The Bay, Marcy's new living room drapes and everything but what she came to discuss. I didn't know how to get her to open up to me, so I took a leap and threw it out there.

"I'm trying to figure out how to make a new life for myself without Matthew. He blames me every day for ruining his life." I sucked in a breath, "I want to leave him."

Marcy inhaled sharply and her hands shook as she placed her coffee cup on the tray. "I was sure Matthew was abusing you, Portia. I've seen your bruises and the way that he treats you—now you have a broken arm." She pointed at my sling. "I recognized the signs and guessed you couldn't talk about it anymore than I could. I'm all out of options and I'm thinking about going to a support group." Her voice cracked and she whimpered, "I am such a mess, could you possibly go with me?"

"A support group. Not something I was considering, but of course, I'll go with you," I said, "I had my suspicions about Bob. Has his drinking increased?"

"He's been angry about something the past few months and there is nothing I can do to placate him. He says it's business, but he's never been this undone over work issues. More is going on with him, but he never confides in me. I'm in the dark."

"Maybe we'll find a way out at the group meeting," I said. "When is it?"

"They meet at seven every Tuesday at the YMCA."

"Won't Bob wonder where you are?"

"No. Bob has a poker game every Tuesday. I'll be back before he comes home. What will you tell Matthew?"

"Umm . . . I'll say I'm taking another cooking class. He makes me go to those every now and then when he thinks my cooking isn't up to par with his Mother's."

Marcy smiled, "Thanks so much. This means a lot to me. I should go."

"Have a quick tour of my garden first. The spring flowers are just starting to bloom."

After a short walk through the yard, Marcy smiled, and I noticed the tension release from her shoulders.

"What a beautiful bed of lily of the valley. It fills that whole back corner, and the fragrance is so delicate. I could stand here and inhale that scent all day," she said.

"My favorite. It spreads like wildfire. I can give you a few roots if you like."

"Oh, I would love some. I have a perfect shady spot for it."

I dug up three plants, wrapped them in damp paper towels in the kitchen and zipped them into a plastic bag.

"Thanks so much, Portia. You made me feel a lot better."

I walked her to the front door, "I'll pick you up at six thirty tomorrow night. Thanks again for the casserole."

CHAPTER SIX

MY hands shook as I set the table for Matthew's dinner. The shepherd's pie was sitting ready in the warm oven. I finished the salad and left it on the table covered in plastic wrap with a note telling him where I was. I opened the fridge to grab the salad dressing when the phone rang.

"Checking to make sure we're still on for tonight," Marcy said in a whisper.

"I'm almost ready. Why are you whispering?"

"Bob is upstairs changing his clothes for poker night."

"I'm leaving shortly." I dashed upstairs to change, took my pain meds, sucked in several deep breaths, grabbed my purse and keys and drove to the west end of the city to pick her up.

It was ten of seven when I pulled into the Winterstein's driveway and saw no sign of Bob's vehicle. Marcy was dressed in black slacks and a frilly yellow shirt, but she was hesitant at the door.

"What if Bob finds out I went to this meeting?"

"He won't find out unless you tell him, girl. We certainly don't have to go unless you're absolutely sure you want to. You can change your mind right now."

"I do want to go," she said as she got into the Jeep. "Support is what I desperately need. My own family is so far away in North Bay."

THE meeting was held in a small, poorly lit, musty smelling room at the west end YMCA. There was seating set up for about thirty people, but half the seats were empty. Marcy was nervous and objected to sitting close to the front. We sat in the back row on folding chairs to observe. I was surprised to see how normal everyone looked. I guess I was expecting to see bruises, black eyes and bandages everywhere in the crowd. I almost felt out of place with my arm in a sling.

"I don't want to say anything," whispered Marcy, "I just want to listen."

"Fine with me—I don't want to say anything either."

A tall, older woman, perhaps in her late fifties, strode to the front of the room and introduced herself. She was dressed casually in a black skirt, beige sweater and low heeled shoes. She reminded me of the librarian at my high school.

"My name is Mae Julianne and I thank you all for coming," she said softly. "I know for some of you, coming here for the first time tonight is a huge step to take, and I know you're frightened."

After a short recap of her life as an abused wife, she focused on how she turned her life around and now tried to empower other women do the same.

"Do we have a volunteer for our first speaker?"

"I'll start." A tiny girl with short, jet black hair stood up and slowly made her way to the front of the room. She was wearing torn jeans and a hoody over a white short-sleeved T-shirt. Standing at the front, she slid off her sweater and exposed the black and blue blotches on her scrawny arms. The left side of her face was bruised and her left eye swollen shut. I gasped, and Marcy took my hand.

"My name is Darlene, and I'm abused. I've lived with my boyfriend, Doug, for seven years and we have four kids. After he lost his job at GM, we managed on unemployment and my Walmart paycheck while he looked for another job without any luck. Now he's stopped looking for work. He says nobody is going to hire him, so why bother. He spends his days lying on the couch, at the race track, drinking in a bar or doing drugs. He gambles away what welfare money we have and drinks the rest."

She paused and took a deep breath before she continued. "This week he beat heavy on our oldest son, Nathan—gave him a broken arm and a bloody nose. Told him he deserved it. When I told him, I was taking the kids and leaving, he grabbed hold of my neck and choked me. Said he would finish the job if I mentioned leaving him again." She lifted her chin to show the bruises on her neck.

The room was silent.

Mae helped Darlene back to her seat. Marcy looked at me, her blue eyes full of tears. "Let's go, Portia, I can't take any more of this."

I fumbled in my purse for tissues and we both wiped our eyes on the way out of the room.

"Do you want to stop for a drink or something to eat?"

"No thanks, I think I'll just go home. I feel so bad for those people," her voice cracked. "I should get into the house and change before Bob gets back."

I pulled into her driveway. "Call if you need anything. Promise."

"I promise." She gave me a little wave as she walked up on her porch.

Driving home from Marcy's, pressure in my chest made it difficult to breathe and I had the onset of a migraine. Thoughts of Matthew's reaction to my note were making my stomach turn.

I'd noticed posters on the wall at the Y for women's self-defense classes. I made a mental note to take a couple during the upcoming week and hoped I could convince Marcy to join me.

AS I pulled into the driveway, I gasped. Matthew was sitting on the porch steps with a drink in his hand waiting for me. Never had he done that before. I was shaking as I got out of the car and walked towards him.

He stood up and put his arm around me as we walked through the front door. "So . . . what did you learn to cook tonight, sweetheart?" he glared at me through glazed eyes.

"Apple strudel," I said, the hair standing up on the back of my neck.

"Make me some now," he said, grabbing me by the wrist.

"I'm tired, Matthew. I don't want to make any now."

"I said, *make it now.*" With a lot of force, he pushed me into the kitchen. I hit my broken arm on the door frame and screamed.

I ran into the powder room and locked the door. "Come out of there, Portia. I know you weren't at any cooking class. What's his name, Portia? Where did you meet him? You're cheating on me, I can feel it." He pounded on the door.

Hours later, my arm still throbbing from the bump I had given it, I silently opened the bathroom door, slipped into the living room in the dark and pulled a blanket over me. The pounding of my heart was the only sound I could hear.

CHAPTER SEVEN

I made Matthew's breakfast in the same rumpled clothes I had slept in, not daring to go up to the bedroom until after he left for work. He never spoke a word to me and averted his eyes whenever I was near him. He read the paper, ate his eggs, drank his coffee and left.

As soon as the Mercedes was out the driveway, I bolted upstairs and ran a hot bath. After dressing and cleaning up the kitchen, I poured myself another coffee and blew out a big breath. Something had to be done about Matthew and time was not on my side. A plan was what I needed, and I needed it immediately.

My phone rang and I didn't recognize the number. "This is Scarborough General Hospital calling. Your friend, Marcy Winterstein, asked me to call when they brought her up to our floor this morning. Could you possibly come to the hospital? Fourth floor nurses' station and ask for Nurse Fraser."

"Oh, my God, is she hurt? How bad is it?" I choked back a sob.

"Mrs. Winterstein was able to dial 911 herself and told the paramedics she fell down the stairs. We can fill you in when you get here, Mrs. Talbot."

"I'll be there as soon as I can. Thank you for calling."

She did NOT fall down the stairs by herself.

My hands shook as I struggled with my sweater. How badly was she beaten this time to have them admit her to the hospital? My stomach roiled.

During the drive to Scarborough General, I tried to calm myself, but failed miserably. This was partly my fault. There must have been something more I could have done to protect her.

As the elevator door opened on the fourth floor, I took a deep breath and braced myself for the worst.

Not even close.

Nurse Fraser escorted me from the nurses' station to room four eighteen. I gasped for air. My legs dissolved under me. I grabbed onto the bedside table to hold myself upright. Nausea rose in my throat as ringing filled my ears. I dropped into the chair beside the bed and put my head between my knees. After the dizziness passed, rage filled the void and the intensity of my hatred for Bob was overwhelming.

Marcy's delicate heart-shaped face was not the same one I had said goodbye to the evening before. Now a deep shade of violet radiated over her skin, her mouth swollen with traces of dried blood caked on her lips, her sparkling blue eyes buried in mounds of purple tissue. She lay motionless.

That fucking low life will get his.

I took Marcy's hand in mine.

Nurse Fraser came into the room and checked the monitor. "She's been heavily sedated for the pain and won't be fully aware for a day or two."

"How serious are her injuries?" I ventured.

"Are you family?"

"I'm her sister," I said, swallowing.

"She has broken ribs, one rib punctured her right lung, broken wrist and multiple bruises. We won't know how serious the head injuries are until the swelling subsides. I'm sorry that's all I can tell you right now and you can't stay long. She needs her rest."

"Could you tell her I'll be back tomorrow if she wakes up?"

"I will," Nurse Fraser said.

SHORTLY after one I arrived home and went straight upstairs to have a nap. I needed a clear head. If I didn't do something, I'd be the next one in the hospital or the morgue—it was that simple.

At four I started preparations for dinner. I set a lovely table with his Matthew's Mother's heirloom cloth—he always loved it when I served dinner on it. I arranged a fresh bouquet of lily of the valley on the table and took a few of the leaves and stems into the kitchen for another recipe.

I spread out a sheet of plastic wrap, ground up the lily of the valley until some of the little white bells had become a white liquid and set this aside in a container. Then I made Matthew one of his favorite dinners—meat loaf with mashed potatoes, and cauliflower with cheese sauce—just like his mother used to make him. *Almost.* For dessert I made crème caramel.

He arrived precisely at six forty-five and sat down at the head of the table. I poured him a glass of wine.

He looked at the table setting and smiled, "Finally, you're shaping up."

"I'm trying to be what you want me to be, Matthew. I truly am." I said as sweetly as I could.

"About bloody time." He smiled as he noticed that I

made a lot of his favorites.

We ate dinner in relative silence. He had seconds of everything. I cleared the table and served dessert with coffee and his favorite liqueur.

He wiped his forehead with his napkin. "Holy hell, it's hot in here. Turn the air on."

I got up to check the thermostat and hid my smile. "It's set at seventy. Just like always."

"Thing must be broken. Call somebody tomorrow." He pointed a manicured finger at me. "Don't forget."

I won't forget, Matthew.

I cleared the dessert dishes. After rinsing his plate and cutlery in the kitchen sink I bent down to load the dishwasher. I was putting away the Clorox when I heard a clatter in the dining room.

Matthew had knocked his wine glass off the table. His face was flushed and blotchy. "Get me some Advil. I have a brute of a headache."

"Sorry to hear that, *darling.* I'll get you some." I sauntered down the hall to the powder room and found the Advil in the medicine chest.

By the time I returned to the dining room with a glass of water and the capsules in my hand, Matthew was slumped over in his chair. "I feel sick," he whispered, barely audible.

When I held out the water to him he grabbed my wrist. I pulled back, but he clung tightly to my arm pressing his fingers into my skin.

"What . . . did . . . you . . . do?" he gasped.

His grip relaxed as he grabbed for his chest and groaned. With drool slobbering out the corners of his mouth, he crashed onto the floor upending his chair. He rolled over onto his back, let go a blood curdling howl of pain and fixed his blue-eyed gaze on the Tiffany chandelier.

Don't worry, Matthew. I'm here for you..

I made my way to the kitchen, picked up the phone and dialed 911.

Less than ten minutes later, eight to be exact, the response team rolled down Hawthorne Lane with sirens wailing. I rushed to the front door in frantic haste and let the paramedics in. They were already scrambling across the porch with a gurney and all of their equipment.

"It's my husband, Matthew," I cried. "He collapsed." I sat down at the dining room table and laid my head down on my arm.

The paramedics rushed to Matthew's side to assess him. "Did you start CPR, Ma'am?"

I raised my head and mumbled, "No, I'm so sorry I couldn't. I have a broken arm."

While my mind spun, I could hear them talking to each other in subdued voices. The young man, Jake, was tall and blonde. His partner, Chelsea was petite with short dark hair.

"Absence of vital signs. No pulse. No respiration."

Jake ripped Matthew's shirt open and the buttons bounced across the hardwood. "Starting CPR." They worked on Matthew for what seemed like ages, taking turns. He didn't respond.

"Defibrillator," Chelsea said.

Jake plugged the pads into the connector. "Clear!"

I peeked out from under my arm and saw Matthew

jump.

"No response . . . again," said Chelsea.

They repeated the process and Matthew refused to breathe. He was always stubborn.

"Ma'am, your husband is not responding. We're transporting him to the hospital. You can ride in the ambulance or you can follow in your car, if you are up to it."

"I want to go with Matthew." I dabbed at my eyes with a napkin.

They strapped Matthew to the stretcher and wheeled him out to the ambulance. I grabbed my purse and followed them out. A couple of the neighbors were standing on their porches craning their necks to see what was going on. Death always attracts a crowd.

Chelsea helped me into the back of the ambulance while Jake jumped into the driver's seat. "We're transporting to Scarborough General," Chelsea said into her radio.

I was in a fog. My mind flooded with endless possibilities for my life without Matthew. I could do anything I wanted to do. Couldn't I? This would take a bit of getting used to. The wailing of the siren quickly brought me back to reality. I straightened my face before anyone saw anything other than a horror-stricken wife. I played my part.

Jake wove through traffic and ran stop lights all the way to the hospital. He whipped the ambulance into the loop in front of the emergency entrance and screeched to a stop. The siren died, the back door of the vehicle flung open and Matthew was whisked away. I climbed out and followed as quickly as I could.

There was no sign of him when I reached the front desk of the emergency room.

"Can you tell me where they took my husband, Matthew Talbot?"

"Talbot. Exam room six. Straight down the hall," the receptionist said. "Wait in one of the chairs in the hall until the doctor comes to find you."

I sat outside room six for what seemed a lifetime, but finally a doctor came out and pulled the curtain closed behind him. "Mrs. Talbot?" he asked. I nodded and he introduced himself, though I didn't hear a word. "Mrs. Talbot. Come this way, please. We can use my office."

He helped me to my feet and escorted me into a small room down the corridor. He sat me down and then perched himself in front of me on the edge of his desk. He had a kind face, filled with compassion. Considering his age, he probably had years of experience delivering bad news.

"Despite our best efforts, our attempts to revive your husband failed. Even though he was a relatively young man, sometimes the heart just stops. Sometimes there is no apparent reason, nor explanation, but I promise you, his passing was very quick. I'm so sorry, for your loss."

He sat quietly and I listened to the blood pumping in my head.

"I . . . I can't believe he's gone," I sobbed, shaking in earnest. My mind whirled, everything around me muted as if I was trapped in some bizarre, distant dream. "It's over. So fast. That's it?"

The doctor placed a firm hand on my shoulder. "It's natural to be shaken, Mrs. Talbot. It will take some time for things to sink in. Death comes when we least expect it and is never convenient."

Sometimes it is.

The doctor helped me call a cab and walked with me to the lobby. As I rode home in the taxi, my hands continued to tremble and my stomach wanted to return my dinner. Somehow I managed to pay the driver and step out of the cab onto legs that would barely hold me. I fought to get control of myself and barely got inside before I fell apart.

WHOW knows how much later, I pulled myself together. My first order of business was to prioritize what needed doing and work my way down the list. While I waited for fresh coffee to brew, I cleaned up the mess in the dining room then made my list for the following day. The appointments could be made in the morning, but tonight I had to find the insurance policy.

Matthew was incredibly organized, and I knew all of his important papers were filed in the study. I had never been welcomed in there, but no one was watching me now.

The wooden filing cabinet stood against the wall opposite the monstrous roll-top desk that had belonged to Mister Talbot Senior. Made of solid oak it must have weighed five hundred pounds. When I pulled open the pencil drawer, a set of keys was the first thing that caught my eye. I jingled through the ring, trying each one. One for the desk, one for the filing cabinet and two more that didn't fit anything in the room. Those would bear investigation later.

The top drawer of the filing cabinet had neatly labeled folders in alphabetical order. All I had to do was go to 'I' and there was insurance information. I glanced over my shoulder as I removed the Manila folder and took it over to the desk. The file contained the usual forms—car insurance for both cars, home owner's policy and life. I was surprised to see there were two policies on me. The one I knew about for seventy-five thousand that Matthew had bought when we were first married, but why two?

The second one was for three million dollars and had been purchased by my loving husband only a month ago. My stomach turned.

Was he planning to kill me?

A month ago—I tried to think back to see if I could recall anything of consequence that had happened around that time—last week of March. Nothing came to mind.

Matthew's policy was on the bottom of the pile. He had shown it to me when we were first married, bragging that he would always take care of me. The amount was for a million dollars. I held my breath when I looked at the beneficiary.

Oh, my God . . . Portia Talbot. Somehow in the back of my mind, I'd expected him to change that and give the money to the Masons, Shriners or some other charity, so I would be left penniless. I found the agent's number on the covering letter and made a note of it for the morning.

After checking the locks on all the doors, I went upstairs to my bathroom. Scented candles came out of hiding and took their rightful places around the tub. I lingered in the bubbles luxuriating in my eerie freedom, half expecting Matthew to come waltzing through the bathroom door and chastise me. No. My husband would never hurt me again. Some of the tension of the past few days dissipated as I readied myself for bed.

Wrapped in my fluffy robe, I crawled under the duvet and slept like the dead.

CHAPTER EIGHT

A ringing on the dresser woke me. Was it morning? The alarm clock said nine a.m. but it wasn't ringing. Matthew's phone. Shit. How many other details had I overlooked? A shiver ran down my back. I jumped out of bed and stuck my feet in my slippers. It was Thursday morning. A workday morning for Matthew. What was I thinking? Was I thinking at all?

In the kitchen, I started a pot of coffee then called Matthew's office back and asked for Bob Winterstein. Bob came on the line sounding like he'd had a rough night.

"Sorry to bother you so early, Bob, but I have to give you some bad news." I paused. "Last night, Matthew had a heart attack."

"What? Is he in the hospital? How bad was it?"

"The paramedics took him to the hospital, but he didn't make it."

"Oh, Jeeze, Portia, this is terrible. I . . . uh, I can't believe this. How are you holding up?"

"I'm in shock but trying to cope and get things organized for the funeral. Could you notify the proper people in the office? I would appreciate it."

"Of course, I will. I'm having a hard time grasping this."

"Me too. You have no idea." I paused for effect and sniffed. "I'll phone with details of the arrangements later."

Another job done.

I filled my coffee mug, grabbed the Yellow Pages and flipped to the first funeral home listing. Nothing under 'A.' Barton and Barton—good enough. A quick call set up an appointment with one of the Mr. Barton's for ten o'clock and I furnished him with the information on where to claim the body. I grabbed a quick shower, dressed in a black pant suit and arrived at the Barton establishment five minutes late.

Mr. Barton, dressed appropriately in a black suit with a muted tie, greeted me at the door of the converted Victorian mansion. He was a short man with sand colored hair mixed with gray. His skin was pale, but his pallor fit beautifully with his surroundings. I didn't ask which Barton he was, and I didn't much care.

New carpet aroma filled the foyer. The waist-high wainscoting looked original and was stained a rich mahogany. Furnishings were antique and luxurious, and the lighting was Tiffany style. Soft music played unobtrusively in the background. Matthew would be comfortable here.

"Please make yourself at home. Mrs. Talbot." Mr. Barton motioned towards the seating.

I sank into one of the sumptuous tan leather chairs in his office. "Thank you. Lovely artwork," I said, admiring the Georgia O'Keeffe.

Business must be good.

Mr. Barton rhymed off many choices and all I had to do was point. I guess funeral directors use this method, thinking the bereaved have lost a loved one and their minds as well. After every detail was covered, Mr. Barton assured me he was capable of taking care of everything. He provided me with the death certificate and left me with nothing to do but grieve. I had no idea that arranging a funeral could be so stress free.

Thank you, God . . . And Mr. Barton

Next stop, insurance office. My appointment was with Matthew's agent, Camilla Brockhurst. The directory in the lobby sent me to the twelfth floor.

Ms. Brockhurst appeared in the waiting area after being paged by reception and asked me to follow her into her office. She was a willowy blonde with legs up to her neck. Her tomato red blouse was unbuttoned just enough to show generous cleavage. I could see why most men would stampede to buy insurance from her—several times over.

"Have a seat, Mrs. Talbot." She motioned to one of the black chairs in front of her desk.

When I passed her the death certificate and copy of the policy, she stared at Matthew's name and burst into tears. "I'm so sorry for your loss," she blubbered.

Why was she crying? Did all agents react this way?

I was stumped for a moment, and then the other shoe dropped. Did I look like I just fell off the turnip truck? My eyes met hers for a second, and I was sure that she knew I knew. Ms. Brockhurst took a minute and regained enough of her composure to carry on with business. She gave me the appropriate papers to sign and I complied with a minimum of waterworks on my part.

"Your claim will begin processing tomorrow. I can call you when your check is ready for pick up, or courier it to you when it comes from head office or you can opt for a direct deposit into your bank account." She focused her gaze on her pen and avoided looking me in the eye.

"Direct deposit will be fine, thanks." I smiled as I gave her a void check with the account number.

Hope you rot in hell, bitch.

On my drive home, I couldn't help but wonder how many mistresses Matthew might have scattered around town. He'd had plenty of opportunity, late meetings, golf games, working out at the gym. I didn't want to venture a guess or dwell on it. I turned the radio to a country station and smiled as Toby Keith blasted out 'Red Solo Cup.' I sang along and stepped on the gas.

AS I pulled into the driveway, my eye was drawn to the front window. I could have sworn the drapes were open this morning when I left the house. My stomach flipped and I felt prickles up the back of my neck.

I slowly turned the knob on the front door and found it locked. I used my key and pushed the door open. No sound. Maybe my imagination was working overtime. Nothing was disturbed in the living room or dining room, but the door to Matthew's study was ajar. I distinctly remembered closing it after I had found the insurance papers.

Should I call the police? They say never to enter your home if you think an intruder is still inside. Who are 'they' anyway? My hands shook as I gave the study door a tiny one-finger shove.

I sucked in my breath. The room was trashed. All the drawers in the filing cabinet were dumped, folders scattered everywhere, and the desk drawers stood open too. Pictures had been removed from the walls. Somebody was looking for what? A safe? Money? How did they get inside the house? Who were *they* and what did *they* want? Should I call the police?

Do I want the police snooping around? What the hell do I do?

Well, the choices seemed clear, either back out of the room and call the police or clean up the mess and try to figure this out myself. I picked up the papers, sorting them into alphabetical piles and putting them back into the file folders. I read everything as I inserted the documents into their appropriate folders. I gasped when doing the 'B' section and discovered there was an unmarked folder dedicated to me under my maiden name, 'Brownell'.

The file was thin, containing only a copy of my birth certificate, an old report from Children's Aid and a few court papers following my life through the foster system. It shocked me that Matthew had obtained those documents without telling me but it renewed my enthusiasm to pursue it later.

After an hour looking at household bills, receipts and articles cut out of The Wall Street Journal, I was no closer to discovering why someone had tossed Matthew's files. Then again—they might have found what they wanted and taken it. In the end, the room was back to normal, but I was not. My hands were trembling, and every noise made me flinch. The Yellow Pages were sitting on the desk in front of me. I flipped to 'L' and called the closest locksmith, then to 'S" for security listings and called Apex, the first one on the page with a block ad. They promised to send a rep over at four. The locksmith would arrive at three.

I locked up the filing cabinet and was returning the keys to the desk drawer when I noticed the extra keys on the ring again. What were they for? Maybe a lock box or a safety deposit box?

Brian would know. Brian Pickersgill had always been Matthew's attorney. I had to let him know about the funeral and I could ask him.

Thumbing through Matthew's contacts on his phone I hit call. "Brian, I'm afraid I have some bad news. Matthew had a heart attack yesterday." I took a breath and paused. "He passed away."

"Oh, Portia, no. Matt was always lecturing me on smoking and high cholesterol. I can't believe this. He just had a physical a month ago. What happened?"

Was Brian suspicious or am I being paranoid?

"He was eating dinner last night, same as always, and he had a heart attack. The paramedics came right away, but it was too late. They couldn't save him."

"I'm so sorry. Are they doing an autopsy?"

No, thank God.

"No, the doctor said it was a heart attack. Plain and simple."

"You'd better come down to the office. There are some things that I should go over with you. When is the funeral?"

"It will be held on Saturday at Barton and Barton. Two o'clock. I could come over there tomorrow around nine-thirty, if that's OK." I jotted the time on a post-it.

"Of course, come over in the morning and we'll go over Matthew's will. Everything is straightforward as far as I can remember. I'll be ready for you."

"Thank you. Oh, by the way. Do you know if Matthew had a safety deposit box?"

"I'm not sure. Just call the bank and they might tell you. See you tomorrow."

"Thanks." I was sweating when I hung up the phone. I practiced some deep breathing to get control.

I didn't know what Matthew would have in his will.

What did Brian mean, *things I should go over with you?*

The growling in my stomach reminded me that I hadn't eaten anything. The fridge was as bare as the Mojave and I was in no mood to go out. I found three eggs and half a loaf of bread. Scrambled eggs and toast would have to do. I made a new pot of coffee and drank it black while scribbling a grocery list. After putting food in my stomach, I popped two more pain killers. My arm was telling me to rest, but that would have to wait. There was too much to do.

I returned to the study and retrieved the key ring, picked up my purse and headed for the door.

Matthew had been in charge of the banking since we were married. He paid the bills and gave me household money. I never questioned him on anything. There was no need and it would have caused trouble and provoked an argument that I didn't need or want. Now, I was getting a whole new perspective on my beloved.

The bank Matthew used was six blocks away. With my arm aching from driving earlier in the day, I walked the distance.

While the receptionist searched for the manager, she ushered me into a glassed-in cubicle where I waited in plain sight. All of the customers seemed to take turns gawking at me. A long twenty minutes passed, and the manager made his appearance. He was a rotund little man nearing retirement age, dressed in a black pin-striped suit and red silk tie. His high blood pressure gave his face a sunburned appearance.

"I'm Jim Timberman," He extended a stumpy hand. "What can I do for you, Mrs. Talbot?"

"My husband, Matthew, recently passed away and I was wondering if he had a safety deposit box here?"

"Oh, dear, I'm so sorry for your loss. Let me check on that for you." He looked me up and down, left the office for a few minutes and when he returned, seemed noticeably cool. "Could I see the paperwork regarding your husband's passing?"

"I'm seeing the lawyer tomorrow. I'm sure he will provide me with what I need."

"I'm sorry, Mrs. Talbot, but I can't give you any information until that paperwork is in order. Client privacy is very important in our business."

"No problem." I smiled, standing up. "Thank you for your time."

"Again, I'm so sorry about Mr. Talbot."

Part way home, I popped into a trendy boutique and spent an hour shopping for funeral attire. Matthew would want me to look my best. I settled on a black silk suit that I truly loved and bought a wide-brimmed hat that made me look like Kate Middleton. Black stiletto heels added four inches to my five foot six, and the diamond sweetheart necklace was reserved yet beautiful.

The walk home was difficult with one arm aching and the other laden down with bags, but I inhaled large lungfuls of crisp April air and it seemed to clear my head. Once in the front door, I took more meds and went straight up to the bedroom to hang up my purchases. Matthew's clothes and shoes took up three-quarters of the walk-in closet. I had one little corner for my things.

Why was I just noticing this now?

Despite the aches, I flew down to the kitchen and hummed as I opened a new box of garbage bags. I spent the next hour removing every trace of my recently departed from our bedroom. The smell of his cologne on his suits made me nauseous and touching his clothes reminded me of the hell Matthew had put me through, but the more bags I filled, the more my energy surged. Even though it was slow going, it was the most fun I'd had in years with my husband.

When I removed his shoe boxes from the corner of the closet, one felt extremely heavy. I gasped when I removed the lid expecting to see a pair of expensive shoes. A hand gun, a box of ammunition and a bill of sale, dated only a month ago, was in the bottom of the box. I knew nothing about guns, but the receipt listed the weapon as a nine mm Beretta semi-automatic. The gun had been purchased with cash, at the same time as the new insurance policy—Matthew had been ready. What a fool I had been.

It was kill or be killed all along.

After slugging all the tied bags down the hall with

one arm, I let them roll down the stairs to the front foyer. Then I called Sally Ann. They scheduled a pick up for the following morning at nine.

Next, I let Mr. Barton know I had chosen a suit and tie for Matthew and I would drop the clothes by the next day. I didn't give a shit what Matthew wore for his big exit, but a devastated wife would want her beloved to look his best.

The doorbell rang as I hung up the phone. I ushered the locksmith into the foyer and left him to it. He installed new locks on the front and side doors in less than an hour, presented me with the keys and an invoice and was gone.

Not long after, Apex security rang the bell at four o'clock sharp. A short husky dude in a navy uniform introduced himself as Vince Darnelli. His dark hair was cut short and his face was showing the hint of a five o'clock shadow. He wore the same expensive Armani cologne Matthew wore and I fought the stomach lurch.

In the living room we sat facing each other as he pulled brochures out of his briefcase and displayed them on the coffee table.

"I'll give you the info on three of our most popular systems, and then you can make a decision. How soon would you like the installation?" he asked.

"As soon as possible. I find myself a little nervous in this big old place now that my husband is gone."

"I understand. There have been a few break-ins in this area recently. Two weeks ago, I installed a system two blocks from here after the homeowners were robbed."

Vince explained what Apex had to offer clearly and expertly. The system could be installed as early as Monday. If Matthew had been here, he would have insisted on at least three prices before making a decision, but I didn't have the luxury of time on this. My instincts told me something was going on.

"Do you want to take a day or two make a decision?" Vince asked.

"No, I think I'll go ahead with the second system you showed me. It has all the features I'm looking for." I wrote a check for a deposit and signed the contract on the dotted line. "Thank you, Vince. You made this easy. I appreciate your patience."

"Nice meeting you, Mrs. Talbot. I'll be here Monday to supervise the install."

After Vince left, I changed my clothes, drove to the hospital and spent an hour with Marcy. She moaned a little now and then but never woke up. She was still sedated. Tears rolled down my face as I drove home.

WITH the rest of the evening stretching empty ahead of me, my mind was a whirl of worrisome thoughts. Tired of all things related to Matthew I decided to distract myself with finding out more about my mother and my past. From the file in Matthew's cabinet, it was obvious he had paid someone to do a search, and there was nothing in that file that I didn't already know. I had my mother's maiden name, Grace Brownell, and the hospital where I was born—Scarborough Centenary.

I'd come up with a place to start—find out where my mother went to high school and get a copy of the year book. At least I'd know what she looked like and maybe that would be enough. To do that, I'd start by visiting the libraries of the closest high schools around the hospital and see what I came up with. All of this thinking tired me out. I took my meds for my arm and crawled into bed.

CHAPTER NINE

SALLY ANN rang the bell at ten after nine. The driver thanked me for my donation and picked up all the bags from the front foyer. Good riddance to that load. Someone less fortunate would be thrilled to wear Matthew's expensive wardrobe.

I arrived a little early for my appointment at the lawyer's, but Brian was in his office waiting for me. He was an attractive man, six feet tall and slightly chunky around the middle. His dark hair was graying at the temples and he was sporting a neatly trimmed mustache. He stood up and shrugged into his suit jacket when I walked into the room.

"How are you holding up?" He offered me his hand and patted mine.

"I'm a little better today, thanks."

"Have a seat and we'll get started. Would you like a coffee?"

"No thanks, I had two cups at home."

"I didn't have to call anyone else for the reading of the will, because you are the only one named. It's completely straightforward."

"I see. I didn't even know Matthew had a will. He never mentioned it."

"Well my dear, everyone should have a will. Now that you have property and assets, you should think of making one as well."

"I should. I'll put that on my list."

Brian read the document to me confirming that I was the only person named and all Matthew's assets were coming to me: the house, his mother's antique furniture, any money in the bank, the cars, and the property in Maynooth.

"What property? And where is Maynooth?"

"It's a little village in Northern Ontario. The property isn't in the village. It's a fairly large acreage on the outskirts. I think Matthew mentioned a cabin, but I'm not sure on that point. Here's the deed. The survey is attached."

"Matthew never once talked about this property."

"Maybe it was just an investment and he never intended to use it."

"Maybe." I slid the deed into my purse.

Brian gave me some paperwork to take to the bank so that I could access the accounts and the safety deposit box, if there was one, while he finished up with the will. I'd bet changing the will was number three on Matthew's list, right after—buy insurance policy and get gun.

Too bad you didn't have time to do it.

"I'll let you know when everything has been finalized, but it's just a formality. No question."

"Thanks so much. I appreciate getting this out of the way. Will I see you at the funeral?"

"Of course." He nodded with a grimace.

On the way home, I stopped by the bank. The manager, Mr. Timberman, took a quick look at the paperwork Brian had given me and led me back to the vault. He assigned a teller to inventory the box upon opening. She removed the box from the wall and set it on a small table. I took a deep breath, almost afraid to look as she lifted the lid. There was a discontinued Canadian purple thousand dollar bill, a diamond tie pin, an emerald ring and fifty thousand in US funds.

With the inventory list completed, I was allowed a moment of privacy. I look at the items, closed up the box, took it back to the slot and replaced it. I turned my key and the waiting attendant finished the locking ritual. So much for that.

Before I left the bank, I opened two new accounts in my own name, one savings and one checking. They gave me a new bank card and I withdrew some cash for the market and incidentals. On the way out, I also picked up the card of an investment specialist.

At the market, I stocked up on staples. As always I started with the fresh fruit and vegetables, and then realized I could get whatever I wanted. Ten minutes later, my cart was loaded with ice cream, cookies and assorted other goodies forbidden by Matthew. Other shoppers gave me a wide berth in the aisle. Was it the silly grin on my face, or the fact that every now and then I'd start to giggle? At the checkout, I paid and requested a delivery. The delivery boy from the market would bring everything to the house and into the kitchen. My arm would be happy.

When I arrived at home, I was about to collapse into a nap on the sofa when the sound of footsteps on the porch made me cringe.

Please leave me alone.

Ding-dong.

The last thing I wanted to do was talk to anyone. I

peeked through the lace curtain on the sidelight and recognized my neighbor Susan from across the street.

"Hi," she said when I opened the door. "I saw the ambulance Wednesday evening, and I was wondering if everything was okay?"

"Not really." I paused and sighed. "Matthew had a heart attack and died."

"Oh, you poor thing," she made a grab to hug me, and I gasped, turning my broken arm away.

"I had an accident," I said, catching her staring at my sling.

"Is there anything I can do?"

"No, thank you though. The thing I need the most right now is rest but thank you for coming over." I closed the door and locked it, hoping she was not the first of many newly concerned neighbors that would come knocking. I needed a nap.

CHAPTER TEN

THE morning of Matthew's funeral, I allowed myself the luxury of sleeping late. It had been a fitful night, my shoulder protesting my busy schedule of the day before. No need to rush. Mr. Barton wasn't sending a car for me until one o'clock. I lingered in a lilac scented bubble bath until my fingers went pruny, dreading the day ahead. A snail's pace proved to be my top speed. After my bath, I shrugged on my thick terry robe and ventured downstairs. My stomach was doing flips and I didn't see the wisdom in eating. Coffee and pain pills were the only items on the breakfast menu.

For the next half hour, I labored at my antique dressing table, putting on makeup with my left hand, removing it with cold cream and beginning again. The gash over my eye was healing nicely. With cover-up and my large hat, it would be barely visible. Lots of blush and eye shadow, shakily applied, would be my saving grace. My biggest challenge, the past few days, was getting dressed. Easing my arm into the suit jacket was a slow and painful ritual. I could manage without the sling for a few hours—and opted to do so—the fewer questions, the better.

As I was slipping into my new stiletto heels the doorbell rang. Game time.

The mirror in the foyer reflected a favorable image as I donned my hat. The bereaved Mrs. Talbot looked appropriately saddened, yet still managed to look hot. Slumping my shoulders, I opened the front door and greeted Mr. Barton. He offered a number of well-intentioned comments, touched my elbow and escorted me to the limo. We rode the short distance to the funeral home in silence. Mr. Barton proved to be an expert in handling the recently widowed. No doubt he graduated top of his class at mortuary school.

When I entered the chapel where Matthew was resting, I was overwhelmed by the number of floral tributes surrounding the coffin. A large bouquet of lily of the valley placed near the head of the coffin unnerved me. I rubbed my clammy palms together and smoothed my jacket. The air was saturated with fragrance mixed with the faint smell of death. I gasped to catch my breath, faltered, missed my footing and Mr. Barton helped seat me in the nearest chair. I bowed my head forward and closed my eyes. I hadn't expected to feel anything but relief this afternoon, but. . . .

"Mrs. Talbot. Mrs. Talbot. Are you all right?"

The ringing in my ears confused me.

"Yes, I think so," I mumbled. "Where should I be sitting?"

"In the ante-room. It's for the family. Let me assist you."

Mr. Barton helped me up and gently escorted me to the small room to the right of the coffin. I was grateful the area contained a sofa. Standing was not an option.

Before the service began, Mr. Barton came to escort me to the casket. He wanted to parade me in front of Matthew for the final glimpse of my loved one before the lid was closed. Could I do it? I had to. I felt the eyes of Matthew's friends burning holes through me. My hands were shaking, and my legs were made of Jell-O. Bad call on the stilettos. Without Mr. Barton's arm around my waist for support, I would not have remained vertical.

My head was bowed under my large hat, but I stole a peek at Matthew for the last time. He looked like the man of three years ago, serene and contented. Death agreed with him.

A large number of Matthew's colleagues attended the funeral. Some brought their wives, and some came alone. They all offered condolences and expressed their shock at Matthew's untimely demise. I was unable to speak and hoped my silence translated into profound grief in everyone's eyes.

At the end of the service, Reverend Millbury announced Matthew would be cremated the following week. Everyone was invited to the upper level for refreshments and Mr. Barton whisked me upstairs in the elevator to receive the guests. "I'll get you a cup of tea, Mrs. Talbot."

"Thank you. I could use a cup." I lowered myself onto the sofa and shuddered as I saw Bob Winterstein lumbering towards me. "I heard you fainted, Portia, are you all right?"

"I should have eaten breakfast," I said pleasantly, "How is Marcy doing?"

"Better—an unfortunate accident," he mumbled.

"How did it happen, Bob?"

"I'm not sure." He pursed his lips and pretended to

be thinking hard of a good answer. "I had already left for work when she fell."

"Uh huh."

You lying piece of shit. You beat her and pushed her down the stairs before you went to work and we both know it.

With the festivities winding down, I sought out Mr. Barton downstairs.

"Will you need me here Monday for the cremation?" I asked.

"No, but you may attend if you wish."

"Thank you. No. Will you give me a call when the ashes are ready?"

"Yes. I'll call you. Would you like any of the flowers?"

"No, just the cards in order to write the thank you notes. Could you send the flower arrangements to Shady Pines Retirement Home?"

"Of course. The residents will enjoy them. The car is out front, Mrs. Talbot, if you're ready."

The day had been emotional and more stressful than I had anticipated. I went directly upstairs and changed into my sweats. My arm throbbed and my head was swimming, signaling that my pain medication was long overdue. Sitting on the edge of my bed, I opened the bottle, took two with a swig of water and crawled under the duvet.

I woke suddenly—my throat raw from the screaming, my entire body trembling and drenched in sweat. It took me a few moments to realize it was a dream. A gaunt face with sunken eyes had been staring in the bedroom window from the blackness outside. I couldn't shake the feeling that it had really happened. I switched on the lamp beside the bed and edged over to the window. Nothing out there but the wind. Branches of a maple tree brushed against the glass.

I closed the drapes, went into the bathroom and locked the door. My face was flushed. Perspiration dripped down my neck. I slipped off my sweats and threw them on top of the overflowing hamper, silently vowing to do laundry the following day. I cranked on the hot water and stepped into the shower. After toweling off, I caught an unwelcome glimpse of my body in the mirror. Shit, I'd lost more weight. The scale was staring up at me with those big zeroes for eyes. Note to self, remember to eat properly.

CHAPTER ELEVEN

I pulled my robe tighter around me as I descended to the kitchen to forage for food. The wall clock said five thirty. I peered out the window into the darkness squinting to see if anything or anyone was moving. Apex couldn't get here fast enough with the security team. I jumped when my toast popped up and let out a squeal. All I could do was laugh at myself. Ridiculous.

By the time I finished my juice and toast, the Globe and Mail hit the front porch. As I stooped to retrieve the paper I caught a glimpse of a black truck pulling away from the curb. I watched it drive slowly down the street and disappear. Odd. It was early for one of the neighbors to be going to work. Back in the kitchen I distracted myself with the newspaper.

At nine sharp, Apex Security arrived to begin the installation. I put on a fresh pot of coffee and hung around in case they needed anything. I tackled the laundry and cleaned the bathrooms. Being busy with everyday tasks was comforting.

At three-thirty, Vince came into the kitchen with his clipboard in hand. His dark blue uniform was snug on his stocky, muscled frame and I battled to keep my eyes on his face rather than drifting lower. The Armani cologne that I detested on Matthew affected me differently wafting from Vince's neck. Inhaling the scent of him, I sensed warmth in neglected areas and reluctantly returned to reality.

"The system has been installed, Mrs. Talbot. I'd like to give you a crash course on how to activate and disarm."

I nodded. "Let's do it."

Vince showed me the operating basics and it seemed simple and straightforward. I did a couple of practice runs under his watchful eye. The sympathetic dark brown eyes.

"If there is an intruder, the alarm itself may be enough to scare them off. But as well, the call will alert headquarters and response time will be minimal. Some lights around the property have been set to come on automatically at dusk and others are motion sensitive. I think we have all the bases covered. Here's a fridge magnet with my number on it, Mrs. Talbot. Call me anytime, day or night."

"Thanks again." I shook his hand.

The men loaded the rest of their gear in the truck, the system was activated, and I was safe.

Remembering my intention to eat properly, I went into the kitchen and made a corned beef sandwich on fresh rye bread. A couple of pickles completed my feast. Maybe later I'd spoil myself with a dish of ice cream.

My plan for the remainder of the day included only two things: reading and resting my arm. I had replaced the sling and taken the meds, but the pain only subsided completely when my arm was immobilized. At this rate, healing would take another month.

Carrying my coffee into the living room, I searched for the novel I had been meaning to finish. As I bent to retrieve it from the coffee table, the doorbell rang and I jumped. The hot liquid in my mug sloshed over the brim and onto my hand.

Ow. Shit. Get a grip.

I peeked through the curtain at the side of the door, and Bob Winterstein was standing on the porch staring back at me. He gave me a little wave.

What the hell does he want?

I deactivated the alarm and opened the door halfway. "Hi, Bob. What brings you to this end of town?"

"Just checking on you, Portia. Marcy would want me to check up on you and be sure you were okay." His bloodshot eyes were riveted on my chest.

I know you're lying, Bobbie boy. What are you really after?

"I'm doing fine, Bob. Thanks for your concern."

"What happened to your arm? You weren't wearing a sling at the funeral."

"No, I didn't wear it to the service. It didn't go with my outfit."

Bob's lip curled up into a cruel half smile.

"I was just going upstairs to rest when I heard the bell." I hoped he would get the message.

"I won't keep you then. I'm off to the hospital to sit with Marcy."

As Bob pulled out of the driveway, I scored a clear look at the black truck he climbed into. It was definitely the same make that had been outside earlier. *Bingo.*

I closed the door, locked it and reactivated the alarm. Bob was creeping me out.

My sleepiness had vanished, replaced by the nagging

feeling that I was missing something vital. My nap could wait. Maybe the answer I needed was in the study and I'd overlooked it. Still sitting on the desk was Matthew's laptop. Worth a look. I pressed the 'on' button. Anything with a password was safe from my prying eyes. Matthew had never shared his computer with me, and I was a novice. I clicked on email and it opened right up. Wow. Two hundred unopened. After reading the first two, my chest was tightening again. Matthew had a life I knew nothing about and it didn't make me feel better to read about his womanizing in print. Even in death he was able to hurt me. I shut down the computer and closed the lid. If there was a clue in there, I didn't know how to find it.

Might as well clean out his desk. I opened the big drawer in the bottom that was filled with the stock quotes and started stuffing them into the shredder. I don't know why he kept all the old prices anyway. When I reached the bottom of the drawer, there was nothing left but one piece of paper caught at the back. As I tugged on it, I noticed there was a tiny latch almost completely hidden in the back seam of the drawer. With the end of a pen, I undid the hook and a false back loosened.

Down on my hands and knees, with my good arm, I removed the thin piece of wood and set it aside. The hidden space was quite large behind the drawer. Dozens of bundles of papers bound with elastic bands sat neatly waiting. I lifted the top one out and pulled off the elastic. I had no idea what they were—certificates of some sort—something about gold. I found a couple of large

Ziploc bags in the kitchen, packaged the bundles and stuffed them into my purse to take to the bank.

CHAPTER TWELVE

MR. BARTON called as I poured my second cup of coffee. Matthew's ashes were ready to be picked up. I showered, pulled on a pair of jeans and eased my arm into a bulky red sweater with a front zipper, thankful that my morning pain meds were working.

When I got to the funeral home, Mr. Barton was in his office shuffling through papers awaiting my arrival.

"I hope everything was to your satisfaction, Mrs. Talbot."

"Yes, you attended to every detail. Thank you so much." Matthew was residing in his tasteful urn on Mr. Barton's desk beside the bill for the funeral. One neat package.

"This is the urn you chose, is it not?"

"Yes, I believe it is." I had no recollection of what I'd pointed to. I picked up the invoice, pulled my check book out of my purse and filled in the amount.

Mr. Barton accepted the money with a sympathetic smile on his face. "Thank you, Mrs. Talbot. It was a pleasure to serve you."

I picked up Matthew, all that was left of him, and was a little surprised by the weight of the urn. After carrying him out to my Jeep and placing the container on the passenger seat, I headed home with only one stop. I popped by the bank, accessed the safety deposit box and added the two bags of certificates. They would have be investigated later in the week.

I parked the car in the garage, popped the tailgate and moved the urn from the passenger seat to the back forty. "Wait here, Matthew. I'll take you for a ride shortly."

THE weather was warm for the first day of May. April showers had given it up to sunshine and blossom scented breezes—perfect for a drive in the country. The deed Brian had given me for the northern property gave away no clue how to get there. Growing up in foster homes in the city limited my knowledge of Ontario to Toronto and its suburbs only. There weren't many picnics in the country in my childhood. If I found the town of Maynooth, I would have to go the local municipal office and ask for more detailed directions. I changed into a pair of boots, took a warm jacket from the closet and trudged out to the garage.

"We're leaving now, Matthew. Hold tight," I called over my shoulder.

At the corner Esso, I filled the tank, picked up a road map, a bottle of water, a Coke and a couple of chocolate bars. Who knew how long I'd be gone? Maybe I'd be lost for days. I unfolded the map, found the most direct route to Maynooth and headed east on the 401.

Three hours later, I parked in front of the Town office. The tiny brick building attached to the post office was staffed by a short gray haired lady in her sixties or seventies, wearing a blue flowered cotton dress. She greeted me at the counter with a welcoming smile. "Hello, dear, may I help you?"

"I hope you can. My husband bought this property

before he died, and I would like to take a look at it, but I need directions." I showed her the survey attached to the deed.

"You passed the side road a way back, honey. You turn around and go back the way you jus' come. Second side road down, take a right. Third property on that road on the left hand side. Used to belong to an old hermit named Mike King. Might still be a mailbox at the road says King. He died a while back. Was out by the barn choppin' wood and keeled over dead. Still had a tight grip on the axe a week later when the mailman found him. Heck of a mess then. That's probably when you folks bought it."

"Could be. I'm not sure. Thanks for your help." I smiled.

"Any time hon, just doin' my job." She waved as I left the building.

I scribbled down the directions on the side of the map when I got back to the Jeep. Retracing my path, I turned on the second side road and drove slowly until I saw a dented mailbox hanging half off a rotten post. Dried grass and sticks hung out the end indicating a new family had taken up residence. Squinting, I thought the faded lettering could have said 'King', but with that much rust obliterating the writing, it could have said almost anything.

I turned the wheel with some difficulty and started up the overgrown path that might have served as a driveway at one time. When I reached the top of the grade my eyes widened. There, in the middle of a clearing, sat an adorable log cabin with a red roof.

I parked the Jeep and stepped out for a look around. There was a porch across the entire front, furnished with a couple of old church pews. A milk can stood in the corner holding a bird house. I walked up the steps and turned the knob, but found it locked.

Around the back was another lower porch with garden doors coming out from the kitchen. A big butcher's block sat off to one side covered with a scrap of red and white checked oilcloth. There were several outbuildings, a barn with a loft, a board and batten garage, a chicken coop and a green outhouse with a heart cut-out in the door.

I could live here.

Behind the cabin, the woods were dense. A narrow opening through the pine trees revealed a footpath sloping downward. I inched along for several hundred feet before I realized that the path was leading me down to water. Upon reaching the shoreline, I was dazzled by the bright sun dancing on a huge lake. I shielded my eyes with my hand to take in the breathtaking panorama.

The opposite shore was dotted with cottages, boat houses and bunkies. Fishermen in bass boats sat silently in the shady spots trying their luck. A speed boat towing a water skier zoomed by, raising a formidable rooster tail. Boards were missing here and there from the weathered boathouse, and the dock was rotted through in places. Careful where I stepped, I edged out to the end and sucked in a big breath of crisp northern air. It was difficult to comprehend that this was my property. I owned a piece of paradise.

After plodding back up the hill to the cabin, I was

breathless. A big rock provided a temporary resting spot as I drank in the beauty surrounding me. The pungent aroma of the evergreens permeated the air as they stood like sentinels around the cabin. Blue Jays squawked warnings high above in towering birches. A Pileated woodpecker hammered at insects on a nearby maple. Chipmunks chattered brazenly as they scurried in and out of the woodpile. Hounds bayed soulfully in the distance. Nature's abundance had a dizzying effect on me.

I went back to the Jeep and retrieved the urn. "Come on, Matthew. It's time."

Down at the end of the dock, I removed the lid of the urn, took out the sealed inner container and sprinkled the ashes onto the sparkling water. Some ashes floated happily along with the movement of the waves, and others sank beneath the surface and disappeared. There was a huge rock on the shore that I returned to and smashed the urn against it. I picked up every broken piece and threw the shards one by one into the lake.

"So long, Matthew," I called farewell to him as he went to his final resting place.

I trudged back up the path, took a last look around, and reluctantly started for home.

ON the way back, I stopped for gas and ventured into a roadside diner for supper. I paid for my pulled pork sandwich at the cash, ordered a large coffee to go and left a generous tip.

As I turned the Wrangler down Hawthorne Lane, my new security lights blinked a friendly greeting. The living room lamp, set on a timer, glowed through the front window giving the house a cozy, occupied look. I was comforted.

CHAPTER THIRTEEN

AN alarm was ringing in my dream. I awoke and my first thought was disbelief. I wasn't dreaming.

It was ringing. Oh my, God.

I jumped up, grabbed my robe off the end of the bed and ran downstairs to the panel. I felt like an idiot staring at the numbers trying to focus, but I wasn't fully awake and couldn't think what Vince had told me to do. I was standing there in the foyer shaking, when the response team thumped onto the porch. I caught a glimpse of Vince through the curtain and opened the door. I exhaled.

"My men are checking the perimeter. Are you okay?"

"I'm fine. Just a little shaky. I don't know what happened."

"Sometimes, an animal, like a racoon, can trigger the alarm accidently. It happens."

One of the men called from outside, "We're all secure out here."

"Thanks, Pete. The panel says the breach was one of the office windows. See what you can find in there and outside. Check every room in the house and the basement as well."

"Will do, boss."

The men completed their search and assured me that no one had entered the house.

"A couple scratches outside on the frame of the office window."

My stomach flipped. "There was someone out there?" I whispered.

"Probably just a squirrel," Vince said in an effort to ease the tension. "They're capable of substantial damage. Little buggers. I'm resetting the alarm now, Mrs. Talbot. Why don't you go back to bed?"

"I doubt if I'll be able to sleep." I could still feel the tingling in the back of my neck.

"In any case, lock the door behind me," Vince said as he left.

I poured a glass of milk and took it upstairs. My hands were shaking, and my stomach was queasy.

Was Bob trying to get in? He didn't know about the alarm system. Now he does. Maybe I should get a dog. What about the gun? I need to be ready.

My thoughts were jumbled. I needed to think clearly and make a plan. I lifted the gun out of the shoe box and started at the cold steel against my fingers. The weight of it was another surprise—heavier than it looked. I opened the ammunition box and snorted. What a joke. I didn't even know how to load it. First thing tomorrow I'd rectify that. I pulled the duvet over my head and slept fitfully.

AT seven a.m. I made a pot of coffee and searched the Yellow Pages for gun experts, while I ate a bowl of cereal. I wrote down the address of the closest one, wrapped the gun in a tea towel and placed it in the bottom of my purse. Because the ammunition box was heavy, I opted to leave it in the glove box of the Jeep.

I arrived at 'George's Guns and Ammo' at nine

thirty, just as the owner was unlocking the store. He opened the door, flicked the rest of his half smoked cigarette onto the sidewalk and ushered me in with a wave of his huge tattooed arm.

George was an impressive sight first thing in the morning. About six foot three or four and nudging three hundred pounds, attired in a Harley tank top under a fringed leather vest. His jeans rode low under his beer belly revealing only a fraction of his huge belt buckle engraved, no doubt, with words of wisdom. Both massive, muscled arms were covered in ink from shoulder to wrist, one with an eagle holding a rebel flag. His handsome face was tanned and weathered, highlighted by a nasty triangle shaped scar on his left cheek. A red bandana tied around his forehead kept his long shiny black hair out of his black eyes.

The gun shop was small. One display window facing the street contained a few dusty scopes, gun cases and several holsters. The tile floor was filthy—perhaps swept, but never washed. The counter was L-shaped, with the wall behind the cash stacked with ammunition boxes in bright colors, row on row. The adjoining wall held locked glass display cabinets holding many different makes of rifles and shotguns. The handguns and knives were displayed under the countertop glass. A rack in the corner was filled with holsters. The air reeked of smoke.

Here goes nothing.

CHAPTER FOURTEEN

GEORGE ROSS didn't get struck stupid often, but this little lady was like nothin' he'd ever set his eyes on before. With a body men would kill for, raven black hair and steel gray eyes that seemed a lot older than they should for her being in her twenties and all. She was a fucking knock-out.

"Now then, young lady, what can I do for you?"

And what are you doin' in my fuckin' store?

"I know this is going to sound stupid," she hesitated and bit at her lip, "but I don't know how to load my gun. Truthfully, I don't know how to shoot it either. Do you think you could help me?"

George laughed hard, his hand resting on his belly. "Fuck, that's a good one—haven't heard that before."

She chuckled along with him and dug a tea towel out of her purse. She had the sweetest flush of color in her cheeks. After unwrapping her gun, she set it on the glass counter.

"Ah, Beretta, nice. Why did you buy it if you didn't know how to use it, little girl?" When she looked down at the counter her hair fell forward and hid her face from view. He leaned closer.

God, she smells good, too. What the fuck is wrong with you, man?

"Fair question." She laughed but seemed to tense up. "My husband recently died and I found it tucked away in a shoebox in his closet."

George lit up another smoke and blew the smoke away from them. "All right, then, let me show you." He took a box of ammunition from a shelf behind him and opened it. "This gun holds fifteen rounds."

She watched as he removed the magazine and pushed a bullet down into the top opening. "Your turn." He handed her the magazine and pushed the open box her way. "Load 'er up." He held the gun for her while she used her left hand and pushed a bullet down into the magazine like he'd done, then another until all fifteen were loaded.

She blew out a feminine sigh. "Okay, got that down."

George took his time and explained how to use the safety. "When you can see the red dot, the safety is off. Remember that." He demonstrated sliding the magazine back into position. He made her try it and listen for the click, so she knew it was locked in properly. Lastly, he showed her how to use the slide to put a round in the chamber.

"Now the gun is loaded. All you have to do is flip the safety off, aim and fire."

"That's where it gets sticky," she said, "I've never fired a gun. And there's a bigger problem, my right arm is broken."

"What the—why do you want a gun then?" George started laughing again and his ashes dropped all over the counter. "How did you break your arm?"

A look crossed her beautiful face and he caught a flicker in her cool gray eyes. "My late husband broke it for me."

George frowned and shook his head. "Sounds like the

bastard deserved to die."

"So true," she nodded, and carried on without hesitation. "Getting back to my main focus, I think someone is trying to break into my house and I'm scared. I want to be able to defend myself." She paused and blew out a breath. "I must seem pathetic to you."

"Maybe a little, honey bun, but we could fix that. Me and the boys have a range outside of town and I could teach you to shoot. Not as good as me. Hell, nobody's that good. But I could teach you how to shoot a fuckin' burglar."

What the fuck am I sayin? I never take anybody up there— and sure as hell not a woman.

"That's what I'm after. How much an hour do you charge for lessons?"

He barked out another laugh. "You're gonna make me piss myself, sweet cheeks. What's your name anyway?"

"Portia Talbot."

"Fancy name for a fancy girl. I ain't give any lessons before, but if it will help you, I can take you out to the range, set you up and you can fire away until you get the hang of it. I'll sit there and watch you and have a few with the boys."

"Count me in." Her smile lit up her face, even her eyes. "When can we go?"

"I can only go on Sundays when the store is closed. Want to go for a couple hours Sunday?"

My God man, you have lost your fucking mind?

"Sure. Can I pick you up?"

He chuckled at the idea. "Nope. No strangers allowed

out that road. I'll have to pick you up. What's the address?"

Portia wrote her address and phone number on a cigarette pack that George handed her. "I'll buy this box of ammunition and take it for practice."

"You can buy that one, but I'll bring a practice box for the range."

"I didn't know there was practice ammunition."

"I'm thinkin' there's a helluva lot you don't know, little Portia." George laughed and lit up another smoke.

She paid George, wrapped up the Beretta and ammo and stuffed the tea towel in her purse.

"You should be tapping into a shoulder harness, girlie. That towel bit can get old quick. 'Specially if you're in a hurry to off somebody." George chuckled.

"Next time. See you Sunday. I really appreciate your time."

"You talk funny and you make me laugh," he said. "I like you, little girl."

I haven't laughed so much or said that many words to a woman in my whole life. Fuck.

CHAPTER FIFTEEN

MY route home from the gun shop took me past the dog pound. I passed the driveway for the parking area, stopped, backed up and pulled in on a whim. The barking was deafening inside the front door. The uniformed girl standing behind the counter was moving her mouth, but I couldn't hear a word she was saying.

"Pardon? Sorry, I didn't catch what you said," I yelled to be heard above the din.

The name embroidered on her blue shirt said 'Vicky'. She didn't look happy in her chosen field of employment. She repeated, "Do you want a dog or a cat?"

"A dog. But I'm not sure what kind. I'd just like to see what you have and think about it."

"Sure. Come on back." She waved me forward and shuffled off without checking to see if I was following. Through the glass paneled door we went, into a back room filled with rows of cages. The pungent aroma of animals living in cramped quarters encouraged me to hold my breath. First we passed the cages housing the cats and kittens. They were so adorable, reaching their little paws through the wire for attention and meowing in unison.

"We have a lot of Pit Bulls. People aren't supposed to be able to buy them but still do. Then when they don't raise them properly, before you know it, they've bought themselves a load of trouble and they bring them here.

It's illegal for us to put them up for adoption."

"That's a shame." I felt bad for them, all caged up with no hope.

When we got to the larger cages, almost all the dogs jumped up against the chain link doors, barking for attention, except for one down at the end. The big Rottweiler just lay in her pen with her head on her paws.

"How about that one?" I asked.

"Oh, you don't want that one. A Rottie named Angel, what a joke. She growls at us every day and she's anti-social. We're putting her down tomorrow."

My stomach flipped as I looked into those sad chocolate eyes. "Can you let her out of the cage so I can touch her?"

"She doesn't like being touched, but they're your fingers."

I walked right up to her cage and squatted next to the door. After a few minutes of talking to Angel, the dog tentatively stood up and sauntered over to me. She was a big, boxy girl, but I didn't agree that she was anti-social. When her wide, black-and-tan muzzle brushed against the chain of her cage I stuck a couple of fingers through the wire. She licked me and that did it.

"I'll take my chances with her," I said.

Vicky raised a brow and shrugged. "Not a good idea. But if you want her, take her for a week trial. Do you have small children, or other pets?"

"No, I'm alone."

She unlatched the cage and slipped a rope through the dog's collar. "The collar is hers, but you'll have to get your own leash."

"That's fine. I can do that."

Out at the front counter, she wrote up a bill for the dog plus the shots she'd been given. I paid her in cash.

"Thanks, Vicky. Come on, Angel." She was hesitant, but I gave a gentle tug on her leash and she trudged along behind me.

Angel took up shotgun position in the passenger seat of the Jeep, looking out the window. I lowered her window six inches and she tried to shove her head through. I kept lowering it until she could comfortably hang her head all the way out. She put her black nose in the air and sniffed the breeze while her ears flapped, and drool dribbled along the outside of the window.

We stopped off at the market and picked up kibbles for large dogs, biscuits and treats. I also bought her a red leash, a ball and a set of stainless steel bowls.

When I got home, I realized I hadn't bought her a doggie bed. She'd have to sleep on a blanket in my room for now. I disabled the alarm, unwrapped her bowls and filled them with food and water. Then I showed Angel the patio door and left it open while she ran in and out of the yard with her ball in her mouth. Her spirits seemed to have lifted considerably and she hadn't growled at me once. I had a feeling she wasn't anti-social . . . she was anti-dog-pound. I frowned, thinking about her being put down.

When the laundry was folded, I made myself a late lunch and spent the rest of the afternoon gardening in the yard with Angel. When we came in, she munched her kibbles, slurped her water all over the kitchen floor and then went exploring through the house. With her rounds done, she flopped down and took a nap.

While Angel seemed content, I slipped out to the Scarborough Board of Education Office and obtained a list of high schools that were open the year I was born. Next, I picked up a city map and came home to plot my strategy.

Spreading out the map on the dining room table, I marked the high schools by address, and listed them in order of their proximity to the hospital. This could prove to be a wild goose chase, but there might be a chance I would find something.

I started with a phone campaign. Each school secretary that I spoke to, I asked if a Grace Brownell had attended their school in 1985 or 1986. They all said they were busy, but they would look when they had time and get back to me. I'd waited twenty-five years; I could wait a little longer.

At bedtime, I double checked to make sure the alarm was engaged, locked all the doors and went upstairs with the dog at my heels. I spread a folded blanket on the carpet beside my bed and Angel claimed it as her own. My sleep was uninterrupted, and I awoke refreshed.

CHAPTER SIXTEEN

WITH Angel in the yard, I pressed the button on the coffee maker, bolted up the stairs and took a quick shower. I dressed in jeans, a T-shirt, boots and a ball cap. I didn't want my hair in my face while I was shooting.

While I waited for George, I took my mug and a plate of toast and jam out to the patio table and shared with the dog. I was raising my cup to my lips when Angel flashed by me knocking my elbow and spilling coffee all over the table. She charged to the front door and raised a huge ruckus, barking at the tremendous racket out in the driveway. I looked through the sidelight and caught sight of George huffing his way up the porch steps, his Harley idling like a roaring beast out front.

Oh shit, he's picking me up on a motorcycle.

I opened the door with my boot while I hung on to Angel. No mean feat when you have a broken arm. George could see I was struggling and took her by the collar.

"Nice girl," he said, patting her on the head. "What's her name?"

"Angel. I just got her at the pound. Come on in, George. I'll just be a sec." I picked up my purse with my gun and supplies inside, grabbed my jacket, enabled the alarm and said, "Let's go." I made a mental note to clean up the spilled coffee when I got back.

George shoved my purse and ball cap into his saddle bag, gave me a helmet to wear and we were off. I hung on for dear life, but the ride was exhilarating. I loved it. We headed north out of the city, turned onto highway twelve for about half an hour, then took dirt roads until we reached our destination. If this turned out to be a kidnapping, no one would ever find me.

We stopped in the middle of nowhere in front of a rusty old gate hanging by one hinge. George got off the bike, lifted the gate up with two fingers and opened it far enough to squeeze the bike through. Then he got off again and closed it. We roared up the tree-lined cow path to the top of the hill and George parked in a line of other bikes all looking like showroom models.

"C'mon, girlie, let's do some damage." He grinned.

I took off my helmet and jacket, shoved my hair under my ball cap and retrieved my gun and ammunition, leaving my purse in the saddlebag.

"Ready," I said, following George past the shack where the other bikers were hanging out. Some were sitting at picnic tables drinking and others were cleaning their guns. There were a couple of girls in the bunch with nice tattoos sunning themselves.

"Hey, George, where'd you get that?"

"Shut the fuck up, Chopper. This is my sister."

"Where you bin hiding your 'sister', Georgie?"

"I'll blow your nuts off, wiseass."

The whistling and catcalls kept up until we reached the range. I was amused to see that George was a little red-faced. If I'd been alone in this kind of a crowd, I would have been nervous, but with big George at my side, I felt safe.

I unloaded the Beretta and reloaded the practice

ammo under George's scrutiny. He shoved mufflers over my ball cap and showed me where to stand.

"Empty the mag at the target. Then we'll see what you need to adjust."

"I'm shooting with my left arm."

"Suck it up, baby girl. Be the best you can be with what you got. Lots of shooters are equally good with both hands."

"I didn't know that," I said. Truth was, I knew very little about shooters of any kind.

George made me empty the magazine, check the target, reload, adjust my aim and start all over again. After two hours of this routine, my arm shook.

"George, my arm is about to fall off. Can we call it quits for today?"

"Had enough have you? I didn't 'spect you to last this long. Your broke arm must be hurting like hell."

"It is, but I brought pain killers with me. I just need some water."

"No water here, but we'll have a couple brews with the boys, and you can down 'em."

Pain killers and beer. Great combo.

We walked back to the half dozen picnic tables by the shack and I sat down. George got three cold beers out of a cooler and put one in front of me. Then he went into the shack and got gun oil and rags. He plunked his bulk down at the other side of the table, chugged two beers and lit up a smoke. Most of the bikers had gone, but a few were left drinking and yelling insults at each other.

"Nice tattoo," I said to one of the girls in passing. She was wearing next to nothing. Cut off low-rise shorts

and a t-shirt hacked off just below her breasts. A
tarantula was tattooed on her stomach made to look like
it was crawling out of her navel. Interesting.

"Thanks," she mumbled. Conversation was not her
strong point.

I washed my pain meds down with a couple swigs.
Matthew told me that ladies always drank wine. But
tasting that cold beer on a hot day was heavenly.

Fuck, Matthew.

"Now, watch while I clean your gun. You're on your
own after this." George took apart the Beretta, cleaned it
and slowly reassembled it.

I paid close attention, because I knew he wasn't
going to be a happy camper if he had to show me a
second time. "I got it. Thanks, George."

"No sweat, sweet cheeks. Let's split."

The Harley started up with ear splitting efficiency
and we were off. Enamored by the noise, the wind in my
face and the smell of grease and leather, the truth had
been revealed by the time I got home. I was in love with
bikes.

"Thanks for today, George. Want to come in for a
coffee?"

"No thanks. Got stuff to take care of."

He roared explosively out the driveway and up the
street. I could still hear his Harley in the distance when
he hit the highway.

Angel wagged her whole back end as I came in the
front door. I gave her a big hug before putting her in the
backyard, cleaning up the spilled coffee and starting a
new pot. With a new sense of accomplishment, I sat at

the kitchen table and reloaded the Beretta. With only one day of instruction, I was certainly no expert, but the basics were in place.

After taking a quick shower to wash off the acrid smell of gunpowder, I donned my sweats and joined Angel in the yard. At the patio table, I opened the envelope of condolence cards Mr. Barton had given me and wrote the thank you notes for the floral tributes and the donations to Heart and Stroke. My right arm pained while I wrote, and my handwriting was barely legible, but the job was done. Tomorrow, I would drop the bundle in the mail.

Angel and I enjoyed steaks grilled on the barbecue for dinner, and then lounged like couch potatoes in the living room for the rest of the evening. She was my shadow.

CHAPTER EIGHTEEN

I rummaged in my purse and found the card of the investment officer at the bank. After making an appointment for three o'clock, I cleared up the coffee things, snapped on Angel's leash and took her for a walk in the park. A jogging path wound its way along by the river, shaded by mature maples. November was the last time I had run, but I gave it my best shot with Angel easily keeping pace beside me. Breathless, I plopped down on a bench. I was out of shape, but physical activity helped clear my head and took the edge off my nerves. The sun was directly overhead and gleeful cicadas heralded the rising temperature.

Angel and I trudged the three blocks home drenched in sweat.

A cool shower was first on my list, while draining her water bowl was first for Angel. I dressed for my bank appointment in white cotton pants, a red tank top with a white cotton over shirt. I slipped my bare feet into sandals and brushed my hair up into a pony-tail. Much cooler. After a spinach salad and a glass of cranberry juice, I read a couple of chapters of my J.L. Madore novel on my favorite bench outside in the garden.

My appointment at the bank was with a Mr. Donaldson in investments. I was shown into his office at three fifteen. Not impressed.

"Good afternoon, Mrs. Talbot. I'm Simon Donaldson. What can I do for you?"

Mr. Donaldson was six feet tall with dark curly hair and hazel eyes. His face was tanned and slightly weathered but highlighted by a genuine smile. He reminded me of the Marlboro Man with whiter teeth. His red polka dot tie hung loosely, and his gray suit pants were in need of a press.

"Well, I don't know if you can help me at all really. My husband left me some of these certificates in his will, and I was wondering if you could tell me what they are, or what I should do with them." I pulled out one of the pieces of paper that I had found hidden in the drawer of desk in the study. I smoothed out the curl of the paper and passed it over the desk to him.

"How many of these did you say you had?" He raised his eyebrows and his mouth hung slightly open for a moment.

"I didn't say."

"This indicates that your husband had purchased gold when it was at a low, many years ago. The actual gold itself would be held in a vault," he said, "How old was your husband?"

"Thirty-eight."

"These particular certificates are dated before he was born. He must have inherited them or come by them in some other fashion."

"I'm sorry, I have no clue on how he came to have them," I said, "but can they be sold?"

"Definitely, and for a huge profit in today's market."

"Each one being worth how much?"

"Well, the market goes up and down almost daily. Let me see what this one would sell for today." He punched numbers into his computer for a few minutes, while I enjoyed the bank's air conditioning. "The price per ounce this morning was sixteen hundred and forty-five dollars and eighty cents. These were purchased in 1971 for thirty-five dollars an ounce. Today the profit per ounce would be over sixteen hundred dollars. Since this certificate is for a hundred ounces... well you can do the math."

Yes, I can.

"If you need to cash any, I can execute the transactions for you."

My hands were trembling. "Thank you for the information, Mr. Donaldson. You have been more than helpful." I smiled and extended my hand. Perhaps we can do business in the near future."

"I'll look forward to it, Mrs. Talbot. Have a nice day."

I had one of the tellers, show me to my deposit box, where I put the certificate back into one of the bundles. On quick count, ten bundles with forty or more in each. Over sixty million.

Does Bob know about this stash? I don't think so. Maybe Matthew's father hid them in that drawer, and Matthew didn't even know. Matthew was so paranoid, he would never have left them in a drawer. Never. He couldn't have known.

I replaced the bundles, closed the lid, and waited for the teller to lock up after me.

On the way home, I stopped at the beer store for the first time in my life and picked up a dozen cold ones.

Angel greeted me at the door, wagging her back end

like she hadn't seen me in days. Out on the patio, I watched while she rolled on the grass in the shade.

Now that the gold certificates were in the bank, they were safe from Bob, but if he didn't know about them what was it that he wanted?

What game were Bob and Matthew playing?

If it was something that Bob knew was in the house, he might keep trying. Prickles raced up the back of my neck like tiny needles and my stomach flipped. I downed another beer, then made some dinner.

Before I retired for the night, I let Angel out for a short run in the yard, brought her in, wiped her paws and went upstairs. With the loaded Beretta under my pillow and the dog on her blanket beside the bed I felt safer than I had during the past week.

A low growl startled me awake. Angel growled again, long and low. I listened. That familiar creak on the fifth step from the bottom. I stifled a scream as I remembered the gun. I groped under the pillow and laced my fingers around the cold metal of the barrel. Cold clamminess enveloped my body as I fought to keep my dinner down. The safety gave me trouble in the darkness. I moved it, but I couldn't see the red dot. I only had to guess that it was off. Footsteps on the staircase drew closer, paralyzing me. The intruder stepped into the bedroom doorway, his silhouette backlit by the hall window. A hooded figure. Metal glinted in the moonlight. Angel lunged. I fired.

"Ughh.......get your fucking dog off me................son of a bitch......"

Thud.

I switched on the bedside lamp and jumped up. Angel was snarling and tearing wildly at the intruder's leg. I dialed 911, shouted the address and threw the phone down. The man was writhing, cursing and trying to beat Angel off. Blood spurted all over the carpet. While I trained my Beretta on his head, I kicked his fallen gun under the bed. His black hoody was pulled up so I couldn't see his face, but the arm of his cotton jacket was soaked through with blood.

"Don't move or I'll shoot you," I hollered.

"Fuck you. Get this mutt off me," he bellowed.

Angel emitted a low growl while she maintained her hold on his neck, pinning him down.

Sirens screamed down my street and I breathed a sigh of relief but held my aim on the man's head. It sounded like an army arriving in the foyer. Officers rushed up the stairs and burst through the bedroom door.

"Are you all right, ma'am?" A female officer approached, motioning for me to lower my gun while her partner advanced on the intruder. After asking me a few questions, the handcuffs came out and the female officer took my gun and placed it in a Ziploc bag.

"You're under arrest," said the male officer, and informed the intruder of his rights.

Angel relinquished her hold on command and lay on her blanket beside me.

"Good girl," I whispered. "You saved my life."

Angel wagged.

"She probably did," said the female officer. "Did he have a weapon?"

"A gun. He dropped it when Angel bit his leg, and I kicked it under the bed."

"Good thinking. Sounds like you kept your head through all this. You just sit there and rest now, I can tell by your color and your pupils that you're ready to faint."

The female officer crawled under the bed and retrieved the perp's gun. She placed it in a plastic bag and wrote something on the tag as the paramedics thundered up the stairs with a gurney. They knelt down and rolled the intruder onto his back and cut off the sleeve of his jacket.

The female officer pulled the man's hood back from his face so I could get a look at him. "Do you know this man?" she asked me, stepping out of the way of the paramedic team.

"No, I'm sorry. I've never seen him before," I said.

"He's lost a lot of blood. Dog bite on thigh. Gunshot wound, left arm. Start an IV and transport," said one of the paramedics. They bandaged his wounds and strapped him to the gurney while I looked on in a daze.

"He's under arrest, so one of the men downstairs will go with you to the hospital." The male officer in the bedroom said to the paramedics.

They nodded as they wheeled the gurney out the door.

After the intruder had been removed, I inadvertently glanced at the maroon stain at the doorway of the bedroom where his blood had oozed into the carpet. I excused myself and took the opportunity to throw up in the bathroom. When I returned to the bedroom, the female officer made introductions.

"I'm Officer Jane Lombard and that's my partner, Constable Rick McDonald."

"I'm Portia Talbot."

"Are you up to answering a few more questions, Mrs. Talbot?" Rick asked.

"I think so."

"Just tell me in your own words what you remember." He took a notebook out of his back pocket.

I told him everything I could remember from the time Angel woke me with her growling.

"We'll have to take your gun into evidence, Mrs. Talbot. You'll get it back. Do you have a permit for it?"

"Yes, I think so. It was my husband's gun, but he's deceased. I'll have to look for the permit."

"No problem. Can you use another bedroom while we examine this room?"

I nodded. "I'll take some clothes and go down the hall to the guest room." I grabbed my jeans, a T-shirt, clean underwear and Angel's blanket and headed for the door, skirting the bloodstain. "C'mon Angel."

As I passed the head of the staircase, I could hear talking in the foyer. I dressed in the guest room, then descended the staircase with Angel at my heel.

"Mrs. Talbot. Are you all right?"

"I'm a bit shaky, Vince, and my arm is throbbing. I don't know how that guy got in here. I know I set the alarm before I went to bed."

"I can't examine the system until the police are finished with it. I'm waiting for the okay."

"Don't worry about it. I should be safe with all these officers here. Angel was my real savior anyway."

Vince ruffled the fur around Angel's neck. "Good work, girl."

"I'm going to start a pot of coffee. I don't think sleep is an option right now. Would you like a cup?"

"Thanks, no. I'll go home and wait for the all-clear from the cops. I could use a couple hours sleep before work."

Did Bob send that guy to look for something? Why was he coming upstairs?

CHAPTER NINETEEN

AFTER waiting in the kitchen for the police to finish their investigation, and ingesting a caffeine overload, I crashed in the guest room and woke up around noon to the ringing of the phone. I checked the display. Apex Security.

"I'm sending some men over to reprogram your system," Vince said. "The cops gave me the go-ahead. What time is good for you?"

"Anytime this afternoon, I'll be here."

Apex came within the hour and revamped the security panel. They assured me, that it was working perfectly, and I had no worries. That didn't make me feel any better.

I walked Angel, and took a quick shower afterwards. Having to step over the bloody carpet in the bedroom doorway prompted me to arrange an appointment with a flooring company. I picked one at random from the Yellow Pages, booked an appointment and got ready to go to the hospital.

While Angel played in the yard, I cut a bouquet of fresh flowers to take with me. Not that Marcy could see them, until the swelling of her eyes diminished, but maybe the fragrance in her room would cheer her.

Marcy was moaning when I entered room four eighteen. I glanced over at the nurse checking her vitals as I put the bouquet of flowers on the window ledge.

"Her pain meds are wearing off," she said, injecting something into the IV. "Those flowers are lovely."

"They're from my garden." I smiled and picked up Marcy's limp hand. She tried to turn her head to look at me, but the movement made her groan again.

"Don't move. Just rest," I said. For the next several hours, I sat motionless at her bedside while she slept fitfully.

"Bye, Marcy. I'll come back tomorrow," I whispered, and slipped out of the room.

On the way to the elevator, I asked at the nurses' station if Mr. Winterstein had been in to see his wife. Negative on Bob, but Marcy's mother had driven down from North Bay and was staying close by with friends to visit her daughter. I hoped to run into her during visiting hours.

On the way home, I stopped off at the market, before driving to the other side of town to see if Bob was home from work. The black Yukon was parked in the driveway. I pulled in. Bob answered the doorbell with a drink in his hand—nothing new there.

"Portia, what a surprise. Nice to see you."

"Hi Bob." I gave him my best smile. "I thought, with Marcy in the hospital, you might like a little home cooking." I handed him a casserole wrapped in a tea towel that I had made in the morning.

"That's so thoughtful of you. I have been out of my mind with worry since Marcy fell down the stairs." He set the casserole down on the wicker porch table and took a step closer.

Yeah, so worried you didn't even go to see her, you rotten piece of shit.

"Come on in and have a drink with me." Bob reached out his hand.

I smothered a gasp and struggled to keep my composure. "I would love to—I actually have something that I want to discuss with you."

He motioned me into the kitchen and offered me wine. "I'll have a beer if you have one," I said, enjoying the surprised look on his face. Matthew always made me drink wine.

"What did you want to talk to me about, Portia?"

I dove right in. "I don't know what kind of shit you and Matthew had going on or what kind of a game you're playing, but there's nothing in my house of any value—and if you or one of your low life scumbags comes around again, I will put a bullet in you." I drained my beer and left Bob staring with his mouth hanging open.

THE evening was warm with no breeze and the air hung heavy with the fragrance of newly bloomed lilacs in the backyard. I clipped Angel's leash onto her collar, walked to the park, following the river path for an hour. Darkness had fallen and we were both panting by the time we made our way home. Angel lapped up a bowl of water, cleaned up her kibbles and stretched out on the kitchen floor while I fixed myself some dinner.

The ringing of the phone snapped me out of my reverie. I had forgotten the flooring company was sending over a rep with samples tonight. Damn. I was emotionally drained and leaned towards cancelling, but the thought of looking at my blood-soaked carpet for another day spurred me on.

A salesman from Toronto Hardwood arrived a half hour later burdened with his wares. Mike Harrison was dressed in tan casual pants and a dress shirt open at the neck. He looked lean, fit and outdoorsy. His thick, black hair and swarthy complexion accentuated his rough attractiveness. When he spoke, I caught a faint bit of an Irish lilt. Those Irish guys are always such a turn on.

He spread out all of the wood samples on the dining room table and talked about the pros and cons of each. Twenty minutes later, I had decided on oak plank flooring with pegging in a dark stain. When we moved into this house, hardwood was my first choice for replacing the floors, but Matthew wouldn't let me change anything. He said it was a waste of money and he wanted the whole house left the way his mother had decorated it.

Happily, neither he nor his mother was here now.

Upstairs measuring the bedroom, I thought there might be questions, but Mike stepped over the massive bloodstain without a glance in my direction. He took it in stride and no explanation was necessary. None given.

He sat at the dining room table, made a drawing of the bedroom, calculated the square footage and came up with a bottom line price. I agreed, then signed the contract and gave him a deposit. "When would you like this floor installed, Mrs. Talbot? We have lots of this wood in stock, so it's your call."

"How about Friday?"

"Friday it is, then. Ten a.m.? The men will remove and dispose of the old carpet, relocate the furniture and replace it when they're finished."

"I'm relieved. The furniture was going to be a problem for me."

Mike glanced at my sling. "How did you break your arm?"

"Oh, fell in the kitchen. One of those freak accidents," I said with a smile.

Mike nodded, looking at me sidelong and said goodnight.

CHAPTER TWENTY

THUNDER crashed and rain fell in torrents while I drank my morning coffee and searched the Yellow Pages for a cleaning service. For the next few weeks at least, I could use some help around the house. An attractive ad by 'Homeshine' caught my eye and after a quick call I had an in-home appointment for Friday morning. Let your fingers do the walking and someone else do the cleaning.

The humidity after the storm was hanging as heavy as a wet wool blanket. I chose a yellow sundress from my closet and opted to take a sweater in case the air conditioning in the hospital was on full tilt.

When I stepped out of the elevator on the fourth floor, there was quite a commotion around the nurses' station. Two police officers were asking questions and taking notes.

"What's going on?" I asked Nurse Fraser, the only nurse I knew by name.

"Something terrible happened. A neighbor found Mrs. Winterstein's husband sprawled on his front steps and called 911. Apparently, he had a massive heart attack and dropped dead."

I gasped and steadied myself with one hand on the gallery desk. "I can't believe this is happening. Does Marcy know?"

"No, she doesn't." Nurse Fraser game me a look that didn't translate.

"Can I see her?"

"Of course, you can."

For the next half hour, I sat in the green chair by Marcy's bedside and held her hand. I had presumed she was sleeping and didn't want to wake her, but something was very different from the day before. She lay completely still. There was no moaning or groaning from the pain. Nothing. I shivered and sought out Nurse Fraser at the desk.

When I found her, I voiced my concerns.

"Let me call her doctor. He should be still in the hospital."

I returned to Marcy's room and waited for almost an hour watching her lay motionless.

"Mrs. Talbot, this is Doctor Driscoll."

"Would you mind checking on Marcy? She isn't moving around and moaning from the pain like she was yesterday. I'm worried." I said stepping into the hallway.

The nurse closed Marcy's door and the two of them didn't emerge again for twenty minutes. Dr. Driscoll brushed past me as he hurried to the nurses' station and barked out commands. I leaned on the wall, pain pulsing through my temples. Orderlies arrived on the fourth floor and went into four eighteen. Nurse Fraser walked down the hall towards me and the look on her face was not one of pleasant news.

"Mrs. Winterstein is being moved to ICU. She has slipped into a coma," she said. As soon as we have her settled there, more tests will be run. You won't be able to see her again until tomorrow."

I put my hand over my face.

Marcy did not deserve this.

Driving away from the hospital my chest was tight. My head throbbed behind my eyes and my breathing was rapid. An explosion was imminent. I was going to lose my mind.

LOOKING for some kind of a diversion, and not knowing why I was being drawn, I pulled into the Harley dealership on my way home. It wouldn't hurt to look around. Glancing over my shoulder to see if anyone was watching, I pushed the door open and walked into a different world. A bike world. Everything a biker could want. I sucked in a deep breath and held tight to my purse. I wanted it all. Rows and rows of bikes in all sizes and every color of the rainbow sparkled and shone. I found it exceedingly hard to obey the "Don't touch the bikes' sign.

"Can I help you with something?"

I jumped and turned around.

Staring at me was a well-built young man with blond curly hair cascading down into his dazzling aqua blue eyes. "Sorry, didn't mean to startle you," he said softly.

"No problem. I was admiring the bikes and I was in a bit of a daze."

"My name's Billy. If you need help just give me a holler." I watched him return to the desk in the corner.

I left the bike section and headed over to the racks of clothing. Men's. Lady's. Kid's. They had it all going on. In ladies' wear there was a vast array of soft, supple, black leather outfits waiting to be tried on and given a good home. Not in my nature to disappoint—the dressing room welcomed me and my stack of leathers. My pulse was racing. I slipped on a pair of black leather pants that fit like they were made for me. I never wanted to take them off.

The three jackets I had taken from the rack were all fabulous, but I settled on the one with zippers and a little chain dangling from the pocket. On my way to the cash, I passed the boot section and that required more trying on and more decisions.

Black leather boots excited me—where had they been all my life? In passing, I picked up a T-shirt that read 'live to ride' and added it to my pile. It took will power to drag myself to the checkout without more merchandise.

Before I left the store, I took another walk over to the bike section, and strolled between the rows. There were all so beautiful, but I knew nothing about what would be the perfect first bike for a woman of my size. Luckily I had already met someone who would know.

George's Guns and Ammo was only a few blocks from the Harley store, and he would be just the guy to help me with my problem.

"Hey, George," I said as the bell jingled above my head.

George looked away from the customer he was helping and said, "What's up, baby doll?" He gave me a nod and finished up with the man at the counter while I amused myself looking around the tiny store. George packed an extensive array of merchandise into a tight space. The customer left the store and I approached George. He looked wedged in behind the counter wearing a blanket of a shirt that read 'Chrome won't get you home'.

"I'm thinking of buying a motorcycle and I need your advice."

"Fuck. Are you nuts? Look at the size of you," George boomed. "What if you dump it, how are you going to pick it up, sister?" He lit up a smoke.

"That's where you come in. I need you to help me choose a bike I could handle. That is if you have time."

George chuckled. "Shit, this is gonna be good. When do you want to go?"

"Whenever," I said. "And George, I also need to thank you for the shooting lessons. You saved my life. A guy broke into my house and I shot him."

George doubled over laughing and started to cough. He straightened up and his eyes were watering. "You're fuckin' with me, right?"

"Nope, I aimed for his head, but I only got him in the arm. Angel helped out and took a big chunk out of his leg." George's laughter was contagious. "The cops took away my Beretta, so I need to buy another one."

"Fuck, yeah. You might want to put a bullet in someone else." Between smoking, laughing and coughing, George was dying. "You are so fuckin' hilarious," he said, wiping his eyes with his sleeve. "Do you seriously need another gun? Do you want another Beretta?"

"Exactly the same, if you have one. I was just getting used to that one." He unlocked the case under the front

counter and came up with a 9mm just like mine.
"Fabulous," I said.

"Ain't it?" he grinned and handed it to me. "Okay,
Okay. When can I go bike shoppin'? How about
tomorrow night? I close up here at seven and Harley is
open until nine-thirty. I'll meet you over there at seven-
fifteen."

"Perfect. Can't wait," I said. "While I'm here, I
should get more practice ammo for the range." I handed
him my debit card.

"Don't forget, the practice box has the green dot on
it, little girl." He pointed.

"I always forget which is which." I said, giving my
head a shake. "You're the best, George." And I meant it.

CHAPTER TWENTY-ONE

THE bell rang promptly at nine am. When I opened the front door, a happy face was smiling at me. Angel jumped up and down in her greeting mode.

"Hi, Mrs. Talbot, I'm Stacey from Homeshine."

"Come on in, Stacey. Would you like a coffee?" She was five feet tall, dressed in jeans and a purple T-shirt with a sparkling house on the front. Cute. Her beautiful smile lit up her face and her bright blue eyes. Her long, blonde pony-tail bounced as she walked.

"No, thanks, I'm good. I won't take up too much of your time—just a quick look at the house, find out what you need done each week and then I can give you a price."

We did a walk-through upstairs and down, then sat in the living room to chat.

"I can see how it would be hard for you to clean with a broken arm."

"It won't be healed for another two or three weeks yet. That's why I need you."

Stacey arrived at a price I thought was more than fair and said she could schedule me for Friday mornings every week. We discussed Angel, the alarm system and made a list of special things that needed to be done. Very professional. As I closed the door behind her I sighed. Matthew had insisted on a spotless home and now it was just second nature to keep it that way.

Half an hour later the Toronto Hardwood truck pulled into the driveway to install the bedroom floor. After showing the men which room it was, I retreated to the patio with my book and waited until they completed the job. It was a long, beautiful day in the back yard, but when they finished and had replaced the furniture, I went up to take a look. The disgusting blood stain in the doorway was gone, replaced by plank flooring that made the bedroom look twice as big and accentuated the Victorian feel.

"Great job, guys. Thanks so much." I handed the foreman the check.

BEFORE dinner I changed my clothes and tried to locate Matthew's car keys. I hadn't touched his vehicle since his timely demise and now, I dreaded having to clean it out before I took it to the dealership. I popped the trunk and removed a leather briefcase and a small duffle bag containing a few toiletries and two unopened packages of condoms.

Cheating bastard.

The interior of the car smelled like Matthew and the lingering scent of his cologne made my stomach turn. Checking the glove box, I found a few receipts, more condoms and a bottle of Smirnoff's'.

Nothing like being prepared.

On the way to the dealership, I drove through a car wash to freshen up the exterior. I parked the car in front of the showroom window and went in to meet the manager.

Steve Underwood was dressed in a cheap gray suit over a white shirt with no tie. His hair matched the color of his suit and his shoes needed shining. He might have been attractive in high school, but that was decades ago, and the years had not been kind to him.

"I'm interested in selling my late husband's car back to the dealership. How would I go about that, Steve?"

"Did you want to trade it in on something newer?" he asked hopefully.

"No thanks, I have a car already. I don't need two."

"Well, Mrs. Talbot, if you want to leave me the keys, I'll have our mechanic go over it, then I can tell you what it's worth. Can probably have it checked out by tomorrow some time and give you a call, if that's okay."

He closed the deal with a weak and clammy handshake and the dealership shuttle dropped me home.

After a quick bite to eat, I prepared for my bike buying expedition with George. My heart was pounding with anticipation. I changed into jeans, black leather boots and my newly acquired biker shirt. I stuffed my checkbook into my purse, swallowed two Advil, kissed Angel on her furry head and departed for the Harley dealership.

CHAPTER TWENTY-TWO

GEORGE ROSS was leaning on the railing in front of the Harley store, smoking. He'd worn his mirrored sun glasses and black bandana adorned with skulls, tied around his long black hair. He smiled as Portia glanced at her watch to make sure she wasn't late. Nope—right on time. She parked the Wrangler and got out, excitement drippin off her like an illegal substance. She smiled and he waved, flicking his butt into the boxwood hedge.

"Hey, you didn't forget," she said with a big grin.

"Shit. How could I. This'll be the biggest fuckin' laugh of the week," he chuckled, holding the door open.

"Hey, George, long time." The guy behind the parts counter gave George a thumbs-up.

"Hey Billy, getting' any?" Didn't see you at 'The Bend' on the 13th."

"Hell no, had to fuckin' work. Who's your little friend? Hey I remember you."

"Keep it in your pants, pervert. She's just lookin' to buy a bike."

George put a massive hand on her back and steered her over to the bike area. "This is Kenny," he said, pointing to the six-foot, tanned and tattooed lady's man.

"What can I help you with?" Kenny flashed her the smile that left chicks weak in the knees. His long shaggy black hair half hid his black eyes.

Portia was transfixed and temporarily mute and George touched her arm to get her attention. "Do you want to sit on some bikes, little girl? I think we should start with a Softail. Might be the best one for you—a little easier to balance than the Sportster."

"Try this thirteen-forty and we can make adjustments to the bars if we need to." Kenny pointed to a turquoise beauty. "Great size for a lady."

Portia threw her leg over and eased onto the black leather seat. The smell of the leather, oil and grease was heady stuff. The handlebars caused her a problem, her broken arm putting her off balance, but her feet touched the floor easily.

"Feels good. Can't wait until my arm heals so I can ride," she said.

"Need more than that, sweet cheeks." George laughed. "Need a bike license."

"I have a driver's license."

"No good. You need to take the government safety course for bikes."

"Nuts," she said, and Kenny laughed.

"Sit on a few more, so you get the feel of what's right for you." Kenny pointed down the line of shiny models. Metallic silver, Candy Apple Red, Harley Orange. She eyed the bikes like she wanted one in each color.

Portia tested five or six more, finally coming back to the original and sitting on it again. "I love this one. Comfort is good. Color is perfect. I think this is going to be my first bike." She couldn't wipe the grin off her face.

"Let me make a couple of adjustments to the bars and

the seat." Kenny indicated that she should stand up and let him custom fit the bike to her size. He touched her good arm to help her up and George frowned.

Don't mess with her, fucker.

Kenny brought his tools out to do the fine tuning.

"What do you think, George?" she asked, "Is this the one for me?"

"As long as you have the strength for it, hon bun. Wouldn't hurt you none to muscle up a bit if you're gonna ride a lot. If you dump this baby in traffic, you'll be in a fuckin' mess."

"Good idea. I have to strengthen my broken arm when it's healed anyway. How'd you get so smart, George?" she squeezed his huge arm.

"Fuckin' born this way," he laughed till he coughed. "Might as well pick out a helmet and some gloves, girlie. You'll need 'em to take your test."

"Right, so much shopping to do." Portia was in heaven trying on helmets and black leather gloves with George supervising.

"Make sure the gloves are snug," he said, and winked. God, she had a perfect body. He hadn't wanted anyone for a lot of years, and he had tried to put his unfamiliar feelings for Portia out of his head, but it wasn't working.

She made her choices and took the merchandise up to the counter.

Kenny wrote up an invoice. "How much do you want to put down on the bike, today?"

Portia stared into his eyes and hesitated. "I'll put five down and pay the balance when I pick it up." She said handing Kenny her debit card. She picked up her receipt off the counter, "Thanks for all your help, Kenny. As you can see, I'm starting from scratch. If I didn't have George, I wouldn't even have the courage to be here."

"Fuck that sappy stuff," George said, "Let's go celebrate. Always do that when somebody buys a new bike." He put a smoke in his mouth but didn't light it.

"I'm off in five. I'll meet you there," said Kenny.

Fuck, the last thing I need is that little prick near her.

George lit up as soon as he cleared the door. "Follow me. It's not far," he shouted over his shoulder as he headed for his bike. Portia jumped in her Jeep and tried to follow George. His bike darted in and out of traffic like he was threading a needle. Trying not to lose him was a full time job for her. He pulled into the parking lot of a run-down building with one lonely neon sign in the front window. The outside wall facing the parking spaces was covered in graffiti—the kind kids do with spray cans. Two long angled rows of bikes and choppers filled most of the spaces. Portia parked beside one of the two other cars in the lot and got out.

George lit up a fresh smoke and waited until she caught up and fell into step beside him. He held the door open for her and paused behind her as she looked around. The bar was poorly lit, the dim light made dimmer by the thick layer of blue-gray smoke. Toronto's no smoking by-law had yet to kick in at Buck's.

"Over there." George pointed to an empty booth at the back by the pool tables. Nobody paid any attention as he made his way through the crowd and found them a seat. Portia blended in with her Harley T-shirt and her black boots.

"Buck, three glasses and a pitcher," George hollered to the bartender on the other side of the room.

Never brought a woman here before. Fuck, the boys are gonna get mileage outta this one.

Buck's was a normal looking bar, filled with not so normal looking clientele. The place was aged and worn, but homey in a rough-and-tumble way. The floor was wooden, like an old roadhouse—wide planks with pegging. Lighting was poor, but bikers didn't care. They were shooting pool, listening to country music, downing a few cold ones and hanging with friends.

The bartender, Buck, was an older fellow, heavy-set, maybe in his sixties, and knew everyone by their first name. Good for business. He chatted, laughed, poured drinks and ran tabs for dozens of guys at the same time without hesitation. A veteran pub keeper.

George filled their glasses from the pitcher Buck sent over and held his glass up to clink with Portia's. "To the world's newest fuckin' biker," he said, "Drink up, little girl."

She laughed and raised her glass. "Thanks, George. I wouldn't be a biker at all if it wasn't for you. Now I'm making a toast . . . To my best friend."

George raised his glass to touch hers with a wistful look on his face. "If I'm your best friend, baby girl, you haven't got much in your fuckin' life."

"Bingo," she said with a big smile. "Absolutely nothing before you, George. You and Angel."

"Hey, at least I rank up there with the dog." He laughed until his belly shook. "Over here, Kenny." He hollered when he saw Kenny through the smoke cloud. "Another pitcher, Buck." George filled up Kenny's glass and drained the last of the pitcher into Portia's glass.

George's bulk took up the other side of the booth, so Kenny had to sit next to Portia. She scooted over and he sat down reaching for his glass.

"Super colors on your tattoo," she said for openers. The dragon on the guy's arm looked fierce in shades of blue, green and magenta. Portia looked like she might want to touch the tat, but had reined herself in.

"Thanks. Just got it finished a week ago. A lot of hours on this one."

"Did you get it done around here?" she asked.

"Yeah. Ivan's Ink, down on Danforth. He's the best, but wait time is long. I don't know if he's takin' any new people."

George was casting her a sideways glance over his refilled glass. "What the fuck? Now a tattoo?" he asked, and then added with a smirk. "Go wild, girl."

After his fourth beer, George whispered to Kenny. "Watch yourself, stud. She shoots men that get in her way."

When Kenny smiled and gave her a questioning look, he busted up laughing. Portia just shrugged and raised her glass to her mouth.

Crash. As beer spewed everywhere, a biker sprawled across the table, blood gushing from his nose and mouth. His assailant was holding a pool cue to his throat and yelling obscenities that made Portia raise her eyebrows.

In a flash, Buck was on the scene. "Out the back, boys," he grabbed one. George grabbed the other and out the back door they tossed them like two sacks of trash.

"Thanks, man," Buck said to George, giving him a fist bump. "They know there's no fighting in here. I'll ship you over a new pitcher."

The front of Portia's jeans was soaked through and she wasn't feeling any too comfortable. She took it as her cue to leave. "Thanks for your help, George, but I'll call it a night. Night, Kenny." She stood up holding her purse in front of her jeans fiasco.

"Good night," said Kenny. "I didn't catch your first name."

"It's Portia. Nice meeting you."

George shook his head and watched her walk to her Jeep from the back door of the bar. Once she was in the driver's seat of her Jeep with the door closed, he gave her a wave.

She's no match for Kenny.

CHAPTER TWENTY-THREE

RING. RING.

I was having such a good dream starring Kenny; I didn't want to wake up. I groped for the phone on the night table. "Hello." My voice sounded hoarse like I'd been out drinking in a smoky bar the night before. Oh, wait.

"Hi Portia. It's Kenny. Hope I didn't wake you up."

Oh shit. What does he want?

"No. I'm up."

I am now.

His voice was husky and kind of gravelly over the phone. Just hearing him breathe made my heart pound.

"Takin' my ride out for a spin this morning. Want to come along?"

Is he asking me out?

"Sounds like fun. What time?"

"How about fifteen minutes?"

"Not possible. Give me half an hour?"

"I'll pick you up in half."

"Do you know where I live?"

"I got it from the store."

"Great." What the hell. I thought maybe George was giving out my address to his friends since my little confession. I bolted into the bathroom, took a quick shower and threw on jeans, a tank top and cut the tags

off my new leather jacket. I put Angel out in the yard
while I made coffee and popped down a piece of toast.

Ding. Dong.

Shit. Not already. Angel ran past me at top speed,
setting a new world record. From the back yard to the
front door in five seconds flat. Barking at strangers and
protecting me was her life's passion. I couldn't fault her
on that one. I turned off the alarm and opened the door.

There he stood in all his glory, dressed from head to
toe in black leather—a biker god. I was speechless. I
choked out a squeaky, "Hi".

"You look fantastic," he said flashing sparkling white
teeth.

"You too," I stammered and stepped aside to let him
in. The scent of him clad in leather took my breath away.
His tight pants outlined personal assets that I tried to
fight against thinking about. It was a losing battle. He
bent down on one knee and ruffed up Angel's fur while I
gathered myself. Angel growled soft and low.

"Nice dog. I love Rotties." His brown eyes looked up
at me wistfully and I melted.

"I love her too." Kenny waited on the porch while I
locked up.

I threw my leg over the bike and cozied in behind
him, wrapping my good arm around him. He was so lean
and muscular and musky smelling it was unnerving.

"I know you can only hold on with one arm, so I'll
take it easy. No crazy stuff." He laughed and revved up
the engine. We rode east out of town along the lakeshore
for about an hour, the scenery flying by in double time.
The noise of the engine prevented any communication,

but physically I felt connected to Kenny and the bike. Riding into the wind at top speed—what a stress reliever.

Kenny slowed down and pulled into a little white clapboard diner that boasted all day breakfast on the sign out front.

"I'm starving," he said helping me off the bike. "How about you?"

"The fresh air made me hungry." I laughed. Before I knew what was happening he pulled me close to him and kissed me on the mouth.

"I wanted to do that the first day I saw you in the store." He grinned.

"Yeah, that was yesterday." I laughed.

"Actually, I saw you a week ago buying out the store."

"Uh huh."

I think I would've remembered seeing you.

We sat in a booth by the window in the diner and I was pleased with myself for knowing why. Bikers like to keep an eye on their babies. Kenny ordered the lumberjack breakfast and I ordered scrambled eggs, bacon, toast and coffee.

When the waitress brought our orders, I took one look at the mountain of food in front of Kenny and was betting he could never finish it. Wrong. I cleaned up my plate and ordered more coffee while Kenny kept on shoveling food into his mouth. As I watched him eat I wondered if all his appetites were that hard to satisfy.

"Boy, you were hungry."

"Fuck, yeah." He wiped his face with his napkin and sipped his coffee. "That hit the spot."

"I'm going to use the facilities. Be right back."

"Good plan. Long way back."

After I washed my hands, I dug two pain killers out of my purse and downed them with a sip of water. A broken arm was not going to screw this up for me. By the time I came out of the ladies room, Kenny had paid our bill and was ready to leave. He handed me my helmet and we were off.

WHEN he pulled the bike into my driveway he shut the engine off.

Okay, he's coming in.

He followed me onto the porch. "Want a beer?" I asked.

"Fuck, yeah. I could use one." He smiled that drop dead gorgeous smile and my pulse rate picked up. Zero to sixty in the space of one smile.

Angel was bouncing, butt wagging at the sight of me. Kenny reached out a hand to pat her head and then jerked back when she curled her lip and bared her teeth.

"Angel, that's not nice," I said as I slid the patio door open and she raced into the yard. I pointed to the table outside and said, "I'll get the drinks."

Kenny sat on one chair, cocked one leg up on another and lit up a smoke. I couldn't stop myself from staring at him through the glass door. Watching him light up a cigarette and put it between his lips made my underwear damp. I needed to get a grip.

This is not the time to get involved with anybody. Forget it.

I dumped potato chips into a bowl, took bottles from

the fridge, grabbed a couple of glasses and set the works down on the patio table. Kenny pulled on my good arm and I tumbled, laughing, into his lap. He was kissing me before I could protest, and I kissed him back against my better judgement. He gave me his tongue and I moaned.

Ring. Ring.

Saved by the bell.

"I'd better get that," I said.

"Leave it. We're busy," he said, pulling me back. "They'll leave a message."

I regained my balance and shook my head. "It might be important. I'll be right back."

He tightened his grip and shoved his hand under my top.

Warning bells rang in my head and I got to my feet. "I think I better get the phone."

"Mrs. Talbot. This is Steve Underwood here at Mercedes Benz. I have an evaluation done for you based on the year and the condition of your car. We're prepared to offer you sixty thousand. Does that sound reasonable?"

"No. It doesn't. I found the original bill of sale, and eighty-five would be more in line with the black book value."

"The highest I'm prepared to offer is seventy."

"I'm sorry. Anything less than seventy-five and I'll sell it privately."

Steve sighed, "All right then, we have a deal at seventy-five."

Ha! That's what I wanted to hear.

"When can I pick up the check?"

"Should be ready by Monday afternoon."

"I'll drop by Monday and sign the papers." I hung up and went back outside. Kenny had finished his beer and was throwing a ball to Angel near the back fence. "Do you want another?"

"One more, then I should go. I have stuff to do."

I got two more cold ones from the kitchen and took them outside. By the time I had filled my glass, Kenny had chugged his down and was standing up, giving me a look I couldn't read.

"Wow. That was fast," I said, a little puzzled by his change in attitude.

"I've got some deliveries to make," he said, heading for the door.

"Thanks for the ride and the breakfast," I said. "I had a great time."

"Me too." He kissed me on the cheek and was gone. *What the hell was that all about?*

I thought things were going well, but what did I know? I hadn't dated for a long time, and never a guy like Kenny. Maybe he expected sex right after hello.

"ANGEL, want to go for a walk?" A blur of black-and-tan bolted for the door and I grabbed her leash. The answer was always *yes* from Angel. She never let me down. We walked for an hour down by the river, where she growled at other dogs and intimidated a few ducks. Coming up our street on the way home, I could see the outline of a large figure sitting on the porch steps. My stomach flipped before I recognized an unsmiling George, smoking a butt. I unclipped Angel's leash and she dashed ahead of me and licked George's face.

"Hi George. What's up?" I gave him a one-arm hug and sat down beside him. My leg grazed the side of his boot and he shifted his leg over at little.

"Careful. Don't want you gettin'cut." He pulled up his tattered jeans far enough to expose the knife clipped to the side of his boot.

"Good to be prepared," I said, waiting for him to tell me why he had come to the house.

He took out his cigarette pack, fiddled with the foil, and finally lit one up. "Just checkin' up on you, little girl. See how you made out with Kenny." His voice had an edge to it that I hadn't heard before.

"He took me for a ride for a couple of hours, bought me breakfast, then we had a drink when we got back here. That was it. How did you know I went for a ride with Kenny?"

He shrugged. "Don't want you gettin' all crazy over him and then he busts your heart wide open. He done that to a lot of girls already. Got quite a rep. The boys call him, 'Lady Killer Kenny.'" He took a big drag on his cigarette. "That boy needs a steel-toe to the nut sack."

"Huh, I had no idea. I assumed you liked him when he joined us for drinks."

George sighed, "Wasn't gonna' mess in your business, but then I got to thinkin' and said fuck it. Would weigh heavy on me if I didn't give you a heads-up."

I squeezed his arm and he nodded.

I should have known better.

George shifted to face me and flicked his butt into the flowerbed. "I'm shootin' tomorrow. Want to practice?"

"For sure. What time."

"Pick you up at ten." He winked, stood up and headed for his bike.

Back in the house, I sucked in a deep breath and resolved not to dwell on Kenny, or the lack of him. After half an hour on Matthew's treadmill, some of my anger was spent and I headed for the shower. I dried my hair and dressed in white pants and a flowered blouse, checked my makeup and drove to the hospital to check on Marcy.

The nurse on duty told me there had been no change in her condition. I sat by her bed, holding her hand for an hour hoping she would wake up and hoping she knew I was there for her. Before I left, I made sure that the nurses' station had my number on file, just in case.

CHAPTER TWENTY-FOUR

THE ride north to the range on the back of George's Eagle cleared my head, and I directed all of my focus into an extended shooting practice. I picked up my ammo box to refill the mag on the Beretta and George gave me a look.

"What?"

"You mixed up the ammo again, girl." He frowned. "Costing you money."

"Must have grabbed it in a hurry," I said.

My broken arm was stronger and my aim with my left hand was improving. As we plodded back to the picnic tables for a drink, George said, "You're coming along damn fine, young lady. Soon be good as old George." He laughed heartily.

"That's a compliment coming from the master."

George pointed to an empty table and trudged to the cooler to get beer. I sat down, took my ball cap off and shook out my hair. Just as George returned to the table, a bike roared up the hill and parked. A pretty blonde girl dismounted from the bitch seat, then the driver got off, removed his helmet, grabbed her around the waist and kissed her. It was Kenny. I felt the blood rising in my face and the heat of anger spreading through my body like a virus.

"Want to split?" George said, eyeing the newcomers.

"Nope. I'm good." I grabbed my bottle and chugged, sputtering and choking.

George laughed until his eyes watered. "You got balls bigger'n a buffalo. I wouldn't want to be on the wrong side of you, sweet cheeks."

After another round, we mounted up and hit the road.

"Got steaks to grill, George. Stay and have dinner with me," I said when we arrived at the house. "Unless you have other plans."

"Yeah, okay. I could clean the guns while you're cookin'."

George sat on the patio cleaning our guns, drinking and smoking while Angel romped in the yard. She rolled in the grass that needed cutting and brought George her ball at frequent intervals, hoping to induce him to play. I put potatoes in foil and steaks on the grill while I made a salad in the kitchen. The tension Kenny had produced earlier in the day was dissipating.

After George left, I cleaned up the kitchen and went upstairs to soak the gunpowder out of my pores.

CHAPTER TWENTY-FIVE

SHEETS of rain slapping against the bedroom window woke me with a start. My foul mood perpetrated by 'Lady Killer Kenny' had not lifted overnight. Depressing thoughts of a blue Monday filled my head as I pulled on black jeans and a T-shirt, brushed my teeth and tried to tame my hair. I threw the brush down and kicked the front of the vanity. My hair needed help that I couldn't give it with one arm.

After Angel had been outside briefly, we huddled in the kitchen away from the storm and shared toast and jam. A quick call to the salon and I was set for three-fifteen. A new hairstyle would lift me out of the doldrums and distract my every waking thought from Kenny. I finished my second cup of coffee and loitered indoors until the rain let up and I could make a run to the Jeep.

The short drive to the clinic was littered with rear-enders. Why can't people drive in the rain? I had almost forgotten my X-ray, but the kitchen calendar was quick to remind me. The lab technician assured me that my doctor would call and give me an update when he received the results. I couldn't trust myself not to bite her head off, so I smiled and nodded. Life sucks when you have to depend on other people.

You can only count on yourself.

My second stop was Sport Chek. I had been thinking about joining a gym to strengthen my arm but decided to buy a set of weights and work out at home. It takes time and commitment to maximize a gym membership and I was in possession of neither. By working out at home, I would avoid contact with people while I was in a vulnerable state of undress and I wouldn't have to engage in small talk with anyone.

My next stop was the hospital. No change in Marcy. After tossing her wilted flowers into the garbage with the promise of fresh ones, I held vigil at her bedside for an hour and divulged the degrading details of the Kenny fiasco, and how stupid I had been. I knew she would understand. Nurse Fraser popped into the room while I was there and asked me if I had attended Mr. Winterstein's funeral the previous day.

Absolutely not.

"No, regrettably I was unable to attend," I said with what I hoped was a twinge of remorse.

On my way to the parking lot, I passed the emergency waiting room on the ground floor of the hospital and gasped when I recognized Darlene Abernathy, from the meeting at the YMCA. Her small battered body was slumped over in a chair waiting to see a doctor. She was holding an ice pack against her eye and her leg was wrapped in a blood soaked towel. Two children were sitting on the floor beside her chair looking at picture books.

Something had to be done to help that girl.

I stomped out to my Jeep and burned rubber onto the road trying to erase the picture of Darlene from my mind.

Concentrate, girl. You'll think of something.

The Mercedes dealership had my check ready when I stopped in. I signed over the ownership papers and thanked Steve Underwood, giving him my best fake smile. I assured him when I needed a new car, he would be my first choice.

Like that would ever happen.

I was fast becoming a prevaricator of sorts.

Next on my list was the bank. When I lined up to deposit the check, I thought I felt eyes burning a hole through my back. Yep. Jim Timberman was staring at me from his glassed-in office.

Creep.

The morning had been hectic, but with all the errands, my thoughts were temporarily diverted from Kenny. After a grilled cheese sandwich and a bowl of tomato soup, I took a short nap and was ready to go again.

While I waited my turn at the salon, I tried to imagine myself in some of the hairdos that were pictured in the dog-eared magazines piled on the table. In the past, my hair had never once turned out resembling the picture, but with two possibilities in mind, I followed Shea to the shampoo area prepared to take another chance.

"What are we getting done today?" she asked.

I explained my ideas leaving the final decision in her capable hands. "Hope for the best." I laughed.

Less than two hours later, I hardly recognized myself in the mirror. She had darkened my natural brunette color to ebony, added blonde highlights, and given me a trendy, saucy haircut. "What do you think?" she asked. "I love it. You're an artist," I said, fishing in my purse for my wallet and laying a huge tip on her. A celebration was in order. I stopped at the Beer Store, drove through A & W and headed for home.

CHAPTER TWENTY-SIX

THE telephone woke me around nine-fifteen from the best sleep I'd had in weeks.

It was the Crown Prosecutor's office calling to tell me the trial date for the burglar I had shot. Nine months down the road – there's swift justice for you.

Would have saved the taxpayers money if I had finished him.

I dragged myself out of bed and down the hall to work on the new me. The third bedroom upstairs was the perfect size for a workout room. The floor was carpeted in a thick Berber. Matthew's treadmill sat in the corner by the window, leaving the center of the room free for weights. I started with a short routine that was outlined in the weight package, and it was enough on my first day to leave me breathless and sweaty.

After my shower, I made coffee and a fried egg sandwich. I fried two eggs and some bacon for Angel and took her bowl out to the patio. As I sipped my coffee, I looked around the yard and realized what a mess it had become. The grass was long, and the flower beds were in need of attention. There was no way I could navigate the lawn mower until my arm was healed, even though the pain had subsided considerably. I looked up the number of a yard service.

All through the day, my thoughts kept returning to

Darlene and her predicament. How could I help her and her children? I had to attend another meeting and, look at that, my calendar's free tonight.

At six forty-five I took a seat in the back row of the meeting room at the YMCA. The last time I had been here, Marcy was sitting next to me. Tears welled up in my eyes. I watched the door as one by one, the women found a seat. Outsiders might see abused, damaged and helpless women, but I knew better. These women were here to start taking control of something that had spun out of control in their lives and I hoped they all found their way to freedom.

The meeting room itself was depressing, with peeling green paint, exposed heating ducts and sporadic fluorescent lighting. Ms. Julianne had just taken her position at the front to begin the meeting when Darlene came through the door on crutches. One of the women jumped up to hold the door for her and helped her settle in a chair. Again, I thought about Marcy and tears rolled down my cheeks.

It just gets worse and worse. It never stops until it's too late.

Sitting through the accounts of day to day violence and mistreatment was torture. With the telling of each new tale, I relived my life with Matthew in spades.

After the meeting, coffee was served in Styrofoam cups with a few cookies supplied by the Y. The women stood around chatting about everyday topics, forgetting for the moment why they were here. I introduced myself to Darlene, gestured towards her crutches and asked if she needed a ride home.

"Thank you. That's so nice of you to offer," she said, trying to smile. "It would be easier than taking the bus."

I retrieved the Jeep from the parking lot and pulled up to the curb at the front of the building. After helping Darlene into the passenger seat, I stowed her crutches in the back.

"Where do you live, Darlene?" I asked.

"Keele Street and Jane area. I'll tell you where to turn when we get close."

That's a bad area at night, or any other time.

Darlene directed me to an apartment complex that needed more than a facelift. It needed to be torn down. The yellow brick walls were covered in huge black letters, spelling out slogans in spray paint, and the bulbs in the security lights were all smashed. Shady looking men wearing hoodies stood in the shadows in the alleyways between the buildings, possibly waiting for customers. Hookers paraded up and down the street showing off their bustier overflow and their micro minis. A beehive of activity.

"What apartment do you live in, Darlene? Do you have to climb any stairs?"

"No, I'm on the first floor at the back. One-ten. I'm okay. Thanks for asking."

I stopped at the curb, hopped out and went around to the other side of the Jeep.

She struggled out of the passenger seat and accepted the crutches from me one at a time. "Thanks for the ride."

CHAPTER TWENTY-SEVEN

I awoke to an ear-splitting chorus of Angel barking and the doorbell ringing. I groaned, threw on a robe and dashed down the stairs in my bare feet.

Oh, shit. The cleaning girls.

"Come on in. Sorry, I overslept," I stammered.

"No problem. We'll work around you," Stacey said with a smile, setting her cleaning caddy down in the foyer. She bubbled with energy while my body begged for another hour under my duvet.

Note to self. Be dressed before nine next Friday.

Two hours later, Stacey stuck her head out the patio door. "All done."

Clean house smell smacked me in the face when I went through the sliding door into the kitchen to write her a check. The faucet was gleaming, the stove sparkled, and the floors looked brand new. "Fantastic," I said giddily. "See you next week."

KILLING time before my next trip to the hospital, I drove over to the gun shop. I scooped the Beretta from the glove box into my purse and entered the store, making the bell jingle. George was busy at the counter with two burly customers clad in flannel shirts. They hefted shotguns of different calibers for weight and balance and asked George all kinds of questions.

Country music blared from the radio in the back room, and the air hung heavy with smoke.

George winked at me.

The shoulder holsters were displayed on a swivel rack in one corner, so I loitered until George finished writing up his sales. When the hunters left with purchases in hand, George walked over and lit up a smoke.

"What's up, today little girl?" he asked. "Whenever I see you, something is goin' on. I swear."

"Nothing going on, George. Just taking your advice and buying a shoulder holster for my Beretta."

"Where you gonna' wear it to? The mall?" He laughed until he coughed.

"Maybe. Which one should I try on?"

"This black leather one is a Beretta holster and will fit your 9mm. Did you bring the gun with you?"

I fished it out of my purse. George checked the safety, snapped the gun into the holster and helped me try it on. My bad arm continued to cause a range of motion problems, but was improving, bit by bit.

"We'll have to tighten it up. You ain't the biggest shooter I've ever seen." He loved to laugh at his own jokes. "How does that feel?"

"Pretty comfy." I twisted around to get the feel of wearing it.

"You know you need a license to carry, don't you?" George said and scowled.

"Yes, I know. How do I get licensed?"

"Shit. You have to take the restricted firearms safety course. I can fix you up for that one. Just another political pain in the ass. Those fuckers in Ottawa never stop screwin' with the gun laws. They do everything they can to keep me from makin' a decent livin'. They should all be shot and pissed on. Canuck shooters need a guy like Chuck Heston on our side." George took a big drag on his cigarette and blew out a cloud of smoke.

"Okay, sign me up, I wouldn't want to break the law," I said crossing my fingers.

"Fuck, I never know what you're up to, girl. You boggle my mind sometimes."

"Maybe it's better if you don't know." I winked at him and he shook his head. I took the holster off, put the gun back in my purse and walked up to the cash. Neither one of us wanted to mention the Kenny incident, and I was grateful that it didn't come up.

"Are we on for Sunday?" George asked.

"Sure, we are. Sundays with you are my best day of the week."

"Fuck, I know you're bullshittin' me now," he chuckled.

I flashed him a big grin and waved as I went out the door and headed for the hospital.

EACH time I visited Marcy, I expected her to be awake, and each time it came as a shock that she wasn't. I rinsed out the vase in the adjacent bathroom and arranged the fresh flowers I had brought from the garden. For the next two hours, I sat reading to her from Pride and Prejudice, listening to the monitor beep while I waited for something that might never happen.

The nurses came in periodically, checking and

rechecking, blood pressure, temperature, IV, and for what? Nothing was helping Marcy.

AFTER dinner, I walked Angel in the park for an hour. We stood on the river bank and watched the sun paint the sky shades of orange, red and yellow as it disappeared behind the trees. As we padded home thirsty and tired, the street lights came on signaling that evening had descended on Hawthorne Lane.

I rested at the patio table and drank an ice cold Coors, mentally working up to what I knew was another Friday night alone. I curled up with Angel on the sofa and watched Criminal Minds reruns.

CHAPTER TWENTY-EIGHT

ANOTHER day, another kick at the can.

I lounged in bed until after nine, listless from the boredom of the previous night. Angel insisted I get up and open the patio door for her, forcing me to face the day before I was ready for it. The workout room called my name but glancing at the weights from the doorway wore me out. While the coffee was brewing, I scooped the weekend Globe from the front porch and flopped down on the sofa. An hour later, I rallied and cooked a proper breakfast.

The yard service arrived and the girls, decked out in matching pale blue shorts and T-shirts were eager to trim, cut, weed and water. Angel kept me company in the kitchen while the girls worked outside. With the weather so warm and inviting, I didn't blame her for pouting. She flopped down on the mat by the door and heaved a heavy sigh.

After the girls had worked a small miracle outside, they left promising to return the following week. I enjoyed a brief tour of the property with Angel, inhaling the aroma of freshly cut lawn, admiring weed-free flower beds and perfectly trimmed hedges. It was glorious.

Trees were budding and the garden was alive with all the pastel shades of spring. Doing especially well was the unobtrusive bed of lily of the valley in the back corner. I enjoyed my coffee on the patio table, inhaling the fragrances of lilac, crocus and cherry blossoms. Angel rolled in the freshly cut grass, chased a feisty gray squirrel and jumped in the air to bite hovering bumblebees. All was right with the world.

After cleaning up the kitchen, I soaked in a hot tub of bubbles and was for the most part rejuvenated for my trip to the hospital. I picked a large bouquet of flowers and wrapped half in waxed paper for Marcy. The rest I displayed in a vase on the kitchen table.

Marcy's bed was empty when I entered her room, and I burst into tears. My stomach wrenched and ran to her little bathroom. After vomiting up my breakfast, I sat on the toilet seat until my legs would hold me. I splashed cold water on my face and dabbed it dry with a scratchy paper towel from the dispenser. Sucking in a deep breath, I ventured out to the nurses' station and questioned one of the staff.

"When did Mrs. Winterstein pass?" I asked.

"Oh, sorry dear. I didn't see you go in there. We moved her to long term care on the eighth floor. Just a sec. I'll find her room number for you."

My knees almost gave out and I had to clutch the edge of the desk.

"Okay, Mrs. Winterstein is now in room eight twenty-two. Are you all right? You look a little pale."

"I'm fine, thanks." I released my death grip from the corner of the desk and started for the elevator. On the eighth floor, the layout appeared identical to the other floors, making it easy to find Marcy's new room. I collapsed in the chair beside her bed and wept. An hour later, when the tears stopped, I gathered myself, hid my red eyes with sunglasses and drove home.

CHAPTER TWENTY-NINE

I was sitting on the front porch drinking coffee when George pulled the Screamin' Eagle into the driveway for our Sunday outing. Thoughts of seeing Kenny at the range had bullied their way into my head, but I quickly discarded them.

"George, do you want a coffee before we leave?" I called to him as he dismounted.

"Okay, I could use one." He lit up a smoke and sat on the porch steps.

I filled two mugs in the kitchen and let Angel bounce out the front door to greet George.

"Hey girl, don't lick me to death." He laughed, as Angel covered his face with kisses.

I handed George his coffee. "She loves you."

"She's the only one," he said with a frown.

"Not true."

George gestured to my jacket. "How's the holster working out, little girl?"

"Beats having a gun in the bottom of my purse wrapped in a tea towel."

After we finished our coffee, I put Angel back into the house, set the alarm and we took off for the range. Since this was the third Sunday I had shown up to practice with George, no one even gave me a second glance. I was old news.

My aim had improved considerably, and George beamed as he pointed out how much closer my shots came to the bull's-eye on the targets.

"You're the new fuckin' Annie Oakley. That's what you are. I'm gonna' call you Annie." He winked at me.

"Only because I had the best teacher," I said, heat rising in my face.

George gathered up the ammo boxes and I picked up the guns. Up close to the shack, we threw our stuff on a picnic table under a tree. The day had become hot and humid and the mercury was still rising. My shirt was sticking to me like the winner in a wet T-shirt contest, and my hair hung damp and stringy on my neck. When George came back with our drinks, his face was beaded with sweat. Not the best weather for a big guy like him.

"Sit down, George. You look like you're going to have a heat stroke."

"No fuckin' kiddin'. I think I might." He sat down and chugged his first beer.

My first went down easily as well, and I started to cool off a little.

"Let's clean the guns later," I said, noticing how tired George looked.

"Yeah, let's," he nodded.

George wasn't saying much, and his breathing seemed more labored than usual. My concern for him was occupying my full attention and I didn't notice Kenny pull in on the other side of the driveway. He hollered over to George and I turned my head.

Was that the girl with him last Sunday? I don't think so. George was so right about him.

George noticed me looking at Kenny. "Bothering you, sweet cheeks?"

"Nope. I'm steering clear of that disaster area."

"Fuckin' right. That could be a bad thing gettin' a helluva lot worse."

"You are a wise man, George."

He winked and went back to the shack. I had intentionally avoided looking in Kenny's direction since he arrived, just to be on the safe side, but I heard yelling and cursing and glanced over. He and his new girlfriend were having a noisy disagreement. She kicked dirt at him, yelled an insult and stomped away from the table. He grabbed her arm and yanked hard to pull her back towards him causing her to stumble and lose her balance.

She recovered, swung her free arm and smacked him across the head. He jumped up and punched her in the face with such force, she fell backwards and cracked her head on the edge of the picnic table. She lay screaming in the dirt where she landed, her hand over her face and blood gushing out of her nose between her fingers.

I was on my feet and running before I thought better of it.

"What do you think you're doing?" I hollered. I knelt down to help the sobbing girl.

"Stay out of my business, Portia. The same thing will happen to you."

"Not likely, you worthless piece of shit." As I spit on his boot, a huge arm wrapped around my shoulder and gently ushered me back across the road.

"Can't leave you alone for one fuckin' minute, can I?" George chuckled.

"Kenny hit that girl and it pissed me off," I said stomping around the table.

"I can see that, little girl. Your face is red, your hands are shakin' and there's fire blazin' in those gray eyes."

George gathered up our gear, packed it into the saddlebags and we mounted up for the ride home. The wind blowing hard in my face helped clear the malicious thoughts of Kenny from my head. If George hadn't warned me about Kenny and his ways, that could have been me stretched out in the dirt with a bloody nose or worse.

Thank God I had George.

CHAPTER THIRTY

I folded the paper, tossed it on the coffee table, and padded barefoot to the kitchen to refill my coffee mug. I popped a bagel into the toaster and sat down to tackle the stack of unopened mail I was avoiding—mostly bills that I sorted into a separate pile to be paid later.

One envelope had the return address of Matthew's insurance company. I sucked in a breath and inserted the tip of the letter opener. Inside was a statement showing the amount that had been deposited in my account along with a polite letter offering the company's condolences. I exhaled a big breath.

Imbued with newfound energy, I showered, put on makeup and dressed for my trip to the bank. I dug out my torn and ragged jeans that were earmarked for yard work, topped them with a paint-stained black t-shirt. I gelled my hair and pulled on black motorcycle boots. If Jim Timberman wanted something to stare at, he was going to get it, the stupid fuck.

As I walked through the glass door of the bank, more than a few heads turned in my direction. Jim glanced up from his computer and raised his eyebrows as I strutted past his office. I smiled, giving him a wave as I joined the line. The teller updated my account and printed out my balance with a questioning look. She eyed me up and down, then politely inquired if I needed an appointment with an investment counsellor. With one of my best smiles, I declined, saying I would take care of it myself. I withdrew the cash I needed, shoved it into my wallet and made my exit.

On the way home, I stopped into the Harley store to pay the balance on my bike. Thinking Kenny might be working, I steeled myself for an unpleasant encounter of the worst kind, but the store manager, Jackson, was at the desk.

He was a muscular, good looking guy in his thirties, tanned, with dark hair and big brown eyes. His right arm was tattooed with a python winding its' way down towards his wrist. Extremely life-like, I couldn't keep my eyes off it. He wrote up a receipt for the full amount and I paid in cash.

"We offer free delivery," he said, gesturing to my sling. "If you want, I can drop your bike off tomorrow morning."

"That would be so helpful. I hadn't figured out how I was going to pick it up." I escaped from the store without a further Kenny incident. No need to go looking for trouble.

WHILE I munched on a sandwich at the kitchen table, I searched the phone book for the Oakwood Apartments in the west end of the city.

"Oakwood Management, can I help you?"

"Yes, I hope you can. I was thinking of renting in that area and I wanted to find out firstly, if you had vacancies and secondly, what the monthly rent was for your largest apartment."

"Right now, all of our suites are occupied. Our three bedroom units rent for nine hundred a month. Would you like me to put you on a waiting list?"

"No, not today, thanks. I'm just making inquiries."

Nine hundred a month for that dump?

I finished my coffee, changed my clothes for a visit to the hospital and left the house.

After spending a couple of hours reading to Marcy, my mood was less than cheerful. I stopped into the gun store to see George and perk myself up. He was sitting on a stool smoking, waiting for a customer to make up his mind on a hunting knife. He grinned when I walked through the door.

"I have news," I said. "My bike is being delivered tomorrow. Can't wait."

"Before you take it out on the street, you'll have to take the course and get your license, little girl." George put on his best serious face.

"I'll book it today. I promise." Two more customers came into the store and moseyed up to the counter to speak to George. I gave him a wave and left.

Before going home, I pulled into the parking lot of the bank down the block from my usual bank and went in. I bought a bank draft in the amount of ten thousand, eight hundred dollars. When I returned to the Jeep, I put the money into an envelope with a note saying, 'Darlene Abernathy - apartment one ten - rent in full for one year.' The drugstore next to the bank had a post office in the back, where I sent the payment by express post to Oakwood Apartment Complex Management Company.

This wouldn't help her with her abusive husband, but

she could possibly kick him out and still have a place to live with her children.

CHAPTER THIRTY-ONE

I spent an hour in the garage rearranging Matthew's golf clubs, his ten speed bike, and other toys I should have disposed of by this point in time, to make a space for my new Harley. I made a mental note to call Good Will for a pick up.

At nine-fifteen the black and orange Harley trailer backed into the driveway, giving the neighbors their morning eyeful. I stood on the grass while Jackson skillfully unloaded the bike. It was easy to see he had unloaded many before mine. He rolled the bike into the garage, flipped the kick stand down, and then motioned for me to join him. Man, he had a gorgeous smile.

"Do you know much about bikes?"

"Nope, I'm a newbie." I said. "I have a lot to learn."

"Okay then, I'll point out the different gauges and tell you what they're for, so you won't be boggled right off the bat." He laughed. "Why don't you sit on the bike while we do this?"

I threw my leg over the bike and got comfortable. The smell of the new leather filled me with a sense of euphoria and pasted a permanent grin on my face. "Okay, I'm ready."

Jackson was a patient man and thorough in his demonstration. By the time we finished, I had touched every part of the bike and could name most of them.

"Time to start it up," he said. "Go ahead."

I turned the key and it started on the first try. That throaty Harley 'rumble' filled the garage and most of the neighborhood. I looked at Jackson and grinned as I squeezed the gas and revved it.

After I turned off the engine, he handed me a thick book and said, "Here's the owners' manual. Even though we've gone over the basics, it wouldn't hurt if you read the book as well. Especially the trouble shooting section. If you have a problem on the road chances are you can fix it yourself, if you know what to do."

"What if I get stranded?"

"As long as you have a phone and CAA, you're covered. Make sure you have the plan that has free towing." He laughed.

"Sounds like experience talking."

"When you ride a chopper like I do, you're always breaking down." Jackson shook my hand and thanked me for my business. As he walked back to the Harley truck I couldn't help but notice his tight jeans. Nice butt. I sighed.

After lunch, I took my coffee into the garage, sat on the bike and reviewed all the parts with the manual in my hand. Left hand – clutch, right hand – front brake, back brake – foot brake. The turquoise paint glistened, the chrome gleamed, and my heart fluttered every time I looked at it. I started it up again, just to listen to the rumble.

Department of Transport informed me where the weekend course would be held, when I called to reserve a spot. I called George at the store, told him that the bike had been delivered and asked him to come for dinner after he closed up.

He arrived around seven-thirty and we chilled on the patio with a couple beers.

"I booked the training course for Saturday. My arm is healed enough to ride if I'm careful."

"You know, little girl, you use one of their bikes to learn on. You don't want to be dumping yours anyway 'n scratching the shit out of it the first day. You'll dump it soon enough."

"I thought I would have to take my bike. They didn't give many details on the phone." I walked over and checked the meat on the grill. "Almost ready."

"I didn't tell you this before, 'cause I didn't want you getting' a big head n'all, but your cookin' is pretty fuckin' good, little girl."

I laughed out loud, "Gee, thanks. I think."

George cleaned up his steak, in no time flat, ate two baked potatoes, three cobs of corn and a heaping side of coleslaw. Then he made short work of half the apple pie I picked up at the bakery.

"Room for coffee?" I asked

"Maybe later." He lit up a smoke and leaned back in his chair.

Angel was lying on the grass, happily gnawing on a steak bone, while I drank my coffee.

George lit up another smoke, pushed his chair back from the table and got to his feet. "Let's go see the bike."

CHAPTER THIRTY-TWO

SUNLIGHT streamed across my bed cradling me in a golden river of warmth. When I opened my eyes, I stretched both arms without thinking, and there was no pain. Today was going to be a good day.

Angel ran downstairs and waited, wagging her stubby tail, at the patio door until I caught up to her. I turned off the alarm, unlocked the door and left it open to the morning breeze. She sprinted to the back fence like the devil was behind her. I smiled at her enthusiasm, turned on the coffee maker and went to retrieve the paper from the front porch. The street was all but silent at that hour of the morning, the air crisp and fresh. The tree buds had exploded into leaves the color of wet frogs, and the crab apple blossoms were glorious shades of pink, plum and fuchsia. Calmness seeped like warm butterscotch syrup through my veins.

After skimming through the paper, I poured my second cup of coffee and resigned myself to tackling the bills that had piled up. Matthew had always paid them somehow on the computer, but he never showed me how to do it. I wrote the checks one by one and put them into envelopes the old fashioned way. Maybe some people liked getting mail. What did it matter?

I showered and dressed in a white skirt, white tank top, a black button-down shirt, and slipped my feet into white sandals. My face was tanned from the shooting range, needing very little makeup, just lip gloss and a little blush.

Before leaving for the hospital, I cut a large bouquet of flowers for Marcy's room, wrapped the stems in wet paper towels, then plastic wrap and put them on the front seat of the Jeep. I grabbed my purse, sunglasses and keys and locked up.

When I stepped out of the elevator on the eighth floor, there was no one at the nurses' station. *Odd.* As I made my way down the hall, I could hear sounds of activity coming from Marcy's room. I started to run, almost crushing a nurse into the door frame when I reached eight twenty-two.

"What's happening? Did she wake up?" I cried.

"Could you wait in the hall, please? You can't come in here right now." One of the nurses called to me over her shoulder.

"I want to see her." I tried to push past the nurse guarding the door. She made me do an about face and go back into the hall.

"Wait here just a couple of minutes. I'll be back to talk to you." She went into Marcy's room and closed the door, leaving me leaning on the wall.

Five minutes later, three nurses and a doctor came out and closed the door behind them. The doctor took a step towards me and I knew by the look on his face, Marcy was gone.

"Mrs. Winterstein passed away. I'm very sorry."

My legs gave out and my body slid down onto the cold tile floor. I gave myself up to the blackness and let it enfold me.

"Open your eyes, dear. Take a sip of water." A nurse held a paper cup up to my lips.

I choked on the water she offered, as I struggled to stand.

"Don't rush yourself, dear. Just sit on the floor until your head clears."

After lounging on the tile like a limp rag, for another five minutes, I managed to get to my feet with a little assistance. I sat on a chair in the waiting room until I was recovered sufficiently to walk to the nurses' station.

"May I ask why Mrs. Winterstein died?" I asked the nurse in charge.

"She succumbed to her brain injuries. I'm sorry."

Bob murdered her. That's what you should be saying.

When I got down to the parking lot, I sat in the Jeep for half an hour and cried before I was able to drive home.

I skulked through the house like a zombie. With the drapes closed and the doors locked, Angel and I huddled together in our misery like two lost souls. I didn't eat. I didn't sleep. Nothing eased the pain. Nothing quelled the anger.

The only call I took was from Marcy's mother telling me that her memorial service would be in North Bay on Friday. I jotted down the particulars and assured her I would attend.

Late in the afternoon, I made an effort and drove two blocks to a small florist shop in a strip mall close by. I ordered white roses for Marcy and wrote the message that I wanted on the card.

On my way home, I made a quick stop at the gun shop to see George. He always managed to make me feel better. He was finishing his bank deposit and getting ready to close up when I walked in. The air in the shop was heavy with smoke and the pungent smell of gun oil.

"Hey, little girl, why the sad face? You look like you been cryin'." With a heavy scowl, he walked over to the door, turned the lock and pulled down the blind.

"My friend Marcy died. Her husband, Bob, beat her up and then pushed her down the stairs and she died from her head injuries. She's been in a coma for a long while," I sobbed. "That bastard killed her."

George wrapped his massive arms around me and let me cry until I was cried out. When the tears finally stopped he kissed my hair and pulled me back to look at me. "You okay now, baby girl?"

I nodded. "Better—I have to drive to North Bay for her funeral on Friday."

George's face clouded over. "What about Angel?"

"She can ride along for company. I'll stash her in my hotel room while I'm at the service."

"Take your piece. Beautiful, single girl alone on the highway. No fuckin' good."

"I'll throw it in the glove box, and I'll have Angel for backup."

"Never even heard a growl outta that one. Don't know if she would help out or run."

"She would help out. Already did."

"Good to know."

CHAPTER THIRTY-THREE

HIGHWAY eleven was endless and boring in the gray pre-dawn hours. I drove through Tim's for steaming hot coffee, a breakfast sandwich and a couple bottles of water for Angel. I munched on my breakfast as I drove. Angel rode shotgun with her head hanging out the window and her little black ears flapping in the breeze. The mere sight of her enough to ward off predators, but just in case, I'd followed George's advice and stowed my Beretta in the glove compartment.

Farther north, the highway was socked-in with an early morning mist, and even on low beam, my headlights weren't making the way any clearer. Everything was shrouded in gray. I was squinting to see the white line, when a massive dark shadow appeared directly in my path. I slammed on the brakes. Angel rammed into the dash, barking and growling. We came to a jolting stop three feet from the back end of a moose. The massive animal turned her head, regarded the Jeep with disinterest and lumbered down into the ravine at her own speed. I sucked in a deep breath, gave myself a moment to stop shaking and resumed driving. Moose encounter of the first kind.

We passed the 'Welcome to North Bay' sign around nine-thirty and I followed the directions the Marriot had provided when I made my phone reservation. Angel and

I checked in to our ground floor room and unpacked. I filled up her bowls with kibbles and water, then spread out her blanket beside the bed. She flopped down, put her head on her paws and gave me the 'where are we?' look.

After a hot shower, I changed into a black suit, put on make-up and left Angel to her own devices. The hotel had graciously printed map-quest directions for me, detailing the most direct route to the funeral home.

It was a newly constructed building on the outskirts of North Bay, with a lobby big enough for a large hotel, plush carpets, quiet secluded seating areas for smaller groups and every amenity imaginable. The chapel chosen for Marcy's service boasted lavish arched windows.

The casket was closed. The arched cover buried in a sea of white roses, perfuming the air with their delicate scent. A framed photo of Marcy in happier times, was the only reminder of why we were gathered. When I looked at her smiling face in the silver frame my eyes welled up. I'd never met Marcy's mother in person, but noting a family resemblance, I wiped away my tears and introduced myself to the woman in black, standing near the head of the coffin.

"Oh, my dear, Marcy has talked about you so many times." She covered my hand with her own, her eyes glistening with tears. "You drove a long way to be here. I thank you for that."

"I wanted to be here," I mumbled.

The service was short and gut wrenching. Both of Marcy's older brothers spoke about growing up with her and how they loved her. At times they couldn't speak at all, strangled by grief for their sister. Most of the people attending were friends and relatives from her home town and they were not taking her death in stride. Not by a long shot. Judging by the angry expressions on the faces of the male members of her immediate family, I was certain they did not believe for a second that she had fallen down the stairs on her own.

Afterwards, during the reception, Marcy's mother and I spoke again. She explained that Bob's family was disposing of the house and contents, and there was no need of her making another trip south to Toronto. She seemed relieved not to be dealing with Bob's parents. After saying my goodbyes and promising to keep in touch, I returned to the hotel.

Angel was thrilled I was back. She probably thought in her little doggie brain that she was destined to spend the rest of her days booked into the Marriot with no room service. I found her leash, changed into sweats and Adidas, and took her for a run on the hotel grounds. She sniffed around all the forsythia bushes, tangling up her leash and muddying her paws in the flower beds. I had to rein her in, take her back to our room and clean her up. Those white towels and face cloths were not intended for dog paws.

Driving home from North Bay gave me hours to reflect on Marcy's tightly knit family. Images of Charley and Phil, her two older brothers, holding their mother's hand and comforting her, all pulling together, and being there for each other in a time of tragedy. Thoughts of my childhood in foster care came bubbling to the surface. I had not been with any one family more than a year or two—always struggling to fit in with new parents and siblings that weren't my own and never quite making the transition. In order to survive, I hadn't allowed my feelings of loneliness and longing for family to surface. But now that I was a grown woman, with time on my hands, it might be the perfect time to probe a little deeper into my sketchy past.

Night had fallen when I pulled the Jeep onto Hawthorne Lane and into my driveway. The security lights illuminated the perimeter of the property, and I started unpacking the Jeep in the garage. Angel emitted a low growl that sent a shiver snaking down the back of my neck.

"What is it, girl?" I patted her head and surveyed the garage. I gasped, "Oh, my god. No. Not my bike." I dropped my bag on the floor and took a closer look. Someone had scratched the word 'bitch' into the turquoise paint on the back fender. Tears rolled down my cheeks. My first thought was *Kenny.*

Would he be that mean?

How could he get into the garage without setting off the alarm? I retrieved my overnight bag and carried it with Angel's bowls into the kitchen and called George's cell.

"What's up, kiddo. You home now?"

"Just getting in. Found a surprise waiting for me in the garage. Someone broke in and scratched up my new bike."

"That fuckin' prick. I'll kill that son of a bitch. I'm coming over."

"Thanks, George. I'm a bit freaked." I hung up the phone and started to fill the coffee carafe with water. My shaky hands clunked the pot into the faucet. The glass shattered and sent a shard into my left hand. I let out a squeal and held the cut under a stream of cold water until the bleeding stopped. After I dried my hand and applied a bandage, I glanced up and saw the Apex fridge magnet.

"Apex. Mrs. Talbot, are you okay?"

"Vince, I was out of the city all day and returned to find that someone had broken into the garage and damaged my motorcycle. Could that happen without setting off the alarm?"

"No, impossible, let me check the log . . . Okay, I see it here. The alarm went off at your address this morning at seven-ten a.m. A team was dispatched to check it out. When they found nothing, they secured the premises and reset the alarm."

"Why didn't you call me on my cell?" I snapped.

"We did try your cell several times, but it says here, the call didn't go through. Was your phone turned off?"

"I was at a funeral." I hung up, questioning the validity of paying for a high-priced security system when the benefit I derived from it had been zero thus far. Better to have a gun and a dog. I cleaned up the mess in the sink, took two mugs out of the cupboard, and boiled the kettle to make instant coffee.

Ten minutes later, Angel bounded for the front door when the rumble of George's Harley echoed in the driveway. She had become quite attached to George, and she wasn't the only one. George lumbered into the foyer with fire in his eyes and his face flushed. "Let's see it."

I led the way through the kitchen to the garage.

He snarled. "That's it. I'm throwin' down."

I was shaking. George was a formidable sight when he was infuriated, a side of him I hadn't been privy to before. He pounded his right fist into the open palm of his left hand and stomped back into the kitchen. I poured the coffee and took the carton of cream out of the fridge.

"I can have it repainted," I ventured, not knowing if I should speak.

"That's not the issue. That fuckin' low life shit has to be taught a lesson."

"So, you think it was Kenny?"

"You bet your ass it was him, but don't you worry about a thing, sweet cheeks. I've got this covered."

Tears welled up in my eyes. Nobody had ever stood up for me in my whole life. I hugged George and buried my face in his neck.

"Don't cry, little girl. He won't be comin' anywhere near this house again. Guaranteed. Guaranteed by George." When he pulled back he chucked my chin and winked. "I need a smoke if I hafta think. Let's take the coffee outside."

I slid the patio door open and we stepped out into the warm night air. Angel bolted into the yard, found her ball, and did laps around the fence like a dog possessed.

I laughed. "She's happy that you're here. Can you tell?"

"She'll be happy for a while then, 'cause I ain't leavin'. Not until this Kenny thing is taken care of anyway."

I raised my eyebrows, "Really?"

"Fuckin' right. That arrogant little prick don't let go when he doesn't get his way with a woman. You ain't safe, little girl."

"I thought he was getting even with me for helping that girl up at the range last Sunday."

"I don't think that's it." George shook his head. "Lots of girls that have dumped Kenny have had accidents and worse. Not maybe right away, but in time."

I leaned forward and held my throbbing head in my hands as my stomach swirled.

Lady Killer Kenny.

"Go to bed, baby doll. You look wrecked." George went back into the kitchen and motioned towards the living room. "I'll sleep down here tonight."

"Why don't you sleep in the guest room? You'd be more comfortable."

"Fuck. I'm not here for comfort. I'm here to keep you alive."

This is bad.

I couldn't shake the worry that George could get hurt if Kenny came back. I took a blanket out of the hall closet and spread it on the end of the sofa.

"Good enough. Show me how to turn on the alarm. I have to leave at seven-thirty to open the store."

"Lot of good this has done lately," I said, as I showed George the code and the sequence. "A complete waste of money."

"Never fuckin' know. Might give you enough warning to grab your gun and get ready."

"Let's hope so." I plodded up the stairs.

CHAPTER THIRTY-FOUR

SLEEP had been sporadic at best, waking through the night with terrifying dreams of Kenny stalking me, coffins covered in dying flowers and empty chairs at my funeral. I forced myself out of bed, shrugged on a robe and went down to the kitchen to make breakfast for George. He was already up, sitting out on the patio smoking. When I opened the door the morning humidity hit me in the face. "Going to be a hot one."

"Good thing I got air at the shop," George said, "or I'd have to serve customers naked. That'd be bad for business." He chuckled. George lumbered up the stairs to get ready for work while I made his breakfast and made us both an instant coffee. He returned a few minutes later with his hair damp, his clothes from the day before looking a little rumpled.

After breakfast a stone cold expression crossed his face, "Let's sit outside. I need to talk to you." He picked up his mug, moved out to the patio table and lit up a smoke. He always needed a smoke to do his best thinking. I took a seat across the table, studied his face and waited.

"This is what we're gonna do. You're gonna pack your stuff and go to that cabin up in butt-fuck nowhere with Angel for the rest of the week. Give me a chance to sort out that little fuck, Kenny. Then we'll talk about when it's safe for you to come home."

I nodded. "That's doable. I could use a break and there are things that need my attention up there anyway." I paused. "But it feels a bit like I'm running away."

"I want you to run away. It will make my end of things a lot fuckin' easier. Take your piece and wear the holster all the time. Don't let your guard down for a second. Lock this place up tight after I leave and don't come back until we talk. Understood?"

"I understand. Do me a favor, George. Don't get hurt because of me."

"That won't happen. I'm not as stupid as I look and Kenny is big in the looks department, but he ain't long on brains."

"You have my cell number. There's no landline up there that I know of."

George got up. "I have it. I'll call when I have something to say." He winked and headed out to his bike.

After my shower, I dressed in cut-offs and a t-shirt and packed what I thought I might need for three or four days in the North Country. On top of my clothes, I placed the holster containing the Beretta, and shoved a whole box of ammo down the side of the suitcase.

Downstairs, I packed Angel's food, treats and water bottles for the trip. Not sure how I was going to gain entrance to the cabin, I rummaged through the desk drawer in the study and tossed the key ring into my purse. If one of those mystery keys didn't work, I'd have to come up with a different plan when I arrived.

I gave Vince at Apex Security a quick call to tell him

I would be out of town for a few days. I set the alarm and locked the house up tight.

Angel jumped into the passenger seat with enthusiasm. She loved riding shotgun, especially with the window down. The day was gearing up to be a scorcher, but as long as we were moving, with the wind blowing through the Jeep, it was bearable.

THIS time around, I had no trouble locating the cabin. Since my first visit, the grass and weeds at both sides of the driveway had grown high and shaggy, almost hiding the narrow entrance from view. I stopped and peered into the bird's nest in the mailbox. Three blue eggs. I smiled to myself. My own baby birds. At the top of the hill, I parked and let Angel out to explore while I tried the keys in the front door. No luck.

Circling around to the back, a startled chipmunk jumped out of the grass, and I let out a shriek. I tried the key in the lock, turned the knob and presto, the door opened into the kitchen. My kitchen. I still had trouble believing this was my cabin. It felt more like I was breaking and entering. Angel ran up onto the porch behind and squeezed ahead of me through the door.

The kitchen played out like a page from a log cabin magazine. The table was early Canadiana, three wide pine planks forming the top with turned legs underneath. The chairs were a matched set of pressed-backs carved in a wolf pattern. On the left wall, a Hoosier cupboard had been restored and held assorted pieces of Fiesta ware and a few stoneware crocks. The fridge and stove were reminiscent of the twenties or thirties, reproductions nestled between natural pine cabinets.

I stepped further into the space and passed a fieldstone chimneywall separating the kitchen from the living room. The latter was furnished with rustic pieces and early Canadian dough boxes. A refurbished grain scale did double duty as a coffee table, and all of the mullioned windows were draped in homespun hung on black iron rods.

Angel ran into the bedrooms sniffing and exploring, while I checked the fridge and stove for power. The hydro was on.

When had Matthew been up here last? Where were the bills going?

After unloading the Jeep and putting away the groceries, I dropped into one of the weathered wooden chairs on the back porch. This far north, the temperature was a few degrees cooler and the breeze eliminated the breathless humidity of the city. I relished being holed up here for a few days. Angel romped through the evergreens, chasing brazen chipmunks and rousting unsuspecting rabbits out of the brush piles. With the serenity of my surroundings and the warm May sun shining on my face, I dozed off in my chair.

When I woke, I grabbed for my cell phone. I had forgotten to let George know that I had arrived safely.

"Hey, little girl, what took you so fuckin' long? I thought you'd be there way before now."

"Sorry, George, fell asleep on the porch. I'm here. Everything is good."

"Sit tight up there. Call me once a day at the store to check in. Got it?"

"Got it." I ended the call.

Somebody cares about me.

After dinner, I filled up my mug and ambled down the path with Angel to watch the sunset over the lake.

I wondered what George was going to do to solve the Kenny problem, but decided I really didn't want to know.

CHAPTER THIRTY-FIVE

ANGEL'S barking woke me from a deep slumber. The room was dark, and I strained to see her at the other side of the room. Her paws were on the window sill and her nose was squished against the glass. She punctuated her barking and whining with low throaty growls. I stumbled out of bed and grabbed my gun. Standing behind her, I squinted to make out the cause of her distress. Through the gloomy predawn mist, I could make out a large shaggy form lumbering away from the porch towards the trees.

"Oh my nerves, Angel, it's a bear." I patted her on the head and pulled her back from the window and got her a doggie treat from the kitchen. Reluctantly she settled down on her blanket. "You can't go out right now. Not a good idea."

I tried for a few minutes to go back to sleep, but it was a lost cause.

After the sun came up, I made coffee and sat on the back porch watching Angel sniff over every inch of ground the bear had covered. As the day started to warm, black flies swarmed around my head and attacked my neck. I had to retreat indoors, an opportune time to explore the barn.

An old two by four cradled by hand-hewn wooden brackets held the double doors closed. After I lifted the splintered beam, one of the doors swung half open with a squeak of protest while the other stuck in the dirt. A barn swallow swooped over my head, chirping her annoyance at my intrusion. I ducked as Angel plunged fearlessly past me into the dim interior.

The air hung stagnant with mixed aromas of dried straw and moldy hay, punctuated with more than a trace of horse manure. Slits of sunlight squeezed through the cracks between the shrunken barn boards creating eerie patterns on the beams and the bales of straw.

An old John Deere tractor with patchy green and yellow paint, and a torn seat was covered in a thick blanket of dust and grime. Antiquated tools hung on rusty nails along one wall. Two shovels, a hoe, a rake, four axes, a saw, and something with a short handle and a sharp curved blade that I didn't know the name of. A rickety ladder with one rung missing, invited me to climb up to the loft and explore, but I saved that adventure for another day.

The back corner was dark, and I squinted through the gloom to see the pile of old furniture covered with a ragged blue tarp. As I lifted a corner to take a peek, a mouse scurried out and ran over the toe of my boot. I shrieked, dropped the tarp, spun around and ran for the door. Angel passed me in hot pursuit of the little rodent, but she was no match for mouse speed. I propped the working door open to let fresh air and May sunshine work its magic.

When I went back into the cabin to make a sandwich, I gave George a call.

"Gun shop," he answered with a growl.

"Just me, checking in," I said. "There was a bear prowling around outside last night."

"Keep your gun handy. You should really have a shotgun up there for varmints. Look around, see if your old man had one."

"I will. Anything new?"

"Looked around for the fucker last night, wasn't at any of his usual spots. Probably heard I'm gunnin' for him and he's crawled under a rock somewhere."

"Maybe he won't do anything else, George. That could have been a one-time thing with the bike."

"You believe that, sweet cheeks, then I'm a male model." He laughed until he started coughing.

"You're right out of GQ, George."

"What the fuck's that?"

"Never mind."

"Stay away from the bears and call me tomorrow."

"I will."

The remainder of the day, I amused myself snooping around the cabin, looking in drawers and cupboards, searching for treasures. As long as we were married, I had never known Matthew to go hunting, but I found several hunting knives and boxes of ammunition in various kitchen drawers. Under the bed I found a Browning shotgun. Maybe everything came with the property when Matthew bought the place. Maybe not. The existence of the cabin and the purpose it served raised a lot of questions that would never be answered.

The bathroom and the kitchen needed a thorough cleaning after months of neglect. My search of the closets for a vacuum came up empty, but I discovered an old push-broom and swept all of the floors. Satisfied with my efforts, I took a little break. I grabbed the camera I had unearthed in one of the drawers and walked down the hill to the dock with Angel.

The sunset the previous night had been amazing, and I had been wishing for a camera. After finding a digital model that I knew how to operate, I was anxious to see if I could capture some of the colors I missed the evening before. I kicked my sandals off, rolled up my pant legs, and dangled my feet in the water while I waited for the sun to go down.

Angel paddled around the edge of the shore, snapping at dragonflies and frogs as they jumped off the lily pads. As I stared of into the distance the sun dropped considerably, leaving the sky wrapped in ribbons of pink, orange and crimson. If my limited photography skills captured the breathtaking display over the water— even in a small way—the pictures would be worth keeping.

CHAPTER THIRTY-SIX

GEORGE was having a quiet day at the gun shop. Wednesdays usually were a gun cleaning day. Nothing else to do.

Thoughts of Portia filled his head when he should have been thinking of other things. With each passing day, thinking of her and wanting her in his life, occupied more and more of his waking hours. He could still smell her perfume faintly, from the last time she'd been in the shop. He could close his eyes and picture her beautiful face, her long black hair and her perfect twenty-something body.

George counted the float, made up the bank deposit, locked up and left. Part of the day—a small part—when he wasn't thinking about Portia, he planned what he was going to do about Kenny, and how he was going to keep her safe.

His feelings for Portia had resurrected memories from the past—memories that had been buried and better forgotten. Twenty years before, George had been in love with a girl belonging to another biker in the club, and he knew from the beginning he was letting himself in for heartache. Years later he still felt the pain when he thought about her. After that, he vowed he wouldn't let anyone get close to him again, and no one had until Portia. He wasn't about to let scum like Kenny Portsmith hurt her. She was way too good for that little shit anyway.

He finished his smoke as he reached the Screamin' Eagle, parked on a patch of dirt behind the store. He admired the skulls that Rusty had recently air brushed on the Black Crimson, and double checked his saddlebag for the tools he needed for later. Yep, he was gonna fix Kenny good. He threw his massive right leg over the leather seat and turned the key. The noise from the big Harley engine ratcheted through the warm spring night like machinegun fire. George smiled and squeezed the gas.

The parking lot at Buck's was half full. George lumbered to his regular booth in the back by the pool tables and raised a hand to Buck behind the bar. Buck poured a pitcher, picked up two glasses, ambled over and sat down across from George.

"What's new?" he asked, pouring a glass for George and filling one up for himself.

"Not much. Seen Kenny?"

Buck raised his eyebrows. "Not today, but it's early. He'll be in, shoot a couple of games, push some chicks around, get drunk and start a fight. What do you want with that punk?"

George shrugged and lit up a smoke. "Might as well make some cash while I'm waiting. Who wants a game?" he hollered—trying to be heard over Miranda Lambert belting out 'Fastest Girl in Town.'

"I'll kick your ass for twenty." Jimmie, one of the regulars shouted.

"We'll fuckin' see," George said slamming his

twenty down on the corner of the table.

Five games later he picked up his hundred bucks and waved at Buck for another pitcher. "Made some tip money." He laughed and laid a twenty on Buck.

George returned to his booth and lit up a smoke.

"Hey Kenny, how's it hangin'?" one of the hopefuls yelled.

George turned his head. Kenny settled into in a booth with three girls. The one Kenny had hit at the range the week before, still sporting her black eye, and two others. *Don't them bitches ever learn?*

George waved to Buck, took a walk down the hall to use the facilities, and slipped out the fire door at the back. There was only one security light over the exit, leaving most of the parking lot in the shadows. Nobody would dare touch the bikes, unless they had a death wish. Bikers were their own best security.

Kenny's baby girl was parked near the brick wall of the building next door. George easily spotted the red and orange flames on the black paint. He sauntered over to his Screamin' Eagle, pulled on leather gloves and picked a pair of side cutters out of the saddle bag. A couple of quick adjustments later and he called it a night.

CHAPTER THIRTY-SEVEN

A crash of thunder woke me, and I rolled over to see big brown eyes staring at me a few inches from my face. Angel rested her head on the edge of the bed, whining.

"It's okay, girl. Storms don't last long. It will be over before you know it." I gave her a pat on the head. However, that proved to be wishful thinking on my part. Rain poured down in torrents all morning, while Angel paced from the front door to the back and I consumed a whole pot of coffee.

I put in my daily call to George at the shop after I finished breakfast.

"Hey, little girl, what's happening in the far fuckin' north?"

"Pouring rain today, pretty boring."

He chuckled. "Long as you're safe. Suck it up."

"I found a shotgun under the bed. You were right, Matthew did have one. Says Browning on it and there's little ducks etched on the magazine."

"Expensive gun, load 'er up in case that bear comes a knockin'. If a bear or a porky shows up, don't let Angel out."

"I won't. How are you making out?"

"Makin' progress. Gotta' go. Got a customer. Call me tomorrow." He hung up.

Making progress?

I wondered what that meant.

The rain slowed down a little in the afternoon and turned into an all-day drizzle-fest. I stared out the kitchen window until cabin fever got the best of me. Donning a yellow slicker, I found in the closet, I jumped into the Jeep, drove into town and searched for a photo shop. Not noticing one on my first pass down the main drag, I asked the bank teller, while I was withdrawing cash, if she knew of one in town.

"Sure," she said. "Go back to the hair salon. The hairdresser's husband, Wilbur, has a photo shop in the back of her salon. Does good work, too."

"Thanks, I'll try there," I said, stifling the urge to laugh.

On the back wall of Hair Works, I spotted a sign that said Photo Shop, with a crooked arrow pointing through the door. Walking past all the ladies having their hair cut and colored, I approached the counter in the back room, and handed the memory card to a man I believed to be Wilbur, the hairdresser's husband. His hair hung long and stringy over his shirt collar. She definitely wasn't wasting any of her talents close to home.

"Which ones do you want prints of?" he asked.

"I don't have any idea what's on the card before my pictures, and I'm not familiar with the camera, so just print all of them and I'll pick them up tomorrow."

"Okay, be ready by noon at the latest."

"Thanks," I said and retraced my steps through the salon.

CHAPTER THIRTY-EIGHT

GEORGE locked up the store and headed for Buck's. A couple of guys had snagged his regular booth, so he grabbed a bar stool and nodded to Buck.

"What's up, big guy?" Buck said pouring a draught.

"Nothin', slow day at the store. Trout season's open and everybody's fishing, so unless the assholes start fishing with guns, I'm fucked till the fall."

Buck hooted and slapped his belly. "Too bad for that. You should close up for a couple weeks and take a holiday."

"What the fuck would I do on a holiday?"

"Jesus, George. You could ride across the states or ride up to Alaska. Something big."

"The only big thing I'd get outta that would be a big sore ass," he roared.

Buck laughed and went to serve another customer. When he returned, he said, "Hear what happened to Kenny?"

"Nope, what did the little shit do now?" George took a long drag on his smoke.

"He was riding home last night from here, took a corner too fast and drove head first into a ravine. Heard he banged up his pretty face real good."

"Always a smart ass, that one. Rides like he's Evil Knievel. Guess he got off lucky. Could have been killed."

"Yep, could've been worse, all right. He ain't dead. Just in the hospital. Some of the girls been in to see him. Cryin' n all that shit. OPP saw a light down in the ditch and called 911."

"Lucky for him." George scowled.

CHAPTER THIRTY-NINE

"YOU can come home today, if you want." George said, "Should be safe for a while."

"Can you tell me what happened?"

Did I really want to know?

"Kenny got wasted and dumped his fuckin' bike. He's in the hospital."

"Is he badly hurt?"

"Don't know, little girl. For your sake, I sure as hell hope he is," George grumbled.

"I'll pack up and come down this morning. Talk to you later."

I packed my clothes, locked up, closed the barn door and Angel and I were homeward bound, but first I stopped in town to pick up the pictures from the photo shop. All the chairs were full in the salon—ladies with standing Friday appointments, I guessed. As I passed their chairs, I gave a smile and a wave. Most didn't even acknowledge my presence—apparently used to the through traffic.

My pictures were sitting on the counter in a brown envelope with an invoice attached. The hairdresser's husband gave me an odd look as he fumbled in the cash drawer for my change. I smiled and thanked him.

The weather had brightened considerably, and I fished in my purse for my sunglasses. Approaching the city, there was a marked increase in humidity, and by the time I pulled into the driveway, my shirt was sticking to me and Angel's tongue was hanging out.

Tossing my stuff into the front hall, I noticed that the house smelled fresh and piny. It was Friday. Homeshine had been and gone. I loved those girls.

Angel went straight to the patio door and stood wagging her stubby little tail, waiting for me to unlock it. I filled her bowl with cold water and put it outside the door, then grabbed a cold beer from the fridge and joined her outside.

I called George. "I just got home. If you're busy, I won't keep you on the phone."

"Nope, store's fuckin' dead right now. Drive a sane man nuts."

"Maybe you should have a sale or something to boost your cash flow."

"Fuck. I could do that." He chuckled. "Want you to call this guy and get him to pick up your bike. He's gonna' repaint it in HiFi Turquoise, an old Harley color. Be better than new when you get it back."

"Thanks, George. It makes me crazy when I think about my bike. Such a mess and I haven't even ridden it yet." I wrote down the number on a scrap of paper.

"Ask for Rusty. I'm gonna' look around the shop and see what I can put on sale without losing my shirt."

After George hung up, I called the paint shop and had an interesting conversation with Rusty. He assured me, because I was the boss' old lady, he would move my paint job to the top of the list and pick my bike up on Monday morning. I laughed out loud.

The boss' old lady? What the hell did that mean?

I wandered back into the kitchen. The fridge door beeped, and I realized how long I'd been staring at the empty shelves. My mind kept wandering back to Kenny and his accident.

Was this my fault?

I showered and changed into a short denim skirt and a lime green tank top for a trip to the bank and market. As I entered the bank, I could see Jim Timberman in his glass cubicle with a customer. He seemed totally engrossed in whatever he was doing, so it took me by surprise when he looked up, grinned and winked at me. I forced a smile and proceeded to the teller.

After withdrawing the cash I needed, I asked for access to my safety deposit box. I emptied the entire contents into my purse, told the teller to cancel the box and left the bank.

Down the block at the competition, I opened all new accounts and signed the paperwork to transfer all funds to my new bank. They gave me an access card and a new safety deposit box. In private, I stuffed all the gold certificates into the box and locked it up.

Fuck you, Jim Timberman. Whatever your game is, you can play it alone.

At the market, I stocked up on steaks and potatoes. No telling when Kenny would get out of the hospital and George would insist on being my bodyguard again. I popped into Home Outfitters and picked up a replacement for my broken coffeemaker and then headed home. Bring on the weekend.

I set up my new appliance and brewed a pot. I poured

myself a cup, picked up the brown envelope from the photo shop and plopped down at the patio table. Tipping up the envelope by the corner, the glossy contents slid out. Focusing on finding my sunset pictures, initially I didn't absorb the images in the other photographs. It was the glimpse of Matthew that caught my attention. I took a good look at what was going on in the picture, my stomach turned. I leaned over and vomited on the grass.

When I returned from splashing water on my face in the bathroom, I took a deep breath, spread the pictures out and took a second look. Matthew was naked in bed, in various poses, with numerous women in different hotel rooms. In the photos where I could see his face, he had that same controlling gleam in his eye that he always had in the bedroom. There was one exception. In the half dozen pictures where he was coupled with a tall lanky blonde, he appeared to be genuinely happy. Happiness was never a commodity he shared with me.

There were also dozens of revolting pictures of Bob in living color, with different women. The photos were taken in the same hotel rooms as the ones of Matthew.

Maybe Bob had been after the pictures all along. Another question I'd never be able to answer.

Tears rolled down my cheeks as I piled the photos on the patio slab and ignited them with the barbeque lighter. As I watched them incinerate, I recalled Matthew's many 'business trips' during our marriage and again I berated myself for being such a longsuffering idiot. My four sunset pictures were amazing. I shoved them back into the envelope and returned to the kitchen.

CHAPTER FORTY

I showered and dressed before dawn, trying to ready myself for the torturous day ahead on the Provincial motorcycle training course. I force-fed myself a bagel and washed it down with orange juice. No amount of makeup could cover my blood-shot, red-rimmed eyes. My grief for Marcy had not subsided one iota and if Bob hadn't died of his own accord, I would have killed him for what he did.

Thankfully, my helmet would hide my face most of the day. I tugged on my Harley boots, picked up my gloves, helmet, jacket and purse and then tossed it all into the Jeep and departed for Centennial College parking lot.

Surprisingly, despite my trepidation and foul mood of the morning, the day was fun. Being out of doors in the sun on the bikes and navigating through the pylons with the other students lifted my spirits.

The instructors were patient, thorough and not too critical. By the end of the day, with only one small burn on the calf of my leg from the exhaust, I was riding like a pro—more or less—well, riding in any case. Mission accomplished.

When I left the training course, my depression, brought on after discovering more of Matthew's infidelity, hung over me like a heavy black cloud. The rest of the day was looming long and empty in front of me. I changed into a pair of jeans and drove over to the gun shop.

George's face lit up when I walked through the door. "Hey, little girl, didn't expect to see you. What's up?"

"First day done." I said, "I'll finish it up tomorrow morning."

He grinned, "Oh, shit, now you'll be following me everywhere—I won't have a minute's fuckin' peace."

"You got that right," I smiled. "Didn't want to go home and hang around by myself—thought maybe you could use a little help getting ready for your sale."

"Sure, I can. I'm putting these red tags on all the boxes of ammo. You want to do that?" He handed me the pricing gun.

"I do," I said with a smile.

"Think I'll put an ad in the paper. Maybe you could write the ad and make a sign for the window. Your English has gotta' be better n' mine." He chuckled.

We worked together the rest of the afternoon. I dusted the shelves, swept the floor, and Windexed the display window inside and out. The store took on a festive air, decorated with the signs and banners. The highlight of the front window was my kindergarten artwork reading 'Summer Sale' in red letters.

"That does it," said George. "We're fuckin' ready as we'll ever be."

"Hope the customers stampede in here on Monday and clean you out." I laughed.

"If they do, it'll be thanks to you, sweet cheeks. Let's celebrate."

Saturday night at Buck's was a biker event. It was barely seven when we arrived, and the place was filling up quickly. George's regular booth was occupied, so we claimed the first empty one available and sat down.

"It's packed in here tonight," I said.

"I think Ol' Buck is having a band tonight. Guys are getting here early to get a spot. Can't see a waitress—I'll go to the bar."

The decibel level of the country music was sky high and yet the words were barely audible over the rowdy crowd hollering and laughing. A blue layer of smoke hung low and thick, my lungs were protesting, and the evening had just begun. At least I wasn't sitting at home alone.

George returned with a pitcher of beer and two frosty glasses.

"I ordered cheeseburgers and fries. Kitchen's busy, so the food will be slow."

I took a long swallow and nodded. "That's okay. I want to have a drink first, anyway, before the food comes. I'm turning into a biker bitch, George."

"That'll be the fuckin' day." He grinned and lit up a fresh cigarette. "You ever smoke?"

"No. I thought about it. Some of the girls I hung with at work smoked on their breaks, but Matthew made it crystal clear he wouldn't tolerate me smoking. He said smoking was a dirty habit and would eventually kill me."

"What killed him? You never mentioned it."

"Not smoking." I laughed hysterically and downed the rest of my beer.

"You're fuckin' crazy." George chuckled and filled

up my glass.

The waitress arrived with our burgers and fries. She slammed a caddy on the table filled with ketchup and condiments and turned to leave.

"Sheila, another pitcher when you get a minute," George said.

She saluted him with the bird. "Get it yourself, George."

"I'll go," I said.

"No, you won't. I don't want you parading around in front of these assholes. That'd cause a fuckin' riot for sure." He laughed and went to the bar.

When George came back, I had devoured half of my food. "This is really good. Best burger ever."

George was quiet while he finished his food. He refilled our glasses and said, "Are we shootin' tomorrow?"

"Hell, yeah, but I have day two of my course. I won't be done until after lunch." I tipped back my glass and giggled when the world spun a bit. "I think I'm getting drunk."

"You can't be drunk yet. You've only had three."

"That'll do it. I'm not a pro like you."

"Well, slow down, little girl. I want to hear this fuckin' band before I go. Heard they had a half decent banjo picker. Hey Buck," George yelled. "What time's the band starting?"

"Nine. Ten more minutes." Buck held up ten fingers.

While we waited for the band to finish setting up, one of George's buddies walked by our booth and stopped to chat. "Heard Kenny's getting out of the hospital tomorrow, thought you might want to know." He winked at George and gave him a punch in the shoulder.

"Appreciate the info, Donnie." George shook his hand and nodded.

My hand started to tremble, spilling a little beer over the side of my glass.

"Don't," George said covering my hand with his. "Everything will be cool, baby girl."

Looking into his big ole brown eyes, my eyes welled up. "Nobody ever cared about me before, George. Nobody." I reached over, touched his face and he kissed my hand.

Just then the band broke into an ear-splitting rendition of 'I Love this Bar' and all the bikers let out a roar of approval and I had to laugh.

"That's better," George said, looking relieved. I guess comforting weeping members of the opposite sex wasn't his forte. When the band broke after their second set, I took a trip to the ladies room to test my state of sobriety. Steady as a stone. Good.

When I returned, George was paying the tab and tipping Sheila. "I figured you'd be gettin' ready to leave," George said. "Can't have you tired and hung over at your course."

"That doesn't mean you have to go. You're a better party animal than me, George. Stay and have some fun with your friends and enjoy the banjo dude. Angel's been in all day, and I need to feed her and take her for a walk."

"I'll walk you out. That parking lot is black as hell. Don't want you getting kidnapped."

When we reached the Jeep, I opened the driver's door and turned to say goodbye to George. His massive arms enveloped me in a hug. It surprised me how natural and uncomplicated it felt.

I kissed him on the cheek. "Thanks for everything."

CHAPTER FORTY-ONE

THE next afternoon, George was leaning on his bike having a smoke before our ride. He couldn't light up while riding—too much wind he said—so I puttered around while he got his nicotine fix. He looked good today in his leather jacket and a bright red bandana tied around his long black hair. For a second, I thought I could smell cologne.

Couldn't be.

We mounted up and gave the neighborhood their Sunday dose of noise and excitement as we roared up Hawthorne Lane. Riding was my freedom. All my worries disappeared into the wind. My broken arm was so much better now, I could wrap both around George. Just feeling his size and strength gave me comfort.

It was getting close to four when we arrived at the range. We had a late start after I completed the remaining hours of my training course. George parked the bike and we ambled down the hill to the target area. The sun was high in the sky and the temperature was in the mid-eighties, with no discernable breeze. I left my jacket and helmet on the bike and carried my ammo box in my hand. George was watching me load the magazine with an odd look on his face.

"What?"

"You brought the wrong ammo again, little girl.

Remember I told you to look for the little green dot on the box? I don't have any practice 9mm with me."

"Does it matter if I use this?"

"No, it doesn't matter. It just costs more,"

"That's okay. It's just one day. I'll suck it up."

We didn't practice as long as usual because of the heat. George's hair hung wet around his neck and his black Harley shirt stuck to him.

"I need a cold one," he said after less than an hour of shooting.

"Me too. I am melting." I wiped my forehead with the back of my hand. We holstered our guns and plodded uphill towards the shack. George was breathing heavily by the time we reached the top of the grade.

I carried the nearly empty ammo boxes over to one of the picnic tables and sat down, while George fetched beer from the cooler. My arms were already red and tingling from the sun, and I was sure they would blister later. When George returned, I picked up my bottle and held it against my face then took a long drink. "Oh, I needed that."

George laughed and chugged his first right down. He was picking up his second bottle, when the rumble of an approaching bike ripped like a razor through the silence of the sultry afternoon. George stared at the newcomers with a puzzled look on his face. The bike was a black Electra Glide Classic with two people aboard. When the passenger took off his helmet, I gasped and looked at George. It was Kenny. He had hitched a ride with another club member.

Kenny's face was blended shades of purple and blue,

and he had a scab covering a gash over his right eye. He was walking cautiously and favoring his left leg. He looked over at George and gave him the finger, before sitting down with his pal at a table on the other side of the driveway. A couple of girls scurried over to his table like flies to honey. What a chick magnet the guy was.

As I looked back to George, I studied his face. He wasn't showing any sign of emotion, just staring in stony silence. "Should we leave?" I asked.

"Nobody makes me leave before I'm ready," he snarled.

I sipped my beer and watched the girls across the way throw themselves at Kenny. They were kissing the bruises on his face and rubbing his sore leg. He was laughing and lapping up the attention. He waved his empty bottle in the air and two girls ran to the cooler like their asses were on fire. He was putting on quite a show.

I turned my gaze back to George and he read in my eyes that I wanted to get out of there. "Had enough of that fuckin' garbage?" he asked.

I nodded. George wiped the sweat off his forehead and got to his feet. Grabbing the ammo boxes from the table, I followed him across the dirt driveway towards his bike. Our route took us past Kenny's table. There was no way around it. I held my breath and didn't look at Kenny or the girls lolling around him. We were only a few feet from the Eagle when Kenny yelled something at George that I didn't quite catch. I was hoping against hope that he would keep walking and ignore the insult, but that was not the way George rolled.

He turned, exhaled, slowly sauntered over to Kenny

and grabbed him with one hand by the collar of his jacket. In a blur, Kenny spun out of George's grasp, pushed back from the table, pulling a knife from his boot. Steel flashed in the sun as it ripped through George's arm.

"You stupid fuck," George spat, clutching his blood-soaked arm. "I'll kill you for that."

Kenny laughed and lunged again, plunged his knife deep into George's left thigh and knocked him off balance. George hit the ground with a thud and before he could recover, Kenny straddled him. The knife was biting into George's throat when I heard the gun shot.

Kenny twisted off George in violent recoil and collapsed into the dirt. The area around him was spattered with a mass of flesh, blood and brains. Part of his face was missing. The bullet had ripped through the back of his head and exited though his eye socket.

Bikers came running out of the shack with weapons drawn and pushed the girls out of the way. A couple of guys helped George get to his feet. He limped towards to me, his hand clutching his arm, blood oozing between his fingers and a dark stain radiating around the rip in his jeans. "Thanks, Annie," he said with a grin.

It was at that moment I realized I was frozen in my stance, still aiming the gun. I drew in a breath, as George forced my arm to bend and pried my fingers from the grip. I stood there while he holstered my Beretta.

"We have to bandage your arm and get to a hospital," I said blinking and trying to focus. "And Kenny . . . we should we call an ambulance." My breath was coming in short pants.

"No need. You finished him, baby."

I sucked in a big breath, tasting gun powder on my tongue while it burned the inside of my nose. "We can't just leave him there. We have to call the cops . . . or something." My hands shook as my lunch made an attempt at a return visit and I definitely needed a bathroom.

"Or something, baby doll. That's it." George went into the shack and spoke to his boys. He came back with a towel wrapped tightly around his arm, held in place with layers of duct tape. "The boys said you're a fuckin' dead eye. We're good to go. You drive."

"Me?" I asked wondering how in hell I could manage it. My mind was racing, my skin was crawling, and I needed to vomit. Now I had to remember how to start the bike and drive it home with a passenger on the back. George got on behind me and wrapped one arm around my waist. The heat from his body oozed through my back. The towel on his arm was soaked with blood and the smell of it caught in my throat.

I turned the key and the big Harley answered with a deep rumble on the second try. I put it into gear and eased it out to the road. On the gravel side road, I had problems with balance because of all the weight behind me, but once I reached the paved highway, I improved.

As we approached the first town on our route home, George directed me down a couple of back streets to a white frame house.

"Go around the back," he hollered over the roar of the engine.

I veered the Harley towards the back porch and

parked. George leaned heavy on me and I helped him through the rear door into a tiny emergency room fashioned in the sunroom of the old house. "Hey, doc," George yelled.

An old man appeared in the doorway with a drink in his hand.

"You cut up again, you old bastard?" he growled and set his drink down on the window sill. He gathered up what he needed for the stitches before he took the towel off George's arm and motioned for George to sit in the only chair. I turned my head while the cleanup was going on, but it wasn't enough. The smell of blood and the trauma of earlier events ganged up on me and I stepped out into the backyard and threw up in the long grass beside the fence.

A few minutes later, George came out of the examination room sporting a clean white bandage, grinning and dying for a smoke.

"Let it go, Annie. It's done. Now, let's get home and forget about it." He winked at me.

The air was much cooler on the second half of our journey, and I was much calmer. After throwing up, I was a new person. Almost. It was early evening as I navigated the Eagle into my driveway and lowered the kickstand with the toe of my boot. George limped over and plopped down on the porch steps.

He exhaled. "These fuckin' stitches are hurtin' like hell."

"The freezing must be wearing off," I said. "I'll get my pain killers and be right back."

I unlocked the door and punched in the code as Angel

flew past me to get to George. She covered his face with kisses, then ran huge circles around the front lawn. I returned with the pills and sat down. "I'm worried about what those guys are going to do with Kenny," I said. "And what about those girls? Are they going to go to the cops?"

"Definitely not. Won't happen. Best if you don't know anything about it, sweet girl. Pretend it never happened."

"I don't know if I'm that good at pretending." I grimaced and clenched my teeth.

"You saved my life. He would've cut my throat in a heartbeat, and he wouldn't have given it a second thought. Then they'd be digging a six foot hole for me." George leaned over and kissed me on the mouth. I put my arm around his neck and kissed him back.

"That was nice," I said.

"Yep."

"Stay here tonight and I'll drive you to the store in the morning."

"Plan A."

George wasn't himself. Color had drained from his face and his boisterous demeanor had become languid and silent. He'd lost a lot of blood and needed to rest. "Let's call it a night." I walked into the house with George and Angel on my heels.

After George downed his pain meds, he settled on the sofa in the living room with a pillow and a blanket. Five minutes later he was snoring. I gathered his blood-stained jeans off the floor, threw them in the washer, made a cup of coffee and called the paint guy.

"Rusty Coulter," he answered.

"Sorry to bother you on Sunday, Rusty. I wanted to let you know that I won't be here in the morning when you pick up my bike. I'll leave it in front of the garage door for you."

"That works for me. I'll give you a shout when it's done."

I finished my coffee, threw George's pants in the dryer, and left him a note on the coffee table before I trudged upstairs. It had been quite a day.

I almost lost the only glimpse of family I'd ever known.

CHAPTER FORTY-TWO

WHEN I emerged from the shower, George was stirring downstairs. Angel was already circling the back yard, excited that she had company outdoors so early in the morning. After pushing the button on the coffee maker, I joined George at the patio table. A little of his color had returned, but he looked exhausted. The red laceration on his neck had faded a little, but blatantly reminded me of how close he had come. "Did you get much sleep?"

"Not much. I'm okay. Nothin' to worry about."

I reached out and touched his hand. "Why don't you rest today and let me take over at the store?"

"That would be the sensible fuckin' thing to do, honey, but I'm bullheaded enough to work no matter what." He flicked his ashes into the peonies.

"Okay, but I'm insisting on helping. You can sit on the stool at the cash and supervise."

"Deal. And by the way, thanks for the clean duds."

I nodded.

Before we left, I backed my bike out of the garage and left it in the driveway for Rusty, then pushed the Eagle in and locked the door.

I squeezed the Wrangler into the tiny parking spot behind the gun shop and waited for George to limp along behind me and unlock the front door. He made his way behind the counter and readied the float for the cash. I was setting our travel mugs on the counter when the bell over the door jingled and our first two customers arrived.

"Saw your ad in the paper," said a small red-haired man in wire-rimmed glasses. "Need a gun for my son here to learn on."

"We have a good selection on sale, what gauge were you thinkin'?" asked George, butting out his smoke in the ashtray.

"Maybe, twenty, till he gets used to the kick." He punched his son in the shoulder.

"I'm not a baby, Dad. I can handle a twelve gauge. I shot yours more than once." The young man was six inches taller than his father.

The kid looked eighteen or nineteen, but his father treated him like he was twelve.

George smiled and tossed me the keys to unlock the glassed-in display. The son tried several makes and models, hoisting them up to his shoulder for the weight and the feel.

"Dad, I like this Remington 870 the best," he said.

"That's the Express Supermag," George hollered. "Nice gun."

The father raised his brows. "That's a twelve gauge, kiddo. Think you're ready for it?"

"For sure."

"Okay, if you're sure that's the one."

"Would you like a case for your gun?" I asked sweetly, doing the upselling bit. "We have some beauties on sale this week." I steered the young man over to the rotating display and showed him a camo case that would fit the Remington.

"That's cool. Can I get that one, Dad?"

"Might as well. You don't want to get your new gun all scratched up."

"We have the ammo on sale this week as well," I said.

"Better get a box," the father said.

I slipped the Remington into the case and took it over to George and let him write up the paperwork, while I put all the other guns back into the glass cabinet.

After the pair had left the store, George lit up a smoke and sat on his stool grinning. "You're quite the fuckin' sales woman, ain't ya?"

"I'd like to think so." I laughed, cocking my head.

Business was steady most of the day. At noon, I walked down the street and bought subs and Cokes for lunch. We ate on the tiny table in the back of the store that George used for cleaning guns. By closing time, George was fading, although he didn't admit it to me.

"Miller time," he said. I counted the money for the float while he made up the bank deposit and we locked up for the day.

As we trudged out to the Jeep, George said, "Good day, thanks to you, Annie."

"Couldn't say that about yesterday, could you?" I said half joking.

"Not your fault, little girl," he said, easing his wounded leg into the passenger seat.

Pretty much was.

The bar wasn't crowded on a Monday night. We claimed our regular booth at the back and Buck came over with a pitcher.

"Heard you had a spot of trouble yesterday." He pointed at George's bandage.

"A bit." George grinned.

"Quite a story the way I heard it." Buck stared straight at me, eyebrows raised.

"Can't believe the shit you hear, Bucko. Ninety-nine percent bullshit." George answered.

"Think I'll go to the ladies room."

My hands were clammy, and the hair was standing up on my arms, just thinking about what happened yesterday at the range. For George's sake, I was putting on an outward show of bravado, but my insides were globs of Jell-O.

As I came out of the stall and moved towards the sink to wash my hands, one of Kenny's bitches came into the restroom. I recognized her face in the mirror and the look she was giving me didn't say lovin' from the oven. She raised her arm and grabbed my hair.

Before she could jerk my head back, I stomped backwards onto her foot with the heel of my boot and rammed my elbow into her gut. She grunted and released her grip on my hair. I spun around and drove her in the face. The impact slammed her up against the wall and I followed, my right hand pressed against her throat. Blood was coursing down her face, her hands were shaking, and she was making a little mewling sound.

"Don't ever touch me again. You are fucking with the wrong woman." I looked her in the eye until she nodded that she understood. When I turned back to the sink to wash her blood off my hands, she locked herself in one of the stalls. I dried my hands, turned on my heel and slammed out the door.

Thank God for self-defense classes.

"You okay?" George asked when I sat down in the booth. "Your face is kinda red."

"I'm great." I smiled and filled up my glass.

A short time later, the girl emerged from the ladies' room and passed by our table on the way back to her booth. She was holding brown paper towels soaked in blood over her nose.

George glanced up. "What the hell happened to that bitch?" he laughed. "Ain't it safe to take a piss anymore?"

"Guess not," I said, wearing my best 'not guilty' look.

George stared at me a moment, then trigged in. The grin widened on his tanned face. "That's what I love about you," he said, "I never know what's happening next."

CHAPTER FORTY-THREE

BUSINESS was slower at the gun shop on Tuesday, but we made a few decent sales, and George seemed happy with the bank deposit. I had no idea what his financial situation was, and until he confided in me, it was none of my business.

"Ready to rock n roll?" he asked.

I picked up my purse and keys. "Ready."

George locked the store and as we walked through the alley towards the Jeep he flicked his cigarette butt into the blue dumpster. "I need to stop by my place and pick up some shit."

"No problem. Just give me directions, and we're there."

George had never broached the subject of where he lived or anything of a personal nature during our friendship of the past few weeks, and I had never asked.

"My place is a few blocks from here. After I took over the shop, I picked the closest fuckin' dump and rented it."

"How long have you had the gun shop?" I asked.

"Five, goin' on six years. It's a livin'."

Following George's directions, we arrived on a tree lined, dead-end street in front of a white frame war-time bungalow that had looked its' best in the fifties. The paint was peeling, and the roof had patches of shingles missing. The chain link fence surrounding the postage stamp sized front yard was sagging in places and full of holes in others. The front steps had a couple of boards missing and I could picture George crashing through the splintered wood some dark night and breaking his leg. A narrow drive with grass growing up the middle, led to a ramshackle garage with one door hanging open.

"Wait here, I'll be back," he said. I clued in that he didn't want me to follow him inside. Ten minutes later he ambled out in clean clothes with a red bandana tied around his head.

"How did you tie that bandana?" I asked.

"With a lot of fuckin' cursing," he said and chuckled.

"Where to?"

"Your call tonight."

"I have steaks to grill, and cold beer in the fridge."

"Go for it, Annie." He rolled his window down and lit up a smoke.

After dinner, we lingered on the patio enjoying our coffee and the warm June evening. The scent of lilacs had been replaced by the heady fragrance of the orange blossom bushes bursting into bloom. The tulips and daffodils had run their course and my gardening crew had filled the beds with petunias, begonias and pansies in shades of pink, fuchsia and purple.

George lit up a fresh smoke and said, "I think I'll ride my bike to the store in the morning."

"Where's that coming from?" I asked with a frown.

"Don't like takin' help from anybody. Drives me fuckin' nuts." He scowled.

"Your decision, George, do you think you can ride?"

"I've been moving my arm around a bit, and with the pills it ain't too bad."

"Try it. If it doesn't fly, go to plan B."

He snorted, "What the fuck is plan B?"

"Come back here and I'll drive you to the store," I said.

"Fuck. It's not that I don't like hangin' around you. Just used to doin' things myself."

"You're sick of me. I can tell."

"Fuck no." he boomed. "There's nobody like you, Annie. Never will be."

CHAPTER FORTY-FOUR

GEORGE roared out the driveway on the Eagle at seven thirty a.m. with no apparent difficulties and I returned to the kitchen to finish my coffee. The images of Kenny haunted my brain, day and night, but I didn't want to discuss it with George. Talking about it made me relive the moment in living color. The moment that I almost lost George. I couldn't even imagine my life without him.

The phone was ringing as I walked into the kitchen.

"Rusty Coulter here."

"Hi Rusty, how's the paint job coming?"

"Fantastic color. I'm lovin' it. Doin' the last coat tomorrow. Can I drop it off Friday?"

I could tell by his breathing that he was working and smoking while he was talking to me. "Friday's fine. Can't wait to see how it looks."

The rest of the day, I spent catching up on things I had neglected. I called the insurance company and added the Harley to my policy, opened all the envelopes on the hall table, threw the junk mail in the recycling and paid all the bills.

After lunch I rang George at the store to see how he was holding up. "Checking up on you. Everything okay?"

"Busy this morning, but nothin' doin' now. I'm

resting and having a smoke."

"Rusty called. He's bringing my bike back on Friday. Can't wait."

"Maybe we'll ride on Sunday if my fuckin' arm can take it."

"I'm excited for that."

"Wanna meet me at Buck's later? I should be there about eight."

"I'll see you then."

When Angel and I came home after our long walk down by the river, I hopped in the shower and dressed to meet George at the bar. My jeans felt snug on my butt, maybe I had gained a pound. Yippee. I wore a red, white and blue t-shirt with a big Harley crest on my chest. That should make George smile. Checking my makeup in the bathroom mirror, I noticed my hair was looking shaggy and needed a trim. Put that on my list for tomorrow.

GEORGE was sitting in his regular booth when I arrived at Buck's. He looked up and grinned. "You're late."

"Am not," I said, sliding into the booth.

He chuckled and poured me a glass of beer with his good arm.

"How were the sales today?"

"Not as good as Monday, but still better than last week. I'm happy."

"As long as you're happy, George." I smiled.

"Nice shirt." George looked towards the door and a frown replaced his smile. "Cops."

I turned my head to see two men in uniform walking towards Buck at the bar.

"What the fuck do those assholes want?" George said, mostly to himself.

"I guess we'll find out." My stomach did a flip and my hands were visibly shaking. I put my glass down on the table and sucked in a breath.

"Don't go there, Annie. Relax."

The two men had a picture in hand and were systematically going from booth to booth asking questions and scribbling in their notebooks. As they zeroed in on our table, I thought I might pee my pants, hurl, or experience both bodily functions at the same time.

"I'm Officer McNiff and this is Officer Pirelli." They flashed their identification. McNiff was short and stocky, about five eight with rusty colored hair. Pirelli was taller, thin and bald.

"Either of you seen this guy around?" Pirelli placed a black and white, eight by ten glossy of Kenny on the table right in front of me.

Don't lose it, girl.

I studied the photo for a moment before speaking. "Doesn't he work at the Harley store?' I asked, my voice sounding a little husky.

"He does, but he hasn't reported for work all week. His father filed a missing person's report this morning."

"Probably shacked up with some filly," George mumbled. "He's done that before."

"You know him, then?" asked officer Pirelli.

"Seen him around. Quite a ladies man, I've heard. Fuck 'em and forget 'em," George said lighting up a smoke.

"I could charge you with smoking in a public place," said McNiff, pointing a finger in George's face.

George stood up, looked down at McNiff and snarled, "Bring it."

There was a loud scraping of chairs on the wooden floor and the shuffling of boots as the boys trigged into what was going on and stood at the ready.

"Next time," said McNiff, threatening George with a shooting gesture. They moved on to the next table and I made a trip to the ladies' room. By the time I returned, they had finished questioning all the customers and had left the building.

"What do you think?" I asked George.

"They'll never find him. Case closed."

CHAPTER FORTY-FIVE

THE doorbell rang as I was pouring cream into my coffee. Rusty was standing on the porch with a cigarette in his hand. He was about five-nine, muscular build with huge tattooed arms. His dark auburn hair flopped into his brown eyes. His jeans were splattered in a myriad of paint colors of many, many bikes.

"Wanna come out and take a look, Portia? I'm lovin' the color," he said, beaming.

"I do," I said, following him onto the driveway.

He rolled the bike backwards off the trailer and the scratch marks were completely gone. The color was a shade darker than the original, but deeper and richer.

"I love it. That's the HiFi Turquoise?"

"I had some in stock. A lot of people still in love with that color."

"I can see why. You did a great job, Rusty. Looks brand new."

"Thanks," he smiled and turned to walk back to his truck.

"Wait a minute, Rusty. What do I owe you?"

"It's been taken care of."

"How could that be?"

"You have friends in high places," he said and laughed as he jumped into the cab of his truck and turned the key. "Enjoy." He gave me a wave and was gone.

What the hell? *George.* I was just climbing the porch
steps to go in and give George a call, when Homeshine
pulled into the driveway.

Shit. It's Friday.

"Hi, girls." I held the front door open while they
brought in their mops and cleaning caddies. Angel tried
to squeeze out the door while they were trying to get in
past her and everyone was wedged in the door frame
giggling.

"Hi, Mrs. Talbot," Stacey said when she managed to
sidestep the dog.

"Why don't you call me Portia, doesn't make me
sound so old," I laughed. "I'll take a coffee out to the
patio while you girls do your stuff." I called Angel off
greeting detail, and we went into the back yard. Once I
set my mug down, I called George.

"Gun shop," he answered.

"Hey, you."

"Oh, oh, what the fuck did I do?" George asked.

"You know what you did. I didn't get a bill from
Rusty. Why's that?"

"He owed me one. Nothin' more to it."

"You didn't have to waste a favor on me. I was
happy to pay him."

"I know. I wanted to."

"Thank you, George. That was unexpected, but a
lovely gesture."

"What the fuck are you sayin', Annie. When you talk
like that, I get all fucked in the head."

"Sorry, just trying to say thank you, from the heart."

"That's better. How'd it turn out?"

"Gorgeous. I love it. I'll ride it over to the store and show you."

"Don't even think about it. When you ride for the first time, I want to be there in case."

"In case what?"

"Just, in case," he said, letting out a big breath.

"Hey, I drove your bike and that Screamin' Eagle is bigger and heavier than mine."

"Yeah, and I was sittin' right behind your little ass in case you dumped."

"So true," I laughed.

"Customer, call you later."

After the Homeshine girls finished, I made a salad for lunch and toddled upstairs to take a nap. In the middle of a beautiful dream about the cabin surrounded by trees in autumn colors, the phone rang. Groggily, I pressed talk.

"You sound sleepy," said George.

"I was taking a short nap."

"Short?" he said and snorted. "It's ten to seven. I'm leavin' for Buck's. Do you want to meet me for a cheeseburger?"

"Holy shit, I've been asleep for hours. I'll be up all night."

"I can handle that," George chuckled.

"Give me half an hour," I said, heading into the bathroom.

I changed into tight black jeans and a black tube top and threw on a short hot pink jacket. To complete my 'fitting in" look, I pulled on knee high black leather boots. With this outfit on, I'd be sure to blend at Buck's.

When I walked through the door into the smoky blue

cloud, I heard a whistle.

Wow, I'm right on the money.

George glanced up as I got closer to his table, his mouth turning into a full on grin. "Lookin' fuckin' hot tonight, baby girl."

I smiled, pleased that he liked the look. "Thanks. Must be all the sleep I had."

George let beer trickle down the side of my glass while I held it for him. I was staring into his dark eyes wondering if he knew how much I needed to be near him, when I moved the glass and he almost spilled. "Hey," he said with a smirk.

"How's the arm feel today?" I asked.

"Better. I can work with it now. No sweat."

"When do the stitches come out?"

"Don't know. I've got scissors. I'll do it myself."

I frowned. "Do you think that's a good idea? Maybe a doctor should do it."

"Done it lots of times, I'm a doctor."

"Fuck you."

"You wish."

Before I could think up my next come back, Sheila arrived at our table.

"You guys know what you want?" She tapped her pencil on her order pad while she chewed a wad of gum and blew a bubble.

"Two cheeseburgers with fried onions, fries on the side, and another pitcher of Coor's for the lady," he said with a laugh.

"Cause I drank my first pitcher already," I said, handing Sheila the empty.

While we waited for our food, George went over to shoot a game of pool with one of his buddies. I was watching them from the booth and didn't notice when one of Kenny's girlfriends slipped into the seat across from me.

"Hey, bitch," she snarled with her lip curled up like Elvis. "I'm gonna get you for what you did. You won't even see it comin'." She hopped up and went back to her own table before I had a chance to say anything.

George saw her leaving our booth and came over. "What did that ho want?" he growled.

"She wanted to scare me."

"Did it work?"

"Nope. I'm not afraid of her. I can take her."

"Shoot her." George chuckled as he lumbered back to his pool game. When he won, he picked up the money from the corner of the table, stuffed it into his jeans, hung the cue in the rack and came back to eat with me. The cheeseburgers were heavenly. I'd probably gain a pound from the smell of the grease alone.

After George pushed his plate away, I pointed to the table where my little visitor had settled. "What's that girl's name?"

"That's not a girl. That's a fuckin' disease," he said with a scowl, "She's a crack head—calls herself Barbwire, but she ain't no Pamela Anderson. If she gives you trouble, I want to know. Most of the guys have had a run at her and won't give her the time of day. Kenny was about the end of the line for that one."

"Barbwire? Good one. I wonder what they call me."

"Nothin' . . . if they fuckin' want to live."

I raised my eyebrows. "Uh-huh."

George and I finished off our conversation and called it a night. Driving home alone in the dark gave me time to think—I wondered where and when Barbwire might make a try for me.

CHAPTER FORTY-SIX

EVEN though the house was secure and Angel was on guard duty beside my bed, knowing Barbwire was out there waiting and watching made me antsy. I reached under my pillow and felt the weight of the Beretta in my hand. Touching the cold steel of the barrel and flipping the safety off gave me solace. I showered and dressed for the day, donned my shoulder holster, checked the magazine to make sure it was fully loaded and put the gun in place under my denim jacket.

After my initial cup of coffee at the kitchen table, I gathered my thoughts and walked to the back of the garden. The lily of the valley had finished blooming, but the leaves still looked shiny, green and fresh. I picked a few and took them into the house.

It wouldn't hurt to have a syringe ready if I needed it. And what's another needle mark?

I ground up the leaves on plastic wrap and sucked the resulting liquid into the needle. I sealed the syringe in a Ziploc bag and tossed it into my purse.

I took two travel mugs out of the cupboard and filled them with coffee. Extra cream and no sugar in one, just the way George liked it.

Angel jumped into the passenger seat, panting and drooling, but happy to be going with me. I secured the coffee mugs in the cup holders, rolled down the windows and headed for the store. There was no way in hell I was going to sit at home all day waiting for that bitch to sneak up on me. I had tried to help her, and this is what I got in return?

The little bell jingled merrily as I blasted through the door of the gun shop.

'Whoa, little girl. What the fuck is up?" George raised his eyebrows as I set the coffee mugs on the counter. "Those gray eyes are looking mighty cold and stormy this morning. Who's on the hit-list?"

"I didn't tell you last night, but that bitch, Barbwire, said she was coming for me. This morning, I was thinking about what I should do, and decided that I wouldn't wait. I would track her down and deal with her myself. Man, she pissed me off."

"That I can see," George said with a smirk. "What do you want me to do, little girl?"

"You can give me a clue where she hangs out, and I'll take it from there."

George grinned and lit up a smoke. "She hangs with a crowd of fuckin' addicts in a sleazy basement rat hole. She's always with a couple of 'em, and if you think I'm gonna send you alone into that den of losers, you are dead wrong, baby girl. Not happening."

The bell jingled again, and two men came in, heading directly to the counter to talk to George. I bided my time looking in the glass case that held the knives. Maybe I needed a boot knife. Everyone seemed to have one—just in case.

George wrote up his sale and bagged the ammo that the dudes were buying.

"How long is your sale on?" One of them asked as he reached the door.

"End of next week," George answered giving them a wave.

"George, I want to buy one of these boot knives," I said."

"You don't know how to use a knife, honey."

"Could you show me?"

"Never bring a knife to a gun fight," he stared at me with a stone cold look in his eye.

"Okay, maybe not. So... you won't tell me where Barbwire hangs out?"

"Can't. I'd be sending you there to get hurt or fuckin' worse. We'll think of another plan after I close up."

"Come over after work. I'll fix us up some supper." Before I could chicken out, I leaned over the counter, put one arm around his neck and pulled him towards me. I kissed him hard on the mouth and gave him a lot of tongue. He tasted like smoke and beer and Saturday night. At first his lips were tense, but the surprise wore off and he caught up with me. Damn, this man could kiss. "Don't take too long," I whispered hoarsely and let my intentions show.

A look of surprise flickered across his tanned face, before being replaced by a brilliant grin. "How can I work now? Look what you done to me."

I blew him a kiss and winked as I went out the door, kicking a little extra into my hips as I went.

Angel wagged her tail as I hopped back into the Jeep. I had rolled the window down for her, and parked in the shade, but the temperature was climbing, and she was panting.

Driving home, I sucked in a few deep breaths and reveled in the effect George had on me. When I turned on the CD player, my hands were steady, and I had a sense of security I had never known before. He was a little stockier and gruffer than what I had pictured in my head as my ideal soul mate, but Mother Nature was a tricky bitch. If she sent me an overweight biker, who was I to argue? My heart told me he was *the one*.

I pulled the Wrangler into the driveway and let Angel in through the front door. I scooped up the mail from the floor and it landed on the Duncan Phyfe Sewing table in the foyer. Matthew's mother had always fussed over that table, but it was just an old table.

Angel was pawing at the patio door when I walked into the kitchen and I slid the door open for her. The thermostat read seventy, and I turned it down to sixty-five. If I was going to seduce George, I didn't want the house to be too hot. He hated the heat.

I raced upstairs and changed into a pair of super short cut offs and a red tube top, sprayed myself all over with Light Blue and redid my makeup. After years of second guessing myself with Matthew, I was ready to give in to the chemistry with George. I yahooed out loud as I ran down the staircase.

Steaks were soaking in marinade in the fridge while I made a salad and wrapped the potatoes and veggies in foil for the barbeque. I shoved four bottles into the freezer to cool them down quickly, hoping that I wouldn't forget they were there.

Ding-dong.

Oh my God. He's early.

As I stopped for a quick check in the mirror, Angel charged past me into the foyer, knocking me into a table, and upending a five foot potted philodendron. I screamed as dirt and leaves scattered all over the shiny marble tiles.

George burst through the front door. "I heard you scream," he said.

Doubled over with laughter, I pointed to the mess and squeaked out, "Angel."

"Good one, girl," he said grabbing her by the neck and roughing her fur.

"I'll get a broom."

"Got a shovel?"

"In the garage."

After the dirt had been cleaned up and dumped back into the pot, I sighed. "Beer break." I remembered the bottles in the freezer and jerked them out. "Are you early?" I asked, pouring. "I lost track of time in all the confusion."

"Closed up early, couldn't wait," he said wrapping his arms around me. "Do you know how crazy I am for you, baby girl?"

"I was wondering if we were on the same page." I kissed him fervently and held him close, savoring the scent of him . . . leather, gun oil and sweat. I exhaled a big breath.

He grinned. "I didn't know what page you were on—but if this is it—I am so fuckin' on it."

He picked me up as if he was picking up a feather and carried me up the staircase.

"Your arm," I said.

"Don't talk."

George laid me on the bed and gazed down on my body. I smiled and he smiled back, his black eyes sparkling. Sitting on the side of the bed made it awkward for him to unzip my cut offs, but he managed. I moaned as he ran his hands over my thighs, and gently pulled my shorts down. He unzipped his jeans and stepped out of them, then lay down on the bed beside me.

I wanted to rip the rest of my clothes off, but George was setting the pace and taking it slow. He pulled my top over my head and sucked in a breath when he saw my breasts overflowing my purple lace bra. I helped him remove his Harley shirt being mindful of his stitches. His breathing was rapid as I traced the razor wire tat across his chest and kissed the pink mark nearly healed on his neck. Heat radiated from his large, callused hands as he unclasped my bra, cupped my breasts and his mouth claimed my nipple. It was electrifying.

My hand found its' way across his belly to the heat of his groin and caressed his God-given equipment. He shivered, growing thicker in my hand and groaned when I guided him inside me. He thrust long and lazy inside me, filling me over and over, and content to take his time and absorb every sensation. I was so okay with that.

When my orgasm hit, the surge of sensation brought him home too. He roared a throaty cry, his shoulders pitching forward before he lay motionless on top of me, enfolded tightly in my arms. I buried my face in his neck as the tears flowed and I was reborn.

I must have dozed off, because the sound of the

shower woke me with a start. I let out a big breath and smiled. George was with me and I was safe. I walked naked into the bathroom and joined George in the shower.

"Hey, beautiful girl, come on in." He grinned and held his arms out for me.

We kissed under the running water, then laughed like kids on prom night while we soaped and rinsed each other.

My stomach was growling as I dried my hair. I was ravenous. I hopped into sweat pants and a t-shirt and ran outside to start the barbeque.

By the time George wended his way downstairs, dinner was underway. He stepped into the kitchen and encircled me with his massive arms. "You're fuckin' amazing, you know that?"

"No, not me, I've never done anything amazing," I said.

"You just did," he said with a laugh. "Let's go outside. I haven't smoked for hours. I think I'm goin' into fuckin' withdrawal."

"Oh, I thought maybe you quit," I said picking up the bottles and the glasses.

"That'll happen the day they bury me."

"I hope that's not soon. I kind of like having you around."

"I don't know how in hell I got so lucky."

"I'm the lucky one," I said, checking the barbeque.

CHAPTER FORTY-SEVEN

THE bedroom was in semi-darkness when I opened my eyes. The face of the clock was obscured from where I lay, and not wanting to disturb George, I stared at the ceiling and pondered the Barbwire problem.

She wouldn't make a move with George here and I didn't want her to. I wanted that bitch all to myself.

I cuddled up closer to the giant of a man in my bed and felt invincible for the time being. Things could change. They probably would, but I was savoring the moment.

George stirred as I pressed my breasts up against him and he rolled onto his back. I gave the duvet a healthy shove making his body shiver when the cool air touched it. I kissed the inside of his thighs and gently coaxed him awake. He lay still, but his breathing was rapid as he waited and anticipated my intentions.

"Ready, big guy?" I whispered the question and ignored the answer as I straddled him. I reveled as the bulk of him slid inside me, filled me. I moaned, creating a rhythm with each downward thrust harder than the last.

"Jesus, Annie," he panted as he gave it up and gasped for air. I lay limp on top of his sweating body until I could breathe, then rolled off onto my back.

"That's one way to wake a guy up, little girl," he chuckled. "I need a smoke."

I jumped into the shower while George smoked on the patio and let Angel run in the yard. After I dressed, I brewed a pot of coffee and whipped up a lumber jack's breakfast for him. He polished off eggs, bacon and a stack of pancakes and syrup without skipping a beat.

"Are we shooting today?" I wasn't relishing the idea of going back to the range, but I had to face it sooner or later. Might as well be sooner.

"Guess so. Have to talk to a few of the boys."

George was always talking to the boys.

"I'm going to ride my own bike. I can't wait to try her out."

"I hear ya." George chuckled. "Before we leave, I want you to do something for me, honey girl." He headed out to the garage and I followed on his heels wondering what he was up to. He released the kick stand on my bike and gingerly laid it on its' side on the garage floor. "Pick it up for me."

It was awkward and heavy, and it took every ounce of strength I possessed, but I managed to right it. When it was back on its stand, I heaved a big sigh, and sat on the leather seat for a few moments, catching my breath. "My weight training must be paying off. I don't think I could have done that a month ago."

"Good girl," was all he said.

We packed our guns and ammo into the saddle bags, secured the house and roared up Hawthorne Lane towards the highway.

The day was gray and overcast with a threat of rain, but hazy humidity was all that was in evidence when we left the city. As we travelled farther north the wind picked up and cleared some of the cloud cover. My bike drove like a dream—so much easier to maneuver than George's Screamin' Eagle. I was no expert on the gears, and I ground a pound now and then, but I managed. At one set of traffic lights, the bike wobbled a bit, but I kept my balance and didn't tip. By the time we arrived at the range, I was in control and exhilarated from the ride.

We parked the Harleys and ambled down to the target area. Everyone spoke to George and seemed anxious to discuss something or other with him. I couldn't say that I had noticed it before, but he was respected by the other bikers. He set up the targets while I loaded the magazines and we practiced diligently for an hour. Since my arm had healed, I practiced equal time with left and right hands.

"Now that you have your Beretta mastered, we should get in some shotgun and rifle practice." George said as we walked up to the shack. "Make you more well-rounded," he said and winked. "Not that you're not well rounded in other fuckin' areas."

"I'm up for that. This is the only gun I've used, so it would be a challenge."

"Maybe next week," he said.

After another half-hour George packed up to leave. I had avoided looking at the spot where Kenny died last Sunday. The picture was indelible in my mind, and probably forever. I didn't need any refreshers. No sign of Barbwire and her friends here today, but that was no surprise. She must be raising hell somewhere else.

Halfway into our ride home it sprinkled. I was following George and he didn't stop until we came to an overpass on highway twelve. We parked underneath and hung out until the shower passed.

"Smoke break," he said. "Didn't want you riding your first day on slick pavement and scraping up your pretty little ass." He patted me on the behind.

"Thanks. Are you sure you didn't just stop for a smoke?" I pushed him up against the abutment and kissed him—with lots of tongue—until I felt him harden.

"Time to go."

"I'll get you for that."

"I'm counting on it."

AN hour later we pulled into the driveway on Hawthorne Lane and parked the bikes.

"You look tired, George. Why don't you nap and rest your arm until dinner is ready?"

"I am tired. Don't know what it could be, do you?" He winked at me.

"No clue," I said with a grin.

George ambled into the kitchen an hour later. "Must have dozed off," he said with a chuckle. "You can tire a man out."

I laughed. "That's my new job, and I'm liking it a lot."

"You're fuckin' good at your job, Annie."

"Thanks. Dinner will be ready in an hour or so."

"After dinner, I'm gonna' head out. I have some stuff to take care of, and I have an early day at the store tomorrow. Some guys takin' a boar hunting trip to Alabama. They'll be picking up their guns at eight."

George finished his second cup of coffee and got to

his feet. He favored his left leg, but never mentioned it. "Another good meal, baby doll. How'd you learn to cook so good?"

"Matthew made me take lessons. Said he wasn't eating any of the shit I cooked, when we first married. Wanted me to cook like his mother." I laughed. "When I burnt stuff on the stove or in the oven, he would beat me up." I sighed. "It was definitely safer to take lessons."

"Shit." George shook his head and gave me a long hug.

"I'll walk you out." I followed him into the foyer and gave him a lingering goodbye kiss.

"Lock everything up tight and set the alarm. I don't like leavin' you here alone with that fuckin' nut bar running loose."

"I'll be fine. You have your own life."

"Not no more, I don't. You're my life now, Annie."

"I love you, George," I whispered as he disappeared out the door.

ANGEL barked sharply, and I woke with a start. I shivered as I fumbled under my pillow for my Beretta and flipped the safety off. I felt for George beside me with a shaky hand, and when I touched the cold sheets I remembered he hadn't stayed the night.

Angel bolted down the stairs growling low and dangerous. I grabbed my robe, left the lights off and felt my way down the stairway using the banister. The hair on the back of my neck was standing up giving me icy chills. Angel's growling led me to the foyer. She was scratching on the front door. I peeked through the lace curtain on the sidelight and saw nothing. No movement. I cocked my gun, opened the door a crack and peered out into the pitch black void. I sucked in a big breath.

"Nothing out there, girl."

She scratched again on the door and I opened it. I stepped out onto the porch and Angel ran down onto the grass. "I guess you just had to pee." I exhaled as I stood on the steps and looked up at the stars. On a lunge, Angel started towards the street.

"Angel, come back here." I jumped down from the porch to go after her and the world exploded into the fourth of July. Blackness and pain engulfed me, and I felt myself crumple onto the damp grass.

CHAPTER FORTY-EIGHT

GEORGE gazed around his time-worn bungalow and decided it resembled a club house more than a home. The front room was monopolized by a poker table surrounded by a dozen mismatched chairs that would have brought fifty cents each at a yard sale. A worn green recliner with a tattered rip on the left arm occupied one corner, while the west exterior wall sported a boarded over fireplace with a fifty-two inch flat screen mounted on the wall above. The picture window facing the street was covered by a thick navy blue blanket held in place by three inch nails.

The meeting with the club members was winding down when the phone clipped to George's belt rang. The screen showed Jimmie's number.

"Yeah, Jimmie, speak."

"Trouble, boss. Bomb went off on Hawthorne Lane."

"*What?* Where the fuck is Portia?"

"She's down, but not out."

"Fuck Jimmie, how did you let that happen?" George roared, kicked the leg of the poker table and everybody's chips went for a dump.

"I didn't *let* it happen, boss. Nobody came near the house all fuckin' day. They must have planted it on the Jeep somewhere else and used a remote."

"Did you call 911?"

"Yep."

"I'll be right there," he said blowing out a long slow breath.

"What's up, boss?" asked Rusty. "Woman trouble?"

"You have no fuckin' idea. You guys sit tight. I might need you in a while." He jumped on the Eagle, threaded his way down the driveway between the rows of parked bikes and burned rubber at the end of the driveway.

George had a heavy hand on the gas, exceeded the speed limit and reached Annie's street in eight minutes flat. The paramedics slammed the back door of the ambulance just as he got to the end of the driveway. Police vehicles roared down the street with sirens screaming and fire trucks trailed close behind.

George veered the Eagle into a neighbor's driveway, made a quick turn and followed the ambulance to the hospital. He stubbed out his smoke in the sand bucket at the door, sucked in a big breath and prepared himself for the worst.

"Portia Talbot. They just brought her in," he said to the nurse behind the glass.

She looked at her list. "They're prepping her for surgery. Are you the next of kin?"

George nodded numbly.

"Talk to the next desk, through those doors." She pointed to her right.

George walked down the hall thinking he might hurl. "Can I find out about Mrs. Talbot?"

The nurse looked at her sheet. "Are you family?"

"Yes. She's my . . . wife."

"She's been taken straight upstairs," she said. "That's all I can tell you until she's out of the operating room. We'll know more then."

George's knees gave way under him. He put a hand on the counter to steady himself.

"You won't be able to see her for a few hours. You can wait in the family waiting room or come back in the morning. If you leave, let me know how to contact you and I'll be sure to call you as soon as there is news."

The helplessness he felt rose in his throat and turned into fury and blind hate. He had to repeat his cell number three times for the woman before he turned to go.

Hold it together for five more minutes. Barbwire's not going anywhere fast.

He sat on the Eagle in the hospital parking lot, took a couple of deep breaths and lit up a smoke. Then he punched a number into his phone.

"Hey, boss, everything okay?" Billy asked.

"Not yet. Gimme Jackson."

Jackson came on the line. "What's up, boss."

George spat on the ground. "Those fuckin' druggie whores blew up Annie's jeep and she's in the hospital. They're gonna' pay for this."

"Who made the bomb?" asked Jackson. "That army lowlife that lives with them?"

"That's what I figure. None of those bitches could hold a thought long enough to make a sandwich let alone a bomb. Had to be him. I'm sittin' in the hospital parking lot. I should be back in fifteen. Annie's cut up bad, and she's on the operating table right this fuckin' minute."

"Fuck, no." Jackson inhaled. "We're ready boss,

whenever you get here."

"On my way." George revved up the Screamin' Eagle and rode back to his place where the boys were putting in time playing hold-em. By the time he parked his bike in the driveway, he had hatched the outline of a plan.

When he walked through the door, one of the crew jumped up from the poker table and fetched him a beer. He sat down in the green leather chair and lit up a smoke. "We're gonna' wipe out a den of fuckin' vermin," he growled.

THE gray light of dawn was hazed over by a thick layer of fog that had blown in off Lake Ontario. Three bikes, with headlights out, coasted up in front of the crack house and the riders dismounted. The entrance to the basement was around the north side of the condemned building. The windows had been boarded up and there was only one way in and one way out.

The men, dressed in black, wore gloves as they stealthily descended the narrow steps to the lower level. They each chose two passed out addicts and slit their throats while they slept.

George approached the sleeping form of Barbwire. Her scrawny arm was extended in sleep, exhibiting multiple track marks. He poked her in the ribs, and she opened her eyes. Her pupils were dilated and as she stared up at George's face, her expression of surprise turned to one of terror. She opened her mouth in an effort to scream, but George was as fast as lightning with his Tanto knife. He slit her throat in a millisecond. He followed his boys up the basement stairs and they rode off before the sun came up over the horizon.

Back at George's place, everyone stripped down and placed their blood soaked clothes and gloves in black garbage bags. The bandage on George's arm was soaked through with Barbwire's blood and he added it to the collection.

One of the boys was assigned to transport the bag to the range and incinerate it. George showered after everyone left for home and changed into new blue jeans and a Harley t-shirt. He tied a yellow bandana around his neck and scowled as he rode back to the hospital.

After checking with the nurses' station, he found out he couldn't see Annie yet, and took a seat in the waiting room. He closed his eyes and slept for a couple of hours. He woke stiff and sore from the hard metal chair, made for people half his size, and ambled outside for a smoke.

As he leaned on the wall in the smoking area, a pair of cops parked their cruiser at the curb and headed inside. He stayed put. Five minutes later they left.

George got a coffee and walked down past the nurses' station. "Mrs. Talbot?"

"Taking her to recovery now. You'll be able to sit with her in ten." She smiled.

He leaned on the wall and finished his coffee. A few minutes later, the nurse motioned him to join her and she gave him directions to the recovery area.

The large, rectangular room held several beds, all occupied with sleeping patients. Most had a family member keeping a vigil and that was what he was there for as well. He gasped when he saw Annie. She was pale and still. A large gauze pad covered half her face, and bandages wrapped her arms. Her hair was matted with blood and he was grateful he couldn't see her legs. George ignored the tightening in his chest, sat down, took her hand in his, and slept.

A couple of hours later, he got a coffee while Annie was being moved to a room on the fourth floor. He found her new room, four twenty-seven, and took up his position beside the bed.

Come on, baby girl. You can do it.

He looked up as Doctor Casey came in. "Hey, Doc. How's she doin?"

"Are you her husband?"

George nodded.

"Better now, but it was touch and go earlier. She lost a lot of blood from the leg injury and had to be transfused on the table. She's very weak." He checked the chart, and the machines beside the bed. "I have her heavily medicated. She'll sleep most of today."

An hour later, she opened her eyes, looked around the room, and focused on George.

"Hey, Annie, bout time you woke up, baby girl." He kissed her on the forehead and her eyes rolled closed.

CHAPTER FORTY-NINE

GEORGE had Porky open the gun shop for him and take over for the day. Porky knew next to nothin' about running the store, and even less about guns, but George had no choice.

The previous day, George hadn't had time to make any arrangements, and the store remained closed while he spent the day at the hospital.

Before visiting hours, George hopped on the Eagle and cruised by Annie's house to assess the damage and feed Angel. One cruiser was parked in the driveway, along with the crime scene truck. The TV vans that had been there the night before hoping to capitalize on someone's misery had long since vanished—the bombing was yesterday's news. Yellow tape defined the perimeter. He parked the bike at the end of the driveway and ducked under the tape.

"Hey, buddy, you can't be here," one of the crime scene guys hollered out of the garage.

"Won't be here long. Have to feed the dog and make sure she's okay." George walked past the molten mass that once claimed to be a Jeep. The heat was still radiating from the wreckage and he choked on the stench of the smoldering rubber.

Fuck. Look at the mess of her bike. Gotta' get Rusty to pick that up before she sees it.

"No dog here, sir," said the guy examining the Jeep wreckage. "I'm Jerry O'Keefe, the Fire Marshall," he extended his gloved hand.

"Where's the dog?" George asked with a frown.

"Been no dog here since we came," he said.

"When will you guys be finished?"

"I'm wrapping up tomorrow and the cops as well."

George nodded and headed for his bike. He took a quick tour around to Scarborough Animal Control on the way back to the hospital. "Hey," he said to the girl behind the counter. Her name tag read 'Vicky'. The chorus of barking coming from the back room was deafening.

"Can I help you?" she yelled.

"Pick up any Rotties in the last couple days?"

"Nope. Did your dog have a chip?"

"No idea."

He took a business card from the holder and wrote his cell number on the back. "Any Rotties—call me," he said peeling off a twenty and tossing it on the counter.

"You got it." Vicky smiled, and shoved the twenty in her pocket.

George lumbered out to his bike and straddled it. He punched a number into his phone.

"Rusty, we've got a fuckin' problem."

"What is it, boss?" George could tell Rusty was smoking while he was talking.

"Got any more of that color you used on Annie's bike?"

"Fuck, no. Don't tell me this," Rusty hollered.

"Fuck, yes. I saw it in the back of the garage today.

You gotta' get that mother out of there before Annie comes home."

"Fuck, how am I gonna' do that? The cops are swarming all over her place. I took a look this morning on my way to the shop."

"The Fire Marshall said they'd be all wrapped up before tomorrow night. I'll meet you over there around nine and we'll load it."

CHAPTER FIFTY

GEORGE spent the morning sitting with Annie. She was pale and quiet, but she was awake, and he was relieved. The purple bruising was starting to show where she had been hit by flying debris.

"What day is it?"

"Wednesday, baby girl. I should have been here when you woke up—sorry 'bout that."

He picked up her hand and kissed it.

"I saw you here before. I don't know when." She tried to smile.

"Didn't know if you'd remember that," he leaned over and kissed her.

"What happened?"

"It was a bomb. Someone rigged it under the Wrangler. The cops have everything taped off, and they've been there since it happened. Much better for you here. Vince is hanging around, taking care of the security stuff."

"Was it Barbwire?" she whispered.

"Don't know, honey girl. I don't want you to even think about it. Promise me."

"Okay."

"How's the leg feel?"

A nurse came in to check the monitor.

"My leg hurts," mumbled Annie.

"I'll get you something for the pain. You need to rest." She returned and injected something into the IV, then pressed buttons on the machine and left.

"Did Angel come home?" A look crossed George's face, and tears welled up in Annie's eyes.

"Don't cry, little girl. I'm gonna' find her if it's the last fuckin' thing I do. I checked the pound yesterday, and I'll check again today to see if they picked her up. If she was spooked by the blast and ran really far, she might have got lost."

"When can I go home?" she reached out for George's hand.

"Doc will decide tomorrow. I've been checking."

Her hand went to her face and she touched the bandage. "This hurts." She tried to stick her finger under the gauze.

"It's a bad one, Annie, don't touch it." George removed her hand from the bandage and held it. When the doctor came into her room to examine her, George left to check the dog pound again.

HE parked the big Harley in front of the door of the building and stuck his head in.

Vicky looked up from her paperwork and saw him. She shook her head. "No Rotties, only two more Pit Bulls I can't get homes for."

ON Hawthorne Lane, the Eagle rumbled as George slowed down to see if the cops had wrapped up. The crime scene van was still there. He smiled as he looked up and saw Angel bounding off the porch and running towards him.

He parked at the end of the drive and got off the bike. "Hey, girl, you're home." He bent down and ruffed up the fur around Angel's neck. "Bet you're fuckin' starving."

The CSI was loading his kit into the van. "The dog was lying on the porch when I got here this morning. She growled at me a little," he said. "But we made friends soon enough."

"I'm glad she's back. Must have taken off when the bomb exploded." George said.

The guy nodded and climbed into his van.

George fumbled for his key, unlocked the front door and let Angel in. He fed her, and filled up her water bowl, then went into the garage to have a good look around.

The window in the side wall was blown out. The tools that had hung neatly on the wall over the workbench were strewn everywhere. The garage door was scrap lumber. Chunks of it had hit the back wall and gouged the drywall. The frame around the opening was splintered and damaged. The new paint job on Annie's bike was scratched from the flying metal and bubbled up in places from bits of burning debris landing on it. Rusty was gonna' be thoroughly pissed.

GEORGE rode back to the hospital to tell Annie the good news about Angel. He was smiling when he walked into room four twenty-seven.

"You found her?" Annie was grinning.

"She found herself." He told Annie that Angel had

been waiting on the porch when he got there. "I fed her
and she didn't look any the worse for her little getaway."

"How did the house look? Is there a lot of damage?"
Annie asked.

"The garage door is fuckin' toast, and the side
window. Nothin' that can't be fixed."

"What about my bike?" she asked with a scowl. "My
new paint job," her eyes filled up with tears.

"Rusty's picking it up tonight to do a couple of
touch-ups."

"Touch-ups?"

George nodded and changed the subject. He stayed
with Annie until visiting hours were over. "Pick you up
tomorrow, baby girl." He kissed her on the mouth.

RUSTY'S black pickup towing the bike trailer was
backed into the driveway when George arrived at ten
after nine.

Coulter was in the garage with a flashlight surveying
the damage.

"Shit, boss. Did you look at this fuckin' mess?"

"Yeah, I did. Annie was asking me today, and I lied
and told her it needed a couple touch-ups."

"Fuck, yeah, touch-ups." Rusty threw his butt down
and ground it into the garage floor. "I don't have enough
of that Hi-Fi Turquoise. I just know it." He pounded the
wall. Rusty was emotional about paint.

"You'll think of something. I'll help you get it on the
trailer, then we'll chug a couple."

After Rusty left, George locked up. He took Angel
upstairs and they slept like the dead.

The last three days had been rough for both of them.

CHAPTER FIFTY-ONE

MRS. TALBOT, the police are here to talk to you," the nurse said from the doorway.

I nodded.

The officers came into my room and stood by the bedside. "I'm Officer Lombard. Do you remember me, Mrs. Talbot?"

"I do, you came to the house when I had a break-in. I'm still having a little trouble hearing, if you can bear with me."

"Of course, I understand. This is Officer McDonald."

"Uh huh."

"We need to know what you can remember from the night of the bombing."

I took a breath and tried to think. "Angel was barking . . ."

"I understand you found your missing dog?"

"Yes, I'm so happy she came home." I inhaled and began again. "She was barking. I got out of bed and threw on a robe and followed her down to the front door. I had my gun in my hand with the safety off.

I peeked out the front window and didn't see anything. Angel was scratching at the door. I punched the code in for the alarm, opened the door a crack and didn't see or hear anything. I thought maybe she just had to go to the bathroom, so I let her out and stepped onto the porch to wait for her. She started to run towards the street, and I called her . . . and that was it."

"Can you think of anyone who would want to hurt you?" asked Officer McDonald.

I shook my head.

Only Barbwire.

"Have you found anything yet?" I asked.

"The Fire Marshall, Jerry O'Keefe, is investigating. He'll be in touch with you. I think the unit is almost done with the scene, and you'll be able to go home straight from the hospital."

"The doctor hasn't told me when I can leave, but I hope it's soon."

"We're glad you made it," said Officer Lombard.

"Me too," I smiled.

After they left   George walked into my room, smelling like Irish Spring soap. I held my arms out, and he sat on the bed, kissed me and gave me a hug.

"You look a little better. Did you sleep?"

"Like I was drugged, and I probably was. You look clean and fresh this morning. Love the yellow bandana."

"How's your hearing this morning?"

"Better."

"Does anything hurt? Is it time to take pills or anything?" George asked. He looked up as the doctor came into the room. "I'll go get a coffee."

"I'm Doctor Casey. I'm the surgeon that worked on you. I'm glad to see you're doing better, Mrs. Talbot."

"How bad was it, Doc?"

"A piece of metal from your vehicle was embedded in your left leg and required surgery to remove it. It will be tender during the healing process, and you may require a crutch, but the damage won't be permanent." He paused. "However, your face required several stitches and there will be a scar."

"Can I see it?" I lifted my fingers to my face.

He pursed his lips and shook his head. "Let's let it heal a bit longer. You may want to consider plastic surgery in the future."

Or avoid mirrors for the rest of my life.

"Will I be able to go home soon?"

"I'm considering letting you go later today, but you won't be going anywhere until I'm sure you can manage with the crutch.

"I can do that."

The nurses came in later, and I practiced getting to the bathroom with the crutch. They insisted that I try to eat some of the lunch that the kitchen had fussed over and I tried.

George returned with a grin on his face. "Doc signed the papers for you to go home."

"Yahoo," I hollered, "I have to use the bathroom." Before trying out my sea legs without the nurses, I sat on the side of the bed for a moment and did some deep breathing. George put his hand on my elbow to steady me and got the crutch under my arm. I walked under my own steam into the bathroom, washed my hands, then splashed water on my face and patted it with a towel.

When I came out, George helped me dress in the clothes he had brought. The sweat pants were loose and fit over the huge bandage on my leg. He put a t-shirt over my head being careful not to disturb the gauze pad on my face. I sat on the side of the bed, stuck my feet in my runners and blew out a big breath. "Guess, I'm ready."

"I'll check at the desk and see if you can leave." George went into the hall, wasn't gone long and returned with a nurse and a wheel chair.

My head was swimming as the nurse took me down in the elevator and wheeled me to the exit where George had a cab waiting. He lifted me out of the chair and placed me in the back seat of the cab. He tucked the crutch in beside me, and I was on my way home.

At the end of the driveway, George opened the door of the cab to pick me up, and my stomach did a turn. The pungent smell of the burnt rubber and metal choked me. "It stinks out here."

"You called it, baby girl."

He carried me past the yellow tape and in through the front door. I felt like a newlywed—kind of a war zone newlywed, but one all the same. He sat me on the sofa and found a blanket in the closet.

"Hey, you're good at this, big guy." I held my arms out for him and he kissed me.

He grinned. "Never did it before. Must be some natural fuckin' gift."

"Must be." I smiled at him.

"I sent Vince and his crew home. There was nothin' they could do until the garage door and the window are replaced."

"Thanks." Tears welled up in my eyes and I frowned. "I hate it when I'm all emotional."

George laughed, "I'll give you one. You almost got blown sky fuckin' high."

"I'll deal with Barbwire. Don't you worry about her."

"I won't," he said softly.

"Do you want different clothes? I didn't have a fuckin' clue what to bring you."

"These are okay." I indicated the sweats. "Just grab me some underwear and a bra."

"Fuck. I hate touching that stuff. Gets me all crazy." George screwed up his face.

"Well, just go up there and get crazy this one time." I laughed.

Angel got up to follow after George. "Stay there, girl," he said.

"I'm so glad you came home, Angel." I patted her head and she licked my hand.

It was an ordeal getting my underwear on, but George helped me.

"Rusty and Jackson are dropping by. I have some shit to talk to them about."

"That's fine. I'll close my eyes until they get here."

"You don't have to get up, baby girl. I'll talk to them outside."

I woke when I heard voices, wrestled with the crutch until I positioned it under my arm and gave it a shot. My legs felt like I was just learning to walk.

Rusty and Jackson were sitting outside at the patio table smoking. When they looked up at me, I heard Jackson suck in a breath. He lit up a smoke before he spoke. "Glad you're okay, Portia," he flashed me his gorgeous smile.

"Yeah, me too," said Rusty grinning.

"Hey, guys, want some coffee?"

George raised his eyebrows. "I think you should be sittin' down, Annie."

"We're talking about getting' a drive-through at Wendy's," Jackson said.

"Sounds good to me. I admit I am a bit wobbly from my recent adventure."

"You sit there, Annie." George pointed to a chair. "I'll make the coffee and Coulter can do the drive-through."

"Didn't know you could make coffee, boss," Jackson piped up, chuckling.

"Lots of stuff you don't know, dumb fuck," George punched Jackson in the shoulder and knocked him off his chair. "How many scoops do I put in, Annie?"

"Four should do it and fill the water up to the line."

A few minutes later, Rusty returned on his bike with the bags of burgers and fries. He spread it all out on the patio table and we dug in.

"I don't know when I've been so hungry," I said.

"Me neither," said Rusty, polishing off his third burger.

George got the carafe from the kitchen and filled everyone's mug.

"Nothin' better than Wendy's, right, boss?" Rusty taunted.

"Fuck the hell off, you bastards," George grumbled.

"The boss holds the record for eating the most bacon double cheeseburgers," Jackson said with a grin.

"Did you get a trophy?" I asked.

George scowled and lit up a smoke, while the boys laughed and pointed at him. They were still laughing, as they rose to leave.

"We have to work—we can't make our own hours like some people."

I smiled as they walked through the patio door.

"What about the shop, George. Do you have to go to the store?"

"I had one of the boys take the store for today. You were coming home from the hospital, and repairs have to be done here."

"I could take care of it," I protested.

"Nope. I called Eddie and he'll be over in an hour to measure and get started on the garage window and the door frame." He took a drag on his smoke. "I want you to take it easy today, baby girl. Sit here." He pointed to the chair next to him.

He refilled our coffee mugs. My head was pounding, and I was nauseous, but I didn't want George stressing over me. He reached over and covered my hand with his giant paw.

"Once the house is secure and you're up for it, I think we should go up to that cabin of yours and have some down time."

"I would love that, but what about the store?"

"One of the boys can take it for a week. And they can call if they need to. No sweat."

I smiled. "Honeymoon cabin."

"Is that all you think about, Annie?" George put on a fake frown.

"Ninety per cent of the time."

"Hundred per cent for me."

"You have no other thoughts?"

"None," he chuckled.

SOUNDS of voices in the foyer woke me from my nap on the sofa. I yawned, as George brought his friend into the room.

"This is Eddie Nolan. He's gonna' help us out with the repairs," George said. Eddie was a short guy with gray hair and dark eyes. He spoke rapidly and was difficult to understand with his thick Irish accent.

"Hi, I'm Portia. Bit of a mess in the garage, eh?"

"Window is easy to replace. Frame around the garage door will take a bit longer. I know a guy at Garaga if you want his name," he said.

"I'm gonna' sweep up the glass and crap in the garage before Eddie walks around out there," said George as he headed to locate the broom.

"Be careful of your arms, Eddie," I said. "Those edges cut like a razor."

"He nodded, "I'll wear gloves when I clean out the opening. No worries."

After the two of them milled around outside for half an hour, they came in the kitchen.

"Got everything you need, Ed?" asked George.

"Yeah, I'm off to Lowes. I know the lumber manager there and I can get a deal. I'll call you on your cell when I'm on my way back with the goods."

"Roger that," George said as he escorted him to the door.

After I made a trip to the bathroom, George helped me into the study to find the number for the car insurance. He settled back in one of the leather wing chairs.

The folder in the filing cabinet gave me the information I needed, and I sat down at the desk to call. As I started to press the numbers on the key pad, I looked up and George was staring at me, smiling. "What?"

"I just like lookin' at you. You're so smart and so beautiful, I can't figure what you want with me."

I put the phone down on the desk and motioned for George to come closer to me. He sat me on his lap, my arms encircled his neck and I pressed my lips on his and held him close.

"You don't decide who you're going to fall in love with, it just happens when you don't expect it. You can't change it," I whispered.

"No, you can't," he said, kissing my neck. We sat that way for a while, holding on to each other in silence.

When George got up, I completed my call to the insurance company. An adjuster would be dispatched to evaluate the Jeep the following day.

Hope he has a sense of humor.

George was out on the patio smoking when I found him. "Want some dinner?"

"No, just a beer, I'm still full of lunch. You sit down and I'll get it." He brought two bottles out and uncapped them. He poured mine into a glass, with a pensive look on his face.

"What are you so deep in thought about?" I asked.

"The other night, when I got that call about the bomb, I knew in a split second that I wouldn't want to live another minute if you were dead. Scared the shit out of me." He paused. "Never been attached to anybody. Ever. That's why I'm the best at what I do, but I don't see how I can keep doin' it. The way I figure, if I want you in my life, I have to retire."

"That's heavy stuff." I blew out a big breath.

"For me, I never pictured doin' anything else. Fell into 'the life' years ago and I can't even believe I'm thinkin' like this. I'm fucked, pure and simple."

"Well, you took me by surprise on that one, but if money is one of your concerns, you can cross that one off.

"Nope, that ain't it. I have a stash that would be more than enough for both of us. Mostly, my problem lies in who would take over, and how the boys would make out after I was gone."

I nodded.

"Hello," Eddie hollered from the front hall. "I have the material and I'm going to make some noise in the garage."

"I'll give you a hand," George said. "Annie, why don't you go get some sleep."

"I think I will lay down for a bit. Thanks guys." When my head hit the pillow in the front room, I was out.

MUCH later George walked through the door and I opened my eyes. The drapes were open, but the room was dark. "How long have I been sleeping?"

"Awhile." George said, "Eddie finished up the door frame and the garage window."

"I'll get up and make us some dinner." I said sitting

on the side of the couch.

"Like hell you will. You need rest, Annie. I'll make a sandwich or something easy. I have a meeting in an hour."

I stepped into the kitchen to see George staring into the fridge. He glanced up and saw me smile. "See, I'm getting' all fuckin' domestic. Today I was sweepin'. Tomorrow, I'll likely be ironin'."

I hooted. "Pastrami and mustard, okay?" I took the bread out of his hands and started the sandwiches.

He frowned at me, but realized I wasn't one for sitting around. "Fine but keep it simple. It's all good when you make it. I mean that."

I finished the sandwiches, standing on one leg and leaning on the counter. I put dill pickles on the side and George carried the plates out to the patio table. The June evening was warm, and Angel lay stretched out in the grass.

"I'm goin' to say something to the boys and see what happens," George said. "They might have an idea or two."

"No matter what you decide, or what you do in the future, my feelings for you won't change."

George held me close for a long time, then kissed me and left for his meeting.

CHAPTER FIFTY-TWO

GEORGE wheeled the Screamin' Eagle into the narrow driveway at the clubhouse and wove through more than two dozen bikes parked in neat rows. He wasn't looking forward to saying what he had to say to the boys, but if Portia was the prize, then it would be worth it. In his line of work, few men ever based decisions on love—those that did never spoke about it.

Jackson stood up as George came in, strode to the fridge and handed him a beer. "Hard day, boss?"

"Fuckin' long one, for sure," George said.

George blew out a big breath, dropped into the green chair and lit up a fresh smoke. The boys around the poker table stared at him, waiting to hear what was making their leader look so troubled. No one spoke.

George chugged half down, then started. "You boys are a good fuckin' bunch."

Jackson held up his hand. "Stop, boss, don't say it. Don't even think it. We'll work it out some other way."

George looked surprised and then a little pissed. "You don't even know what the fuck I was gonna say."

"I think I do. Could see this comin' the first day you brought her to the range. You're in deep, boss, and we don't blame you. One look at her and you were fucked. Any guy would be, but you've always had our backs and now we got yours," Jackson said. He lit up a smoke and inhaled a big drag.

"I couldn't think of nothin' fuckin' worse than being without my boys, except for being without Annie. The other night, because she's hangin' around me she nearly gets blown to bits. And do you know what she said about that? Nothin'. Fuckin'- nothin'. You guys know better than anybody else, that I know fuck all about women. Never bothered with 'em—always in the way, and all that shit. Then Annie walks into the shop and in ten minutes, I'm fucked for life."

George blew out a big cloud of smoke.

Jackson nodded. "We hear ya, boss. We feel your pain. Well, not really, but just sayin'." All the boys laughed. "Everybody get a fresh drink, we're gonna' hammer this out before morning," said Jackson.

CHAPTER FIFTY-THREE

I put my arms around George's neck when I felt him picking me up from the sofa. He carried me upstairs, undressed me and climbed into bed next to me. The room was dark. I closed my eyes and drifted back to sleep. When I woke the second time, George wasn't beside me and Angel wasn't on her blanket. With the help of my crutch, I reached the top of the stairs and hollered for George—he carried me down and sat me on a chair on the patio.

"Hey," I said, "You sneaked out on me." I put my arms around his neck, tipped his head towards me and kissed him. "How did your meeting go?"

"Better than I hoped."

"That's good." I smiled.

George lifted me over onto his lap and slid his hand up my night shirt and along my thigh. I moaned at his touch and kissed his neck. "Do you want to go back to bed?" I whispered.

"I want you, baby girl, but I don't want to hurt you."

"You won't hurt me, big guy. I swear."

He lifted me up, carried me to the bedroom and made love to me gentle and slow, paying close attention to my injured parts.

The sound of the shower woke me, and I limped to the bathroom door and stuck my head in. "Would you have time to help me take a shower before you go?"

He nodded with a huge grin on his face. "Come on in, baby girl." I leaned on him while he waterproofed my bandage and washed my hair and the rest of me. He dried me while I hung on to the vanity, and then helped me into my robe.

"Thanks. I feel tons better." I kissed him, got dressed and watched him get ready for work. For one big tough biker, George was a gentle, lovable guy.

"I'm training one of the boys, this week to take over the gun shop."

"Who? Do I know him?"

"Porky. You don't know him. He's out of work—not too bright, but I need somebody."

"Uh huh."

"We need to talk later."

I sucked in a deep breath.

"It's all good, Annie. We have to make a plan, that's all. Call me after the insurance dude leaves."

While I was drying my hair, I examined the jagged mark on my cheek. The stitches had started to dissolve, but the cut was red and uneven. It was on the opposite cheek to George's, but it was definitely going to leave a scar. The lacerations on my arms and chest, I left unbandaged hoping they might heal faster exposed to the air. I rebandaged the ones on my feet and put a pair of socks over them to keep them clean. The black and blue marks would fade in a few days, but today they reminded me of my time with Matthew—something I didn't care to recall.

Sweats or a skirt were my only choices—the bandage

on my leg was too bulky for blue jeans. I slipped on a short denim skirt, a turquoise tank top and a pair of Nikes.

I sat down on the porch steps and called George.

"Gun shop."

"Hey, my sexgod, how goes the battle?"

"Fuck. When you say shit like that to me, I get all hot and crazy."

"I'll remember that for future use," I laughed. "Is Porky there?"

"He went out for coffee."

"The insurance adjuster was here. Said he can't do much until he gets a copy of the police report for the files. He asked me if I needed a rental car, but I declined. I'm thinking of buying a Humvee when I'm able to drive again."

"Always wanted one of those mothers—never got around to it," he said. "Want me to drive you to the dealership later and then I'll take you to Buck's for a burger?"

"Sure," I said. "But if I'm going truck shopping, I better lay down on the sofa for a nap."

SOMETIME later, I woke to my cell ringing on the coffee table. I grabbed it half asleep and pressed talk.

"Mrs. Talbot? This is Mrs. Allen at Mowat Secondary School. I'm pleased to tell you that I did find a student named Grace Brownell that attended our school in 1985, and I have an old year book that you can look at if you want to drop by."

"That's great news, Mrs. Allen. I just got out of the

hospital, so I won't be mobile for a couple of days. I'll come by as soon as I can. Thanks again."

My heart was beating fast, and I wanted to go right away, but I just couldn't manage it at the moment. *Finally, I might get to see what my mother looked like.*

AT six-thirty I was sitting on the porch drinking a beer, waiting for George to pick me up.

The Screamin' Eagle roared into the driveway and I motioned him over to have a cold one before we left. "I needed that, baby girl. You always know what I need," he kissed me, and I wanted him right there on the porch. I tried to rein in my hormones, and I fought hard, but I wasn't strong enough. I sucked in a deep breath and stood up, with the help of my crutch.

"Ready?" he asked.

"Umm . . . no." I hesitated. "I need you inside me before we go."

A look of surprise crossed George's face, but he grinned and carried me back into the house, and to the sofa. When I caught my breath, I straightened up my clothes and tried to tame my unruly hair with my hand.

"Sorry, I'm making us late," I whispered.

"You had a damn good reason, baby. Doesn't matter what time we get there."

George placed me on the back of the Eagle. I did up my helmet and wrapped my arms around him. When we got to the Hummer dealership George bent down and kissed me in the parking lot before he helped me off the bike.

I was slow getting up the two, wide stairs and into the

massive, shiny showroom, but slow and steady and all that.

"I have an appointment with Rodney Baker," I said to the girl doing crossword puzzles at the front desk.

Without speaking she blew a huge pink bubble, leaned over and pressed a button on her phone. "Customer," she said without looking up.

I glanced at George and he shrugged. Moments later a tall rangy dude with short cropped gray hair and rumpled clothes strode towards us with his hand extended in George's direction. "Rodney Baker," he said, "how can I help you?"

I leaned into his line of sight. "I called about the black Hummer that you have in stock."

"Oh yes, now I remember." He smiled politely and looked back at George. "Would you like to take her for a test drive, sir?"

George pointed to me and I nodded. "Yes, I believe a test drive would be the thing to do."

While Mr. Baker went to fetch the keys, George helped me out to the vehicle and lifted me into the passenger seat. Mr. Baker piled in the back and with a powerful rumble George headed up McCowan and toward the highway. After he let it out on the highway for a bit, he circled round and then drove back to the dealership.

"I can give you a great deal, sir." The salesman said.

"Probably no better than anywhere else," I said, "if I felt like looking around."

Mr. Baker smiled again but kept his attention focused on the man in the driver's seat. "Will you need financing?"

I watched George set his jaw. He swung around real slow and slid his palm against my head rest. When he was looking the man straight in the eye he spoke low and slow. "I don't need fuck all, mister. The lady is buying the Hummer and if you don't want to talk to her you can shove this deal up your ass."

Mr. Baker flushed crimson as he offered me a forced smile. "I'm so sorry, I didn't realize."

I rolled my eyes and heaved a sigh. "Just give me the bottom line and I'll sign."

"When can we pick it up?" asked George.

"Tomorrow afternoon."

"Done. Let's write it up."

BUCK'S bar was packed on a Friday night. We sat in our regular booth and Buck brought over a pitcher and glasses as soon as he saw us.

"Heard about the bomb, Portia. You okay?" He eyed my face. "That's a nasty gash."

"It'll heal. Then George and I will have matching scars." I smiled.

George laughed and lit up a smoke.

"Saw on the news about those junkies biting it in their beds. Hear about that, George?"

"Nope. Don't watch the news, Buck. Too much fuckin' bad stuff happening out there. Keeps you awake at night." George leaned over slowly, took his knife out of his boot and jammed it into the wooden table beside Buck's hand.

"You guys want food?" Buck asked with a scowl as

he jerked his hand back.

"Cheeseburgers and fries," George said with a grin.

So, that's why George wasn't worried about Barbwire. I knew by the look on his face that a man like him would never let something like that go.

"You're my hero," I said tracing the muscle along his arm.

"I'm nobody's hero," he said with a scowl and drained his glass.

"Before the food comes, I'm going to the lady's room." I picked up my purse as George nodded. On my way back to the table, one of the pool players grabbed my arm, pulled me towards him and tried to kiss me. I let out a cry as I twisted, unsteady on my sore leg. I stumbled against the pool table and sucked in a breath.

"Come and play with us, honey," he slurred as he reached for me.

I gave him a shove. "Don't touch me."

"Aw, come on, sweetheart, be nice."

I meant to smack him in the face, but he grabbed my wrist. My bad leg couldn't take the strain and I screamed as I fell to the floor.

George came from behind, picked me up and carried me back to our booth. After he checked my bandages and made sure I was okay, he turned on his heel and the pool players headed for the back door. Jackson blocked their exit and before long I heard the sound of cracking bone.

George lingered at the back for another couple of minutes imparting words of wisdom close to their faces. The scruffy pool players nodded their heads in unison

and looked like they might piss themselves. After
George returned to our table, they threw money on the
bar and left.

"You okay, baby girl?"

"Bit of pain in my leg. I'm fine. Thanks, George—
didn't see that coming," I said, touching his hand.

"Girl that looks like you, honey—that's always
comin'." He winked and filled his glass.

Buck walked over and set our plates down. "Eat
hearty," he said.

After we cleaned up the last of the French fries, I
said, "You mentioned earlier we needed to talk about a
plan."

"Yeah, we do. By the end of the week, Porky should
be able to run the store, and Jackson and I have worked
everything else out. Next week, we'll go up to your
cabin for a while and see what happens."

"Like a test?"

"Right. A test run. Might be a fuckin' disaster, but
we'll see."

"George, you don't have to make changes in your life
for me. I would never expect that."

"Maybe I want to make a change and now might be
the time."

CHAPTER FIFTY-FOUR

GEORGE left for the shop at eight-thirty while I lingered at the kitchen table nursing my second cup of coffee. The phone rang and it was Jerry O'Keefe the Fire Marshall.

"We finished our investigation yesterday and you can have the wreckage removed from your driveway," he said. "The insurance company will get a copy of our findings. I've already had a conversation with your adjuster, Lionel Bachus."

"Thanks. That's good news. I'll make some arrangements. I'm sure my neighbors don't like looking at the mess or smelling it any more than I do."

I hung up the phone and it rang again. It was George. "Hey, Annie. What's up?"

"The fire inspector called, said he was finished, and the Jeep could be hauled away. Apex called for an update."

"I know a guy with a wrecking yard that will take the Jeep," George said.

"That's one off my list. How's Porky doing today?"

"Not bad. He served a couple customers and he knows how to operate the debit and the credit card machine. He just doesn't know fuck all about guns."

"Compared to you, George, nobody knows fuck all about them."

"Ain't that the truth?" He chuckled. "This afternoon,

I'm putting Porky on gun cleaning detail. If he takes 'em apart and puts 'em back together enough times, maybe he'll get the drift."

"That's a good idea. Maybe he should take some notes for when you're not there."

"Fuck. That's funny. I could just see Porky takin' notes. Shit, you make me laugh."

"That's what I'm here for," I said, "among other things."

"It's those other things I think about all day long."

"I'll show you one of those things if you come home for lunch and give me a ride to the Hummer dealership."

"I'm out the fuckin' door."

George arrived in the front foyer eleven minutes later. "I'm up here," I called over the banister." His tanned face was flushed when he reached the top of the stairs and saw me leaning against the bedroom door wearing only my bandage and a red bandana around my neck.

"Jesus, Annie. You make me crazy." He picked me up and carried me to the bed, paying special attention to my sore leg. Starting at the bandana, he worked his way down the length of my body kissing me, lingering a while around my breasts and continuing on south. By the time he reached my belly, I was dying.

"I need you now, big guy. Please, stop the torture and get inside me."

He laughed against my skin and made me wait until I was worked into a frenzy. When he finally gave in and slid his erection into my heat, I moaned at the perfection of it. My orgasm blew off the charts—if there are charts.

After I was good and content, George filled me with his heat and closed his eyes.

An hour later, I spent a few minutes in the bathroom, and when I came out, I took a peek at George to see if he was moving. Nope, still breathless and exhausted.

"Hey, big guy. Can you give me a ride, or should I call a cab?" I laughed.

"Oh, baby. That was fuckin' unbelievable. I think I'm dead." He let out a long moan.

By the time I had thrown on my skirt and a t-shirt, George was sitting on the side of the bed. "I gotta' cut down on the butts. I can barely breathe."

I kissed him and shoved my tongue in his mouth. "Want to go again?"

"I'm goin' back to work, to rest," he wheezed, picked his jeans up off the floor and slowly pulled them on.

The bank was my first stop, then George dropped me at the dealership and roared off to work. I limped by the Hummer, peering in the windows on my way into the showroom and wondering if it was ready to go. Mr. Baker had told me everything was set when he had called earlier, but I had the distinct feeling he was waiting to see the money. I went to his office and knocked.

"Mrs. Talbot, you're here to pick up your vehicle."

"That's right, Mr. Baker. Is she ready to roll?" I asked with a smile and sat down in the chair opposite his desk.

"Is your husband with you?" he asked, looking past me.

"Sadly no, he's at work."

Mr. Baker looked relieved. "If you could sign the ownership, and pay the amount shown in the bottom box on the invoice, I can give you the keys."

I wrote a check and handed it to him.

He smiled as he stared at the check then passed me the keys and the ownership. "I hope you enjoy your Hummer."

"I'm sure I will."

As I aimed the big black beast down Hawthorne Lane, I could see a flatbed truck backed into my driveway. I parked at the curb and watched as a short stocky guy winched the charred frame of my Jeep onto a truck with 'Andy's Auto Wreckers' in big white letters on the side door.

I walked down the driveway as he finished up. "Hi. Are you Andy?"

"Yes, ma'am. I am. Too bad what happened to your vehicle," he said.

"It is, but I'm happy to have the wreckage taken away. What do I owe you?"

"Nothin' at all. I owe George a favor—happy to take it for you."

Everybody owes George a favor.

I waved as he jumped into his truck and drove up the street. I limped back to the curb and drove the Hummer up the driveway.

Apex arrived at three-forty five to reprogram the security system. The house was secure now, but not the garage. At five, Vince was finished and as he pulled his van out of the driveway, a blue Mini-Cooper drove in with Lionel Bachus behind the wheel. He saw me on the porch and sauntered up the steps to talk to me.

"Mrs. Talbot, I stopped by to tell you that we received a faxed copy of the police report and wrote the Jeep off. Your check will be mailed to you shortly."

"Thank you. I appreciate you dropping by in person," I said. "Can you tell me what the police said about the bomb?"

"They listed the explosive as possible pipe bomb with a remote detonator—most likely cell phone."

I nodded. "Thanks."

After he left, I opened a Coke and went into the back yard with Angel. She emptied her water bowl, then stretched out on the patio stones to cool down. My cell phone rang. "Hey," I answered.

"Hey, yourself. Look, baby girl, I have stuff to do tonight. Won't be there until late. You okay with that?"

"I'll be fine. Vince was here and the alarm's working again. Angel will watch over me."

"That's my girl. Okay, call you later."

I finished my can of pop while I looked up Ivan's Ink in the phone book. I still wanted to get my first tattoo. Ivan was polite, but informed me that the waiting list was long, and I was looking at November fourth before he could give me any time. Disappointed, I booked it and hung up.

CHAPTER FIFTY-FIVE

"I'M coming," I called in the direction of the front foyer. I tried to smooth my hair down but was sure I was going to scare the shit out of whoever was at the door. Glancing through the side light, I saw a good looking young man wearing a uniform, his finger pressing the bell. "Sorry, I'm not fully awake yet. What time is it anyway?"

"It's ten after nine, Miss. You wanted an estimate for a garage door?"

"That's right, I do. I was surprised you guys would come on a Sunday. Can you give me a minute?"

"Sure. I'll do the measuring out here and then we'll talk when you're ready."

"Great," I said as I closed the door and limped into the powder room.

George didn't call. Something must have come up.

After splashing water on my face and trying to tame my hair with just my bare hands—no weapon handy like a brush or a blow-torch, I started a pot of coffee then joined the garage door guy outside.

"What happened to your door?" he asked when he saw me on the porch.

"Bomb," I said with a laugh.

"You're kiddin', right?" He chuckled.

"Nope, my car blew up in front of the garage and the

door has the scars to prove it. "I'm Portia Talbot." I held out my hand. "Eddie Nolan gave me your name."

"I'm Buddy Feldman. Nice to meet you. I've never run into a bombed out door before. Frame looks new. Did Eddie replace that?"

I nodded. Buddy was looking pretty hot in his uniform. His dark curly hair matched his puppy-dog eyes and he had an electric smile.

"Okay if I look around inside the garage? Need to check the rails and the motor. With the door gone, I have no idea if the mechanism still works."

I left Buddy in the garage, went into the kitchen and left the door open. Angel bounced into the garage and barked at Buddy.

"What's your Rottie's name?" he asked.

"Angel."

"Hey, Angel, come here, girl." He rubbed her behind her ears, and she licked his hand. "I have one just like her, but he's a male. Call him Turbo."

"That's a cute name. I'll leave you to it. I have coffee in the kitchen if you would like a cup," I said, moving inside. My cell phone on the counter was ringing. "George?"

"I'm at the shop, baby girl. Sorry, I didn't talk to you last night. I texted you, but you must have been asleep. I had stuff to pick up and now I've got Porky working here unpacking and straightening up the store. He was pissed I made him work on a Sunday, but I want everything done before we go up north."

"Shit, I missed your text. I fell asleep on the sofa and was still there this morning in my rumpled clothes."

"I didn't miss anything where there were no fuckin' clothes?" He laughed.

"You'd be the first call I'd make if my clothes were off," I said, and turned to see Buddy standing in the doorway with eyebrows raised and a glimmer of a smile. My cheeks flushed hot.

"Mrs. Talbot, do you want to see the brochures I brought?"

"Who the fuck is that?" barked George.

"The garage door man."

"I'll be there in ten," he said and hung up.

Buddy spread out his information package on the dining room table, showing all the styles, colors, windows, and hinges available in a garage door. I set a mug of coffee down beside him and took the chair on the opposite side of the table. I was sorting through the colors for the 'North Hatley' when I heard the rumble of the Eagle in the driveway.

Buddy looked up when George blasted through the door with murder in his eyes. Bravely he stood up and offered his hand. "I'm Buddy Feldman, from Garaga."

"Hey, Bud," George said paralyzing Buddy's hand and taking a chair at the end of the table. "Find anything you like, baby girl?"

"This one would suit the style of the house best, I think. "I'm going with the 'North Hatley' in dark sand."

"Good choice, Mrs. Talbot. That style looks amazing on an older home." Buddy nodded, avoiding George's stare. "When would you like the installation?"

"As soon as possible. We'll be out of town this week, but I can have someone here to let you in." I looked at

George for confirmation and he nodded.

Buddy took out his calculator and wrote up the paperwork. When he arrived at a total he said. "How much is your deposit going to be?" He looked at me.

"Since I won't be around when you install the door, it would make more sense to pay for it now." I cocked my head and looked at George. He nodded. I wrote a check for the full amount and handed it to Buddy. "The door and the installation are guaranteed?" I asked.

"Of course, the guarantee is spelled out in your contract." He slid the check into his briefcase, gathered his materials and zipped up his case. "Thank you for your business, Mrs. Talbot." He smiled.

George motioned for me to stay seated, and he showed Buddy to the door.

"He didn't try anything, did he?" George asked when he returned.

I laughed. "He's a salesman, not a rapist. Are you jealous?"

"Fuckin' right. Can't stand it when other guys are staring at you. I know what they're all thinkin'. Makes me want to throw down."

"And what are they thinking?" I said rumpling his hair, running my hand down his scarred cheek and sticking my finger in his mouth.

George didn't answer. He scooped me up, stomped up the stairs and laid me on the bed.

"Do my clothes look like I slept in them?" I laughed. "Cause, I did."

"Yeah, these clothes have gotta' go," he said, undressing me piece by piece.

After we made love, and George lay on his back panting I noticed that his arm was red and inflamed. Kenny's knife had slashed through the eagle inked onto his forearm, and the bird looked eviscerated and sewn back together. The rebel flag the bird was holding in its' beak was tilting badly towards the Mason-Dixon Line.

"Your arm looks pretty raw. Maybe you should go back to the doctor."

"I don't need no fuckin' doctor." George pulled his arm from my grip and clenched his fist.

I gasped and pulled away, my heart racing.

Horror struck, George froze. His dark brown eyes scanned my expression, as his scowl deepened. "Jesus, Annie. You know I would never hit you, baby girl . . . Don't you?"

I tried to relax and blew out a deep breath. "Matthew's favorite place to hit me was in bed," I mumbled.

"Wish that fucker wasn't dead, so I could kill him," George snarled.

I managed a smile and stroked his arm.

"I'm not mad at you, Annie. I'm pissed about the fuckin' tat. It's wrecked."

"Maybe it can be fixed," I said, easing into his lap. "But there's no telling when. I called Ivan today to make an appointment for me, but the earliest one he had was in November."

"Bullshit. I'll call him." George kissed my cheek and sucked in some deep breaths.

"I missed you last night," I said.

"Quick trip to Hamilton—took longer than I figured."

"Want me to fix you something in the kitchen before you go back to work?"

"Fuckin' right."

I threw a t-shirt over my head and went down to get to work. George would go all day without any food. He existed on smokes, coffee and beer. I put together a tray and took it out to where he was sitting at the patio table.

"Hey, thanks." He kissed me and I sat down. "I called Ivan and tuned him up. We're goin' tomorrow at ten-thirty."

"Tomorrow? I thought he had no openings."

"He has one now." George smiled. "What are you thinkin' of getting' done, honey girl?"

"Just a flower, I was thinking lily of the valley. My favorite."

"He can do anything if he has a picture," George said. "He's a helluva artist."

"I'll cut a picture out of one of my gardening magazines."

"That'll do it." George lit up a smoke and held it out to look at it. "I'm cutting back on the butts," he said grinning. "I'm in training."

"That's impressive," I sat on his lap and kissed him. "You'll be a holy terror in the bedroom."

"I'll never be half the terror you are, sweet Annie."

After George went back to the gun shop, I sifted through my stack of gardening magazines until I came up with a crystal clear photograph of a sprig of lily of the valley. I cut it out and put it in my purse for Ivan. Tomorrow I was getting my first tattoo.

Yahoo.

The rest of the afternoon, I did laundry, got the suitcases out of the closet and packed a few things for the week at the cabin. At six, I answered a call from George.

"Want to meet me at Buck's?"

"Sure. What time?"

"Me and Porky are goin' as soon as we lock up. You can come anytime you want."

"Save me a spot."

"You'll always have a spot right next to me."

After my shower, I dressed for the bar in a black denim skirt and a black top that showed a lot of cleavage. I pulled on my leather boots and tried to disguise the angry red gash on my face with makeup. My hair needed cutting, but it could wait a couple of days.

TRYING to find a spot for the Hummer in the parking lot at Buck's was challenging. The frame was wide, and I wasn't used to driving it. I backed up against the building next door, locked it up and limped across to the door of the bar.

The blue smoke layer wasn't so thick on a Sunday night. I could see all the way to the back of the room. George was sitting near the pool tables, but not in his regular spot. I waved at Buck as I passed the bar and sat down opposite George.

Rusty, Jackson and a couple of other guys were sitting in the next booth.

"Hey, Portia," Jackson called over. He flashed me his smile.

"Hi guys. Good to see you," I said.

"You know, you could have any fuckin' guy in this whole place, baby girl," said George, "Probably in the whole city."

"I'm sure most of them have girlfriends of their own," I said.

"Not any they wouldn't dump for a chance at you," he winked.

"Where's this coming from?" I asked.

"Nowhere, just sayin'."

I got up and walked around to his side of the booth and kissed him long and hard. "Fuck them."

"Shit. They saw you do that. Now they're gonna' be all over me. My life is fuckin' over," he said with a smile.

"I can make it worse." I offered.

George groaned. "Those guys try to get under my skin every fuckin' chance they get."

"Want me to talk to them?" I asked, leaning forward so George could get a good look down my shirt.

"Lord Jesus, no." He moaned.

I laughed. "Did you order?"

"Yep, should be here soon."

"Hi Rusty," I said as he ambled over to our table. He looked like he definitely had something on his mind. "What's up?"

"Boys want to have a bonfire tomorrow night before the boss goes on holidays."

"That sounds like fun. What do you say, George?"

"I'll think about it," he said with a scowl.

Rusty nodded and went back to his booth.

"Don't like that idea?"

"Boys can get rowdy. Might be fights. Not a good place for you, Annie."

"But before me, it might have been a fun night for you?"

"Maybe."

I shrugged. "No problem. I won't go. You have fun with your boys. I'm good with that."

George shook his head, his grin widening. "You get me, Annie. I never have to explain things to you. You just get it."

I smiled. Buck strode to the table with two heaping plates of food. "Thanks, Buck. Do me a favor. Bring those four guys at the next table burgers, fries and another two pitchers on me."

"Will do," said Buck.

"Why you doin' that, baby girl?" George looked puzzled.

"They were there when I needed help. It's nothing."

George refilled our glasses and we devoured our burgers. When Buck served the food to the table behind us, the boys gave me thumbs-up and I gave them a wave.

We were almost ready to leave when two suits appeared in the door of the bar. "Fuckin' assholes," said George, "More cops."

They sat at the bar for a few minutes, scanning all of the tables, scrutinizing the customers.

"Lookin' for some poor fucker," George said. "Probably trying to tag some asshole for spitting on the sidewalk or wearing his cut or shit like that."

"No doubt," I said with a laugh and stood up to leave, "You staying?"

"Just to sort out this bonfire shit. Then I'm comin' home."

"That's so nice. You said 'home'."

CHAPTER FIFTY-SIX

"HEY, you're getting good at sneaking into bed. I don't even remember you getting in last night."

I was at the kitchen table with my first cup of coffee when George came downstairs.

"Didn't want to wake you, baby girl. It was late."

"Want coffee?"

"Uh huh," he said with a little glint in his eye.

"What?" I said trying to get a read on his expression.

"Nothin'." He smiled like he had swallowed a fat yellow canary.

I poked him in the gut. "I know you're up to no good."

"Talked to the boys. There'll be no trouble tonight. They want you to come."

I smiled. "They do . . . and how about you?"

"I always want you with me, Annie," he said. "That's why . . . I bought you this." Looking unsure of himself, he pulled a small box out of his pocket and opened it. A huge blue sapphire surrounded by diamonds sparkled on a bed of black velvet. I gasped and stared.

George took my hand and slipped the ring on my finger. "I am so fuckin' terrible at this sentimental shit, but you know I'm crazy in love with you, Annie."

"I love you, George, for always." Tears welled up in my eyes and rolled down my cheeks. I moved over, sat on his knee and put my arms around his neck. I kissed him for a long time while my tears spilled onto his face and made us both wet. We laughed.

"You make me so happy, George," I whispered.

"Never pictured this happening to me. Not in a million fuckin' years."

We made love upstairs before George left for work. He showered, shaved and dressed while I languished on the bed staring at the sapphire on my finger and grinning like a Cheshire cat.

After my shower, with my leg wrapped in plastic, I dressed and was putting the finishing touches on my make up when the doorbell rang and the cleaning girls arrived. They unloaded their gear into the foyer, trying to avoid Angel as she bounced around trying to grab their mops out of their hands.

"Sorry I couldn't make it on Friday," Stacey said, "It was my daughter's graduation."

"No problem," I said, beaming. Nothing was going to spoil this day for me. "I'll put Angel in the yard, so you girls can do your thing."

"Wow. Is that a new ring?" Stacey exclaimed, staring at my hand.

"New this morning. It was quite a surprise."

"Nice surprise." The girls gathered round to get a better look.

"Does this mean you're engaged?" Stacey asked me.

"Umm, more like committed," I said.

"I'd commit to anybody or anything for a ring like that." She laughed.

"Oh, sorry, there goes my phone," I hobbled out to

the patio to answer, smiling at George's number on my screen.

"Do you want to pick me up at the store and we'll go to Ivan's from here?" he asked.

"Oh, my God, my tattoo. I've been so mesmerized showing off my ring to the cleaning girls, I forgot about the appointment. This is such an exciting day."

"Ain't that the truth?" George sounded less than impressed.

"I'll pick you up shortly. I have the picture in my purse," I said as I scoured the kitchen for the car keys.

"As soon as Porky gets back from Tim's, I'm good to go," he said and hung up.

"SHIT. Shit. Shit," I said out loud, as I tried to navigate the Hummer down the back lane behind the gun shop. Branches of the overgrown bushes were scratching at the doors and George would surely think I was an idiot for trying to park here.

The bell jingled when the front door opened, and George's grin turned to a frown when he saw my face. "What happened? You look red in the face and guilty about something," he said.

I shrugged and said nothing.

"Hold the fort, Porky," George hollered into the back room as we headed for the door. "Phone me if those bastards cruise by here again. Cops have been driving by slow all morning. Makes me fuckin' nuts," he said on the way out to the Hummer.

"What are they looking for?" I asked.

"Nothin' *to* look for. Business is legit. Maybe they

figure if they do it enough, I'll run out the door and ventilate their fuckin' cruiser."

"Maybe they're hard up for some crime to prevent." I giggled.

"What in hell did you do here, little girl?" asked George as he ripped at the weeds caught in the driver's door.

"The Hummer is a lot wider than the Wrangler. I'm not used to it yet. Sorry," I said.

"Don't go there, Annie." George put his finger under my chin and tilted my head up to look him straight in his dark ebony eyes. "You never have to be sorry to me for anything you do. You please yourself and I'll be happy as hell. Don't think I ain't seen the way you always try to please people. If that fuckin' bastard was still alive, I'd choke him by the neck until his eyes bulged out of his head, for the way he used you."

"I love you, George."

"Love you too, baby girl." He came around to my side of the truck. "Stick your leg out here for a minute," he said, taking a jar out of his pocket. "Point where you're getting' your tat."

I showed him the spot on my thigh that I had in mind, and he opened the jar. Dipping his fingers into the ointment he covered my skin in slow, slick circles.

"This will take the edge off for you, baby. Should be working by the time we get there."

"Thanks, George—you take good care of me."

George backed the Hummer down the lane and out into the street with no problem. I made a mental note to practice.

IVAN'S INK was less than ten blocks away from the gun shop. George pulled into the gravel parking lot, helped me down from the truck and lit up a smoke. He inhaled a few drags on the way to the entrance then flicked the rest into a sewer grate. "Think you're ready, little girl?" he asked with a grin.

"I am so ready for this," I said, as I limped through the door.

Ivan's shop was compact. Hidden amongst a row of old brick storefronts on Danforth Avenue, he had four stations, one for himself and one for each of the three tattoo artists working for him. The walls were filled with pictures of work he had done in the past, and photos of famous people with tats.

Ivan looked up from a customer he was finishing and smiled when he saw George. He was a small man in his forties, thin and muscular with long dark hair tied back in a pony tail with a red ribbon. He wore wire-rimmed glasses while he worked but popped onto his forehead when he looked up.

"Where the hell have you been hiding? Thought you left the country."

"Keeping out of trouble," George said with a chuckle and nodding at me.

"That looks like a brand new kind of trouble for you, Georgie Boy."

"You got that right, Ivan. Now, she wants a tat."

He pointed to an empty chair. "You two can sit over here. I won't be more than a few minutes."

"Do you have any idea what design you want?" he

asked, taping a wide swath of gauze over the other customer's shoulder.

"I have a picture here of my favorite flower. It's lily of the valley," I said, unfolding the photo. He took a quick glance and nodded as he walked the finished customer to the cash and went over the care instructions. When he came back, I held out my hand. "I'm Annie."

"Ivan," he said, concentrating on the details of the flower. "I don't believe I've done this one before, but it looks simple enough. Love those little bells. Where do you want it? I see that your left leg is bandaged."

"I had some surgery, but it's coming along. For my tat, I'm thinking on my thigh." I pulled the side of my denim skirt up and pointed to a spot on my right thigh. I glanced at George and saw him glaring as Ivan touched my leg while moving my skirt out of his way.

Ivan caught George's expression and smiled. "Oh, yeah, I'm getting the picture here. Loud and clear."

"George rubbed cream on my leg before we came," I said.

"I don't doubt that for a second," Ivan said with a chuckle. "Emla cream?" he asked.

George nodded.

Ivan slipped on latex gloves and opened a packaged towelette to wipe my skin. After he'd made a transfer, he set it in place, and I gave him the nod. When he started the design, it stung my skin like little electric shocks. George paced and smoked during the whole procedure, while Ivan worked and chatted to me.

"That's some rock you're wearing, Annie."

I nodded towards George.

"Never would have believed that could happen. Not in this lifetime," he shook his head.

"Took me by surprise," I said. "Unexpected."

"That's an understatement," he snorted as he finished up and taped a clean bandage over the tattoo. "Leave this on for a couple days. Don't soak in the bathtub for two weeks, and don't touch the scab. Any problems, come right back to me."

"Thanks, Ivan. I love it."

"Oh, I forgot. Don't let that bandit near you for a week." He slapped his knee and chuckled.

"How much do I owe you?" I asked.

Ivan waved my words away, "Consider it an engagement present."

"I don't know how to thank you," I replied. I knew better than to argue with these guys. They were all the same.

"I could think of something, if that brute wasn't here," he whispered. Ivan stood up and shook George's hand. "She's a winner, you old bastard. Tread softly." Before releasing George's hand, Ivan said. "Hold on here a minute. What the fuck happened to your arm? Looks like this eagle was gutted. That was one beautiful piece of work, and now look at it." Ivan glared.

"Stitches," George said.

"I can see they're stitches, you dumb son of a bitch. Come see me when the arm is completely healed."

"Later, Ivan." At the door, George gave him a slap on the back and nearly knocked him over. George navigated the Hummer alongside the curb in front of the gun shop while I tried to peek under my bandage to see the tattoo.

"Annie, get out of there," he said. "I touched one of mine too soon and fucked the color, baby."

"You're right," I said, pulling my skirt down. "Ivan told me not to touch it."

At the gun shop, George got out and I slid over into the driver's seat and kissed him through the open window.

"This is my last day with Porky, so I want to make sure he's down with every fuckin' thing in the store."

"That's wise. Make sure he has your cell number written down."

"Good one. See you later."

I waved and eased the Hummer out into traffic for the drive home. My leg was smarting a little as I walked up the porch steps, and into the house. I started a pot of coffee, made a corned beef sandwich and sat down at the kitchen table to list what I needed for a week at the cabin.

My short skirt showed the bandage on my thigh as well as the bandage over the surgery, so I changed into sweats and a t-shirt for a trip to the market. When I returned home, I left all of the bags in the Hummer that didn't need refrigeration and went upstairs to pack my clothes.

All I needed for the cabin was sweats, jeans, a jacket, clean underwear and toiletries. George hadn't mentioned his clothes. Maybe he needed me to do laundry or something before we left but offering to help him was not an option. Waiting for him to get to it was the better plan.

At six-thirty the phone rang. "Porky is locking up

now and I'll be there in a half. How's the leg? You haven't fucked with it, have you?"

"Never touched it, I swear."

"Figure we'll ride up to the range about ten or so. That good for you, little girl?"

"Yep, I'll make steaks for eight, and I have beer on ice. We might have time for one other thing before we go."

"That's all I thought about all day. Could hardly concentrate on what that dumb bastard, Porky was sayin' half the fuckin' time."

"Can't wait to see you."

I hung up and started the prep work on dinner.

At seven-ten the Harley roared into the driveway, sending Angel into a frenzy. She could hear the bike coming a couple miles away and took up her position in the front hall. When George blasted through the door, she jumped all over him.

"Down girl, you're almost as fuckin' wild as Annie."

"I heard that." I giggled.

George picked me up and whisked me upstairs without answering.

"In a hurry?" I asked watching him pull off his motorcycle boots and strip down.

"You're all I think about, Annie," he said, lying down beside me. "I'm fucked."

"You will be soon," I said and laughed, throwing off my sweats and rolling on top of him.

When we were spent, George sat on the side of the bed trying to catch his breath, while I grabbed a quick shower.

I came out the bathroom door toweling off my hair and saw him sitting in exactly the same spot. "You okay? You look so pale." He didn't answer me, staring straight ahead like he was in a trance. I stifled a cry, sucked in a breath and punched 911 into my cell phone. I threw on jeans and a t-shirt, not taking time for underwear and tore downstairs as fast as my leg would allow. I shoved Angel into the back yard, reached the front door and swung it open wide, just as the sirens rounded the corner. The paramedics thundered across the porch with the gurney.

"Upstairs, first door on the left," I gasped, forcing the nausea down, and holding back tears. I limped up the stairs, panting for breath and gritting my teeth to bear up under the pain in my leg. By the time I reached the bedroom, George was lying on the gurney, staring at the ceiling. Paramedics shot an IV into his arm.

"Please," I gasped, "Don't let him die." My ears buzzed and darkness filled my head.

Someone helped me up from the floor, and gave me water, then sat me in a chair by the window.

"Are you okay now?" one of the paramedics asked.

"I'm fine," I said gasping. "Take care of George."

"His vitals are stable. The hospital will check him out. Do you feel up to riding along?"

"Oh, yes. I want to." My legs were shaky when I stood up, but I grabbed my purse and followed the stretcher out to the ambulance. One of the attendants helped me into the back, and I sat next to George and held his hand. He was staring at the roof of the ambulance, not speaking.

I cast an inquiring glance at the attendant through my tears. She was monitoring George. Her shirt read 'Gail' in dark blue letters.

"Don't worry. He's in shock. He'll come out of it. By the time we get to the hospital, he might be talking to you," she said, layering on another blanket.

The minutes ticked by one by one, as I sat in the waiting room, while a heart specialist examined George.

A nurse came to fetch me. "Mrs. Ross. The doctor would like to speak with you."

Without bothering to correct her, I followed her into examination room four and she introduced me to Dr. Lee. I shook his hand and took a deep breath, dreading the words that were about to tumble out of his mouth and ruin my life.

"Mr. Ross is going to be fine," he said.

"Oh, thank God. I thought you were going to say . . ." Tears rolled down my face.

"Your husband suffered a mild coronary and changes to his lifestyle are obviously the order of the day," he said. "He must quit smoking immediately, and it would benefit him greatly if he could lose at least forty pounds. Has he been under a lot of extra stress lately?"

"Um, yeah, a little," I mumbled with a frown. I glanced at George's face to see if he was listening to the doctor's words or if he was still out of it. He rolled his eyes and I knew he was hearing, but not buying it. "Can I take him home?"

"I would prefer it if he remained overnight, but yes. He can go home, but I want him to rest for the next forty-eight hours, and no sex for at least a week. Have this prescription filled and follow the directions exactly."

George struggled to sit upright on the stretcher in his blue gown and by the grimace on his face, I was sure his second infarction was imminent. "Shit, doc. You're laying some heavy shit on me here. I might have trouble following all these fuckin' rules."

Doctor Lee didn't seem fazed in the least by George's intimidating demeanor and carried on without missing a beat. "Granted, it will be tough at first, but once you start getting into better shape and feeling healthier, you will find it much easier."

"I hear ya'. I'll give it my best shot," George said. He stepped down from the stretcher and shook Doctor Lee's hand.

What the hell was happening here?

After the doctor left the room, George asked. "Did you bring me any clothes, baby girl?"

"I wasn't that bright, but the paramedics rolled up your clothes from beside the bed and tossed them under the gurney."

"Yeah, here they are." George was quiet while he dressed, then we walked slowly out the emergency exit towards the street.

"We need to call a cab," I said. "I should have driven the Hummer and followed the ambulance. I wasn't thinking clearly."

"Don't sweat it, little girl. You did fine. Probably saved my life for the second time in two weeks," he leaned down and kissed me. "Do you have your cell with you?"

"In my purse," I said, plopping down on a bench at

the end of the hospital property and letting go a big breath. I handed it to George and watched him punch in a number.

"Jackson. Need you to pick me up in front of Scarborough General. I'm sittin' on a bench with Annie. No. We're both right as rain. Okay good."

"He's on his way," George said as he wrapped his arm around my shivering shoulders. "It's hotter than the fuckin' hubs out here. Why are you cold?"

"I'm not cold. Still frazzled from your heart attack. We both know it's my fault."

"Don't let me hear you say that again, Annie. I always want the sex as much as you or even more. It's my fault for being overweight and smokin' like a fuckin' chimney. Not yours." A few minutes passed before George stood up and pointed. "There's our ride."

The black and orange truck from the Harley dealership pulled up to the curb and George helped me into the back of the cab. He climbed in beside Jackson and reached into his vest pocket for a smoke. "Fuck. I do that without even thinkin'," he hollered.

"Do what, boss?" asked Jackson.

"Reach for a smoke," George said. "Doc said I had to quit smokin'."

"When?" asked Jackson, unsure of what was going on.

"Now—I'm thinkin' about it."

"Portia, why are you guys at the hospital?" Jackson asked over his shoulder.

"George had a heart attack. He has to rest for the next forty-eight hours."

"Fuck. No way. What caused it?"

"Guess," said George.

Jackson searched George's face and busted out laughing, slapping the steering wheel.

"It's not that fuckin' funny," grumbled George.

"Damn right it is. Sorry, Portia. Wait'll the boys hear about this."

"They're not gonna' hear about it. Are they Jackson?" George punched him in the arm.

"Not from me, boss. Not from me." He chuckled.

Jackson turned the corner onto Hawthorne Lane and pulled into the driveway. "Come in for a drink, Jackson," I said. "I'm definitely having a couple." I unlocked the front door and led the way to the kitchen with Angel bouncing behind me. I fed the dog and turned on the barbeque. Jackson got the beers out of the fridge and poured mine into a glass.

"You better only have one, George. You have to start the medication."

"Yeah, okay," he said.

I put the potatoes and veggies on the grill and closed the lid. "Stay for dinner, Jackson. I have a lot of steak." I sat down and took a long drink.

"Okay, I could eat. And I like your cookin'. No fuckin' around."

"Thanks. What about the bonfire? George is supposed to rest for the next two days. I'm thinking I'll drive him up north tomorrow."

"Is that what you're thinking, little girl?" George asked me.

"Yes. Quiet place to rest and we're going the next

day anyway."

"Sounds good," George agreed, to my surprise.

Jackson said, "I'll give Rusty a call and tell him we're not comin'. The rest of 'em can party on without us."

George nodded. "Those bandits won't even care we're not there."

"The grill smells hot. I'm going to put the steaks on," I said, retrieving the meat from the fridge. "Dinner in eight minutes. George, you have to take your pills and you can't mix them with alcohol."

George held up his empty and grinned at me. I fixed a tray in the kitchen with plates, cutlery, and condiments and carried it out to the patio. The boys made short work of their meal and I cleared away the dishes.

"Sorry, I don't have any dessert, but I'll make a pot of coffee," I said. "Jackson, do you have bike trailers for sale at Harley?"

"Hell, yeah, do you want one?"

"Thinking of trailering the bikes up north in case George wants to go for a ride."

"You are so fuckin' smart, Annie. You're always one step ahead of me."

"I'll load the Hummer in the morning, then come over to the dealership and pick one up."

"I'm usually there to open up around eight-thirty," Jackson said, stirring the third spoonful of sugar into his coffee.

"Okay. I'll try for nine, then come back here, load the bikes, pick up Angel and we're good to go. George, what about your clothes? We need to pick them up."

"Never thought about taking more clothes. Jackson and I have a couple things to lock down tonight at my place anyway, so I'll grab my stuff while we're over there."

I gave Jackson a look, and he piped up, "I'll drive us over in the truck and bring the boss back when we're finished."

"I nodded. "More coffee?"

"Not for me," said Jackson, standing up and stretching. "Thanks for dinner."

CHAPTER FIFTY-SEVEN

AT four a.m. I awoke, removed the book that had slid down onto the duvet and turned off the light on the nightstand. Angel was on her blanket, but George's side of the bed was cold. After tossing and turning for another half hour, I gave up and padded downstairs to make coffee. I took a cup into the living room, sat on the sofa and closed my eyes.

What if George had another heart attack? He's supposed to be resting, not sorting out who- knows-what kind of club problems.

Calling was not an option. I didn't want to interrupt for no good reason. I leaned back into the sofa, exhaled a big breath, closed my eyes and waited.

At six, Angel jumped up and ran to the front door when she heard George.

"I didn't think you'd be up, baby girl," he said.

"Woke up at four and couldn't go back to sleep," I said, wiping my forehead. "Coffee's ready."

"My fault. So many things I didn't want to leave hangin' before we left. It's all good now. Want to go back to bed? To sleep," he added with a chuckle.

I smiled. "Sounds boring, but okay." We trudged upstairs and I had two solid hours before the alarm went off. George was dead to the world, and I was careful not to wake him while I showered, dressed and loaded the

Hummer with everything on my list.

I brewed a fresh pot of coffee and went back upstairs. "Hey babe, do you want to go with me to pick up the trailer, or sleep until I get back?

George stirred and sat up. "Fuck, I'm tired."

"You had a heart attack. Your body is telling you to rest. Sleep until I get back."

I kissed him and gently pushed him back down on the bed.

"Wish you were pushing me back to climb on top of me," he grumbled.

"Couple of days you'll be ripping my clothes off." I laughed.

I hope.

I closed the bedroom door, grabbed my purse from the kitchen and backed the Hummer out onto the street. Mid-June was warm near the lake and the Toronto humidity had been merciful this month.

Ten minutes' drive time took me into the Harley parking lot. I walked through the big glass doors just as Jackson was striding towards the front counter.

"Morning, Jackson. You must be tired." I smiled.

"Fuck, yeah," Jackson replied, "Pulled an all-nighter with the boss. He's worried what could go wrong while he's away, but it won't. We got his back."

"Is something going on, Jackson? The doctor wanted to know if George was under more stress than normal."

Jackson hesitated. "We had a few extra things to sort out, but I think it's all under control."

"Good. Stress is not healthy for him right now. A week away at the cabin will be ideal." My voice cracked and I choked back a sob.

Jackson ran around the desk, wrapped me in his arms and stroked my hair. "Don't cry, Portia. The boss will be okay. He's a tough guy. He won't kick from a little fuckin' heart attack."

"Thanks, Jackson. Don't know why I'm acting like such a girl." I heaved a big sigh. "Let's go pick out a trailer."

"They're lined up around the north side of the building." He pointed and led the way out the side door. "We've got a few different models here, but this is the best double trailer we carry. Welded construction, folds up to take less space in your garage. Not too heavy. Good rubber on it. This is the one I'd buy," Jackson said giving the stainless steel a hefty punch with his fist.

"Sold. Let's hook it up."

"Do you have a hitch on the Hummer?" he asked.

"I don't know." We walked around the front of the building and checked the back end of the Hummer.

"Fuck, yeah—one on there. You know it's illegal to leave those mothers on if you're not using them. Cops love giving tickets for dick-shit like that."

"No. I didn't even know it was there."

"Well, now you don't have to buy one. After you finish at the cash, I'll get Billy to help me and we'll hook you up."

I settled up the invoice and went back to the Hummer while the boys brought the trailer around. They hooked it onto the truck, and I was ready to roll. Jackson walked around to the driver's window. "Watch your corners, Portia. Don't cut the wheel too short. You don't want to

be takin' any curb shots when the bikes are loaded on . . .
and don't worry so much about the boss. He's fuckin'
strong as George St. Pierre."

Whoever that is.

"Thanks, for everything, Jackson." I put the Hummer
into gear and pulled out onto the street. When I drove
down Hawthorne Lane, I passed the driveway and then
tried to back the trailer in towards the garage. Five tries
later, and lots of snickering from the neighbors, I was
close enough to load the bike. When I stepped out of the
Hummer and walked around the hood, I saw George
sitting on the front steps grinning.

"Why didn't you help me?" I punched him in the
shoulder.

"Fuck. It was way more fun watching you." He
laughed. "Nice trailer, baby girl. Top o' the line, no
doubt."

"The one Jackson said he would buy," I said.

"Let's load my bike," George said swaggering
towards the trailer. When he examined my new
purchase, he grinned like a kid. "Oh, fuck. It tilts. I love
you, Annie." He had no trouble loading the Eagle and
securing it in place with the ratchet straps.

My bike was a different story. It was at the paint
shop. George had checked with Rusty and told him we'd
be by on our way to the cabin.

I packed the last minute items from the fridge, water
for Angel and George's duffle bag from the front hall,
and we were ready to rock and roll. I called Apex to let
Vince know I would be out of town, and that I was
having a garage door installation that would require his

presence on Thursday. With the house locked up tight, we were off.

First stop was Coulter Colors, Rusty's paint shop, to pick up my bike. George pulled around the back of the building and parked. He helped me down out of the Hummer and we went in the side door. Country music was blaring loud enough that Rusty could hear it over the sound of the sprayer. He looked up, saw us and turned off the machine and turned down Toby Keith.

"Hey, Portia, how are you doing?" he asked with a grin.

"Better, thanks."

"I finished your bike, yesterday, and it's ready for you. I was going to drop it off, but the boss said this was just as easy."

"Let's load it up," George said.

Rusty had it covered with a tarp in the corner. When he opened the overhead door and pushed the bike out it gleamed in the sunlight.

I gasped and hugged Rusty. "It's beautiful. Thank you so much."

"I know it's a shade lighter, but . . ." he shook his head.

The boys loaded it onto the trailer and while George was tightening the ratchet straps, I followed Rusty back inside.

"What?" he raised his eyebrows under his gorgeous mop of auburn hair.

I pressed a wad of cash into his hand. "This never happened, sweetie," I whispered, as I turned and left.

He tried to protest, but then gave in. "Thanks, Portia.

You're the best."

George drove while I rode shotgun, rested my leg and kept an eagle eye on the bikes. He slowly eased the Hummer out into the street. Angel wasn't used to being relegated to the back seat, but she took it in stride and hung her head out the window all the same. I shoved a Springsteen CD into the slot, and we started our journey with Bruce belting out 'Wrecking ball'. George said he loved it.

In Peterborough we stopped for fuel, snacks and bathroom breaks for one and all. When we reached the dam at Burleigh Falls, we stretched our legs and sat on the flat rocks in the sun and wind. While we watched the kayaks racing in the white water, Angel ran and splashed in the rapids.

George lit up a smoke. I noticed that he hadn't smoked in the truck up to that point, but I was not going to jinx him by mentioning it.

Refreshed, we continued up highway twenty-eight. George had been quiet, staring out the window while I took a turn at the wheel.

"Do you think everything will run smoothly at the club while you're gone?" I asked.

"Why are you asking me that, baby girl?"

"The doctor thought you possibly had added stress lately—I'm concerned because I love you."

"I don't want you to worry about that shit at all, Annie."

"You can trust me, George."

"That ain't it, baby. Safer for you the less you know."

"Okay." I held his hand.

As we rolled into Bancroft, late in the afternoon, I pulled our rig into the Beer Store parking lot. George went in, bought a couple of cases and loaded them in the back.

"Not much farther," I said. "Twenty minutes."

"I like it up here," George said. "Not so many fuckin' people."

"That's true," I smiled. "Not many jobs up here."

George nodded.

North of Bird's Creek, I slowed down, keeping a watchful eye for my side road. When I recognized it, I slowed the Hummer down and eased around the corner onto the dirt road. In my mind, the laneway had been giving me nightmares, thinking about navigating this awkward rig through the narrow opening. I eased into the turn at the old mailbox, stomped on the gas and breezed up to the top of the hill.

I put the Hummer in park and opened the back door for Angel. "We're here. This is my piece of paradise."

"This is the most beautiful fuckin' sight I've ever seen," said George, "next to you, Annie." He encircled me with his massive arms and kissed me. "We're in heaven."

"I'll show you something," I said, grabbing a couple of cold Cokes. George took my hand and I led him through the trees and down the steep path to the edge of the lake. The scent of pine needles floated on the breeze. When he looked up and saw the huge expanse of sparkling water spread out in front of him he gasped.

"This calls for a toast," he said. "To our life together, Annie."

We clinked our Coke cans and sauntered down to the dock while Angel waded in at the shoreline and splashed around sending frogs scrambling off their lily pads.

"All my life I kept working for some fuckin' thing, and didn't even know what it was," George said. "Then you come along and I think I finally know what it is. It's you. But you and this place, together? Over the top, Annie—over the top." He hugged me and held me tight for a long moment.

"I'm happy you like it, George, because I *love* it." I kissed him at the end of the dock, and we lingered for a long time just drinking in the simplicity of it all. "I'm going to unload the Hummer and put the meat in the fridge," I said. "Why don't you and Angel bum around down here until supper is ready?"

"I'll be up soon, honey girl," he said, his black eyes dancing in the sunlight.

After unloading the groceries and our luggage, I made some smoked meat sandwiches, and headed back down to the dock to watch the sunset with George. When I pushed back the branches at the bottom of the path, I could see him sitting on the dock, staring out over the water.

"Hey, I brought you some food."

"You're the best. Did I ever mention that, little girl?" he pulled me down beside him on the splintery old dock. "I lucked out with you, Annie," he chuckled.

"The sunset over the lake is something to see," I said, munching on my sandwich.

We sat on the end of the dock sipping our soda and anticipating the moment that the sun would drop behind the horizon. George sat with one arm wrapped around me and I dangled my bare feet in the water. "I never want to leave this place," I whispered.

"I'm not going to," he said.

I looked into his eyes and believed that he meant it.

After the sun had set and filled the evening sky with a myriad of reds, oranges, and tangerines, we ambled back up the hill to the cabin.

I opened the back door and swept my arm through the doorway. "Come in, George. Welcome home."

He walked into the kitchen and didn't get any farther than the table. He shook his head, pulled out a chair and sat down. "Ever since I was a kid, I always wanted to live in a log cabin," he said. "I can't believe I'm going to get the chance to do it." His voice sounded like someone I didn't even know. I threw my arms around his neck and kissed him gently.

"If you want to fish off the dock tomorrow, I saw some tackle in the barn last time I was here. Lots of interesting stuff out there to rummage through."

"Do you know the first fuckin' thing I thought of when I saw that lake, baby girl?"

"Jumping in?" I ventured.

"No," he chuckled. "A boat. I'm going to buy a Bass boat." He grinned from ear to ear.

"Great idea," I agreed. "Fishing is restful and non-stressful. I wonder if they have any for sale in town. We can ask at the store. That guy Harry, he knows everything and everybody. I saw a sign for worms down there a couple weeks ago."

"I'm pumped, Annie. Never thought I could be so

fuckin' happy. Let's go to bed and celebrate."

"A week isn't up yet, big guy. Not even twenty-four hours." I smiled.

"If I get a big pain, I'll stop. Promise."

"How big was the pain yesterday? You didn't clue me in on the details."

"Like a six foot load of dirt on my chest. I didn't smoke much today, did you notice?"

"Sure did. My eyes are on you twenty-four seven." I laughed and pointed at him with my two fingers. I took him by the hand and gave him the tour. "This is the living room," I pointed. "Actually, half the kitchen. Here's the guest room slash office, bathroom, and our bedroom. That's all she wrote," I giggled.

"More than we need, sweet cheeks. More than two people need."

I stripped the quilts off the bed and left only the cotton sheets. The night was warm and there was no breeze coming through the screens. George took his time making love to me, and he was gentle and sweet. I reigned myself in, so I wouldn't rev him up past a point of no return. Afterwards, we lay on the sheets uncovered and drifted off to sleep.

CHAPTER FIFTY-EIGHT

GRABBING a t-shirt from my bag, I tip-toed into the kitchen and opened the back door for Angel. She glimpsed the striped tail of a chipmunk hurdling over the woodpile, and the chase was on. I paused to press the button on the coffee maker then stepped onto the back porch to watch Angel's crazy antics. As I stood there, shading my eyes from the morning sun, an indigo hummingbird buzzed over my head. "I need bird feeders," I said aloud.

"Hell yeah," a big voice boomed behind me. "You need lots of bird feeders, little girl."

I laughed. "I didn't hear you, George. I was watching Angel and ducking birds. How did you sleep?"

"Best sleep ever—must be the air."

"Must be." I filled two mugs with coffee and carried them out to the porch. George had settled in a chair and lit up his first smoke of the day. He coughed and hacked, broke out in a sweat and his face flushed. I set his coffee on the weathered butcher block next to him and rested my hand on his shoulder.

"I gotta' get into better shape, Annie, for you and for me. I don't want a young, gorgeous thing like you lookin' after some fuckin' old pervert that can't wipe his own ass."

I burst out laughing. "You're a long way from that,

sweetie pie."

"I felt close the other day."

I hugged him. "Well, a new day has dawned, and we're not going back."

George grabbed his phone from his belt when the rebel yell pierced the silence. "Hey, Jackson, what's up?" he asked. "Yep, I'm fine. Annie's treating me half decent and I had the best night's sleep ever. Trailer was fuckin-A. Annie had no trouble, even getting' up the hill with it." George looked to me, and I nodded. "Had an idea last night—no, not that idea, Jackson, you pervert. I'm buying a boat today, for fishing. Yeah, a Bass boat. Goin' into town to pick one out in an hour. Call ya' later."

"I'll make some breakfast, and we'll get moving," I said.

George went into the bedroom to get dressed while I rummaged in the cupboard for the frying pan and got the bacon and eggs started. It crossed my mind that this couldn't be the best breakfast for George, so I made a mental note to buy healthier choices when we went into town.

"Smells good," he said, walking into the kitchen with his yellow bandana tied around his head.

"You're chipper today," I said, loading up his plate and setting it down in front of him. The toast popped up and I buttered it . . . lightly.

"Never felt this good in the morning, Annie. Usually hack and cough until about noon."

"Your color's better this morning, not so ashen."

After George finished his breakfast, I refilled our

mugs, spread raspberry jam on the last piece of toast and took a tray out to the back porch.

"I'll unhook the bike trailer," he said, as he drained his coffee mug and winked. "We might have to tow a boat home."

I can't swim.

I forced a smile and nodded. "That could happen."

Angel jumped into the back of the Hummer and I rode shotgun as George navigated down the narrow dirt path through the trees we called a driveway. "I might chop some of these weeds down, Annie. Make it easier to get this wide mother through here. You mind?"

"I saw a chopping thing in the barn, hanging on the wall," I said.

"Can't wait to check out that old barn, when we get back." George pulled into the gas station half a mile south of our side road. "Might as well get gas while we're here."

When the old fellow finally limped out to pump the gas, George said, "Fill 'er up, Bud. Do you know if there's a marina around here?"

"Yep, there's a couple down Baptiste Lake Road. Just take a right at the 'Y' and keep going until you can't go any farther."

"Thanks." George pulled a wad of bills out of his pocket, peeled off a couple and paid for the gas. "Okay, let's see if we can find us a boat, Annie." He followed the directions given by the old guy, turned at the 'Y' in the highway and headed down the lake road. The patchy asphalt meandered along the shoreline of the lake passing cottages and campgrounds for several miles.

It ended at South Shore Marine, a large property with boat launching, and storage facilities. In front of the storage building, still housing a few boats shrink-wrapped in blue plastic, a large glassed-in showroom held crafts on display for all sorts of recreation and fishing. Without hesitation, George passed by the smaller offerings and gravitated to the classiest looking boat in the showroom—a red and white, twenty foot Bass Cat Cougar perched on a trailer. He ran his hand along the sleek, smooth side of the craft and peered inside.

"Can I help you with something?" A blonde kid in ripped blue jeans swaggered towards us wearing a South Shore Marine t-shirt that said 'Chuck' on the pocket. Angel growled and I pulled back on her leash.

Not standing on ceremony, George barked, "I need a good boat for fishing."

The kid lit up a cigarette and blew smoke out at George. "You don't look much like a fisherman."

"Where's your dad, kid?" George grabbed the smoke out of Chuck's mouth snuffed it out between his finger and thumb. "You're too young to be smokin."

"I'm here," called out a man, hustling through the back door. "Sorry, had to take gas out to a stranded fisherman. I'm Charles Senior." The small salt and pepper haired man pushed back his glasses and held out his hand to George. He frowned at his son. "Can I offer you something from the pop machine?"

"Sure, you got Coke?"

Charles Senior nodded and after a stern look at his boy, the kid sauntered off back toward the office. "So, tell me, you got something in mind?"

George, pointed at the bass boat. "Tell me about this little honey."

"This is the Bass Cat Cougar SP. Special Package from the manufacturer—comes with trailer and trolling motor. Lots of extras. I'll get you the brochure."

Charles Senior returned with the literature, just as Chuck returned with the Cokes. He gave us each one, turned on his heel and left.

"Don't know what I'm supposed to do with him all summer." His father shrugged. "He works as good as most teenagers—hardly at all." He turned and motioned to us. "Come on into my office. You must have a lot of questions if you're a first time boat buyer."

He saw me look at Angel sitting beside my leg.

"Don't worry about the dog, Miss. Bring her along."

The office was a small eight by ten room with a metal desk, one filing cabinet and three chairs. The desk was covered in piles of shiny brochures held in place by elastic bands. The only decoration on the wall was an old clock that had stopped at three-twenty.

George and Charles Senior covered the intricacies of fishing and boating for the next half hour while Angel and I sat and listened. My knowledge of both those subjects was minimal, but I had the feeling that was about to change.

After all the preliminaries had been touched on more than once, Charles Senior said, "Best idea would be to take her out on the lake. Show you how she handles."

George nodded and stood up. "Let's give it a shot."

I took Angel outside and sat in one of the Muskoka chairs in the sun while the men maneuvered the craft down to the water, serviced the motor, and did all the nautical and mechanical things that needed doing.

"Come on, Annie," George was waving to me from the dock.

"I'll wait here," I said, waving back, hoping against hope they'd leave me on dry land.

"Not happening, little girl. I can't go without you."

I locked Angel in the Hummer with the windows down far enough for her to get lots of air and scuffed my way down to the dock.

"I've never been in a boat before," I whispered to George. "I can't swim."

George whipped a life preserver over my head and tied it up. "Just don't stand up, and nothing will happen, baby girl," he said, touching my face. He lifted me off the dock and plunked me down on one of the padded seats.

"This is goin' to be fuckin' amazing," he hollered, giving Charles Senior a thumbs-up. "What size motor did you put on 'er?"

"Two hundred, Merc," Charles Senior said, and George broke into a grin.

We backed up slowly from the dock, turned around, and I was thinking I could handle it, when Charles Senior cranked the gas and we blasted out into the lake with water spraying up behind us a mile high. The front of the boat was up in the air and we were flying. I screamed and hung onto the side of my seat.

George laughed and put his arm around me tightly. "Hang on, baby girl." Covered in spray, his tanned face looked so handsome I wanted to take him to bed. And I would . . . if I ever got back to shore alive.

Charles Senior slowed the boat and motioned for George to take the controls. Without him to anchor me, I froze in my seat with no intention of moving a muscle. George made a wide circle around the lake and then headed back towards the marina and aimed for the dock. Senior jumped out, secured the line, then George lifted me up, placed me on the dock and followed me out.

He wrapped his thick arms around me in a bear hug. "What did you think of that wild ride, Annie?"

"Exhilarating, to say the least," I said smiling and trying to untangle my hair.

"What the hell does that mean?' George asked.

"I was pumped."

"Me too," he had a grin pasted right across his face. "Let's go make a deal, Mr. Senior."

George and Charles Senior headed for the office, while I went back to the Hummer and let Angel out. I walked down to the landing dock so she could get a drink and then joined the men in the office.

"How are the negotiations coming?" I asked.

"We have a deal," said Charles Senior, as he finished writing up a legal-sized document in triplicate. "You'll need a boat license and a fishing license, all government money grabbers, of course. I'll write down where you can obtain those readily. He turned the contract around and made an X where George was to sign. "This is your total here at the bottom, Mr. Ross."

George dug in his pocket, whipped out his bankroll and started peeling off bills. Charles Senior raised his eyebrows as George made neat thousand dollar piles on his desk.

"Is it safe to carry that much cash?' he asked.

"Never had a problem," said George. "I don't do fuckin' plastic."

Charles Senior nodded.

"I don't have any coin, baby. Can you do seventy-nine cents?"

"Forget it," said Charles Senior, standing up and offering his hand. "Close enough. Enjoy your boat, sir. Any questions, here's my card."

George shook his hand, shoved the business card in his jeans and looked towards the dock. "Can you give me a hand to get 'er on the trailer?"

"Of course, back your vehicle down and we'll get you all hooked up."

I threw George the Hummer keys and walked outside with Angel to watch. In less than ten minutes, the boat was secured on the trailer and the trailer was hooked to the Hummer. George stopped for Angel and I to get in and we headed for home. The smile on George's face never faded the whole way back.

"I can see that you're happy," I said, rubbing his leg.

"Keep that up, I'll be even happier. I asked that marina guy where I could launch the boat closest to us and he gave me directions to the public access. We'll put 'er in, then I'll drive across the lake to our dock."

"The dock isn't much of a dock, and the boat house is even worse. Broken boards and the roof might be leaking. I think a reno is in order if we're going to be boat owners."

"Maybe I'll get some lumber, have the boys come up

and help me fix up."

"Maybe you should start over, might not be worth saving if the wood is rotten underneath."

"I'll have a close look when we get home."

"You're so wise."

"I've never had a fuckin' wise thought in my entire life." He chuckled and turned down a road that was signed for public launching.

I dropped George and the boat off and hoped he could find his way across the lake. When we arrived back home, Angel and I made straight for the path down to the water. There were no boats anywhere on the lake, but I was squinting and looking into the sun. From the end of the dock, I saw a tiny speck starting to come nearer and nearer. As it grew larger and larger, I heard the roar of the engine. George was driving standing up and sending up a twenty foot rooster tail of spray behind the boat.

He cut the motor and steered the boat close to the dock. "Tie this rope around that post, Annie," he shouted as he tossed me a line.

The new rope was stiff and thick, and I had trouble tying a knot with it, but I managed. George stepped out onto the dock and hugged me. He stamped his foot and splintered one of the boards. "Yeah, this dock could use a little help, all right."

"The post I tied the rope around is wobbly. I hope it holds."

George wiggled the post. "Holy hell, I better get a hammer and fix that thing."

"How was your trip across the lake? Was it hard to

pick out this one little dock? "

"It was. The shoreline looks so different from the water," he said. "Looks like a solid mass of green and brown until you get closer. Let's go find some tools. I don't want to lose the boat."

We trudged up the hill, and George was breathless when we reached the cabin.

"I haven't had a chance to look in the garage yet," I said.

George struggled with a broken handle on the side door, wrenched it open and I followed him inside. "Look at all the shit in here. The old guy that lived here must have been a hoarder."

"Quite a collection of stuff," I said, looking at the walls hung with tools of every size and shape. "What are those things hanging all along that wall?"

"C-clamps," George shook his head. "Why anybody would need that many clamps is a mystery."

"Wonder where these stairs go?" I said, "Maybe there are more treasures in the attic."

George rummaged through piles of tools on the workbench and came up with a hammer and nails. A thick blanket of sawdust rained down onto the cement floor as he unearthed pieces of scrap lumber. He blew dust off pieces of two by four and nodded. "I can use these to shore up the post." He headed back down to the lake while I went to the kitchen to make lunch.

George breezed through the kitchen door and kissed me as I was finishing up the burgers. "Just in time," I said.

"Never been on vacation before—a lot of eatin' to

do."

"Want a drink?" I said, opening the fridge.

"Sure. I tightened up that post at the end of the dock. I think it will hold the boat unless there's some kind of a shit storm. Do you want to go fishing if we can find some tackle?"

"Is it fun? I've never done it before," I said. "I think I saw rods in the barn last time I was here, but they may be too old."

"I want to see what's in that barn anyway. Might be some good shit."

"What do you consider 'good shit', George? Maybe there's a whole load of it out there with your name on it."

"We'll see," he said, finishing his second burger. "I think these are better than Buck's," he said wiping his face with his napkin. "Come and poke around in the barn with me, little girl."

I finished clearing the table and followed George out towards the barn. Over to the right, a stump with an axe buried in the middle of it sat askew with a few pieces of split wood on the ground. "That's where Mr. King died." I made a face and pointed at the stump. "He was chopping wood when he keeled over from a heart attack."

George frowned. "Who's Mr. King?"

"The old hermit that lived here before Matthew bought the property."

"So that's all his stuff in the garage?"

"Guess it must be."

George propped the one working barn door open so

that we had enough light to see. "I can fix that other door if there's a shovel in here," he said. "Where did you see the fishing rods?"

I squinted and pointed to the back wall. "I think, over there."

"Right, I see them," George grabbed a couple and took them outside to examine them. "The reels work. Let's see if there's a tackle box with some old lures in it." He propped the rods against the door and raised some dust in the far corner of the barn. "Fuckin' jackpot," he hollered and walked towards me with a green metal box in his hand. "We're good to go, Annie."

"What about worms? I thought worms were the weapon of choice for fishing."

George laughed. "Could be—frogs would be better, but lures are okay too. Wow. Look at that fuckin' old John Deere. Love to get that baby running."

"Do you think it would start? Looks like it's been there for years."

"I'll give it a go when we come back."

I moved the rods so that George could close the barn door. "Angel's still in there."

"C'mon, girl," George called her. "We're goin' fishing."

"Will she be okay in the boat?" I couldn't picture her sitting still for any length of time.

"We can train her. You can train a good dog to do anything."

This could be stressful.

"I'll put some drinks in a cooler to take with us," I said, heading for the kitchen. "Take your meds before we go, big guy."

"Good call, baby girl. You're the brains of this outfit."

George and Angel were waiting for me in the boat when I got down to the dock with the drinks. "Angel give you any trouble?"

"Nope, told her to sit, and she did." He held out his hand and helped me step down from the dock into the boat. The boat rocked a little and I almost lost my balance. As quickly as I took a seat at the front, George whipped a life preserver over my head. "Don't worry, Annie. I'll never take you out on the water without your life jacket on."

"Thanks, honey," I said.

George started the motor and backed away from the dock. He turned the wheel and headed out into open water and gave it more gas.

"I picked a spot this morning on my way over here." He pointed out to a spot, shaded by trees growing almost horizontal from the bank. "Might be worth a try." He got the rods ready and handed me one.

I dropped the line over the side and watched the lure sink into the dark water. "How long does this take?"

"Longer than five minutes," George said and chuckled. "We might have to troll if we don't get many bites."

"What's troll?"

"Means start up the engine and go slow dragging the lures through the water."

"Uh-huh. Want a Coke?" I asked, uncapping two and handing one to George.

"Thanks, baby. Perfect day with a perfect woman."

I laughed. "I'm writing that one down."

I screamed and George jumped to his feet. "What the fuck?"

"Help me. Something is jerking my rod out of my hand."

"Give 'er some line."

"What does that mean?" My hands shook. George took my rod and let more line out.

"Here, turn your reel like this, wind it slow and bring in your fish." He handed back my rod and I started winding. "We don't have a net, so I'll just grab the monster when you get it close enough."

I laughed as I reeled in my first fish. As it came closer to the boat, I could see it thrashing in the water. "Wow, it looks big."

"It's a prize winner for sure." George grinned from ear to ear. He leaned over and put his hands on the rod and helped me lift the fish into the boat. "Son of a bitch, baby girl. Look at the size of that mother. Must be a five pound bass."

"Let's take a picture," I said groping for the little camera in my jacket pocket. "Hold it up, George."

"Your fish, Annie, your picture." He gave me the fish to hold and snapped a couple of pictures.

"Maybe we should throw the poor thing back in the lake."

George glared at me. "Don't you want to eat it? Or stuff it?"

"I feel kind of sorry for it." Angel's head was cocked to one side as she watched it flop around in the bottom of the boat.

"It's your fish, so it's your call." His smile dissolved as he worked the lure out of the fish's mouth. "Wish we had a scale."

Oh, what the hell.

"This is your first day of fishing, honey, so let's cook that monster for dinner to celebrate."

"Shit. You're the best, Annie."

We sat out on the lake in the sun all afternoon, fishing and by the time we headed back to shore, my head was nodding.

George touched my arm and I jumped. "We're back, Annie."

"I must have dozed off," I mumbled.

Splash! Cold water landed on my sunburned skin and I squealed.

"Angel," George hollered, "you're supposed to jump onto the dock, not into the water."

She swam back to shore and shook herself. "I'm glad she didn't jump out in the middle of the lake."

George stowed the rods and the tackle box in the dilapidated boat house and carried my fish up to the cabin. He was breathless at the top of the hill.

I touched his arm. "Are you okay?"

"It'll take a while for all that crap to get out of my lungs, I guess, but I've only had two butts today."

"You're doing amazingly well. I can't tell you how impressed I am."

He held me in his arms. "Well, you're the only one that matters."

After we sat on the porch for a bit, George cleaned

my fish and I cooked it for dinner with fried potatoes and green beans.

"Good meal, baby girl. You sure know how to cook fish."

"One of my many talents."

"I'm in love with some of those other talents. I was thinkin' about some of them today in the boat."

I giggled. "Maybe I'll show you one or two of them later."

CHAPTER FIFTY-NINE

GEORGE'S week of rest and relaxation was going well. He was getting up early, eating a good breakfast, catching a few frogs and retrieving the minnows from his trap down at the shore before going out in his boat. Most mornings, I did a few chores in the cabin or in town, and then we would go fishing together in the afternoon. Today, I had gone to the hospital, had my leg checked and the dressing changed. The doctor on call said it was coming along well.

The boat was now outfitted with a net, insect repellent, a cooler and two new rods tricked out with Shimano reels. I wore my ball cap on the lake to avoid sun stroke, but the rest of me was tanning darker each day. There was no way my tan would ever rival the dark coppery glow that George was sporting. He tanned quickly and never burned.

He weighed himself before breakfast and proudly announced that he was down five pounds from the hospital scale. He was counting the smokes that he had through the day and had cut back considerably. Getting up the hill from the water was giving him fewer problems and he assured me that his breathing was improving.

"That trout was cooked perfect, little girl." George said after dinner. "I bought a proper filleting knife and a 'mister-twister' lure today. See what I can catch with that tomorrow."

"Are you getting bored up here in God's country?" I asked.

"Don't think I ever would in the good weather," he said, "so much to do. The winter might be a different story."

"I've been giving that some thought. Want to hear my idea for the cold weather?"

"Stay in bed all winter?"

"That's my second choice." I laughed. "How about we trailer the bikes to New Mexico and buy a little shack in the desert—somewhere up near Santa Fe. Ride all over Arizona, Nevada, Texas and California like gypsies."

"Holy hell, I would love to do that. I'm in," George said with a grin. "Nothin' worse than a Toronto winter."

"Okay. I'll take you with me." I laughed and hugged his neck. After cleaning up the dinner dishes I said, "I'm taking my coffee out on the porch. You coming?"

"Calling Jackson to check on things and then I'll be out."

I finished my first cup and went back into the kitchen for a refill. The air inside the cabin was not the same calm, warm atmosphere it had been earlier.

"Hey, you still talking?"

George scowled at the phone in his hand. "No. We're finished for now. Fuckin' cops have been cruising the gun shop and my place on a regular basis. Makin' the boys nervous. They were in Buck's last night starin' at everybody again too. Bastards."

"What do they want?"

"How the hell should I know? They put pressure on sometimes, hoping to make something happen. Fuckers probably need more arrests for the month of June." He pulled out his cigarettes, put one between his lips and fished in his vest pocket for his lighter. "Forget about it. The boys can handle themselves."

"What does Jackson want you to do?"

George slammed his phone on the table. "Nothin', just letting me know. Now, let's get back to our vacation."

I crossed my arms over my chest. "You seem pretty stressed if nothing is happening."

His dark eyes were dark and filled with emotion. "I said I don't want to think about it, Annie. I wish you wouldn't fuckin' push it."

"Fine, I won't talk about it—or anything else." The bedroom door slammed shut behind me and silenced our conversation for the night.

CHAPTER SIXTY

I woke during the night and reached for George. The sheets on his side of the bed were cold. The room was pitch black as I rose and groped my way to the kitchen. Angel yawned, stretched and followed me. I flipped on the light over the sink. George wasn't in the kitchen or the bathroom. My heart rate quickened, and my stomach flipped.

What have I done?

I pulled the homespun curtain back in the living room and squinted to see the bike trailer on the driveway, but it was too dark. Tears rolled down my cheeks. I didn't need to see the trailer. I knew his bike was gone.

I wiped my face on my sleeve, sucked in a deep breath and fumbled with the coffee maker. That's when I saw the note on the kitchen table.

'Annie, had to go back. Stay here. Call you.'

I blew out a big breath. So maybe George didn't leave because he was mad at me.

Should I stay at the cabin or should I follow George back to the city? I poured myself a mug of coffee and stared out the window into the early morning mist. After my second trip to the coffee pot, I tugged on jeans and a sweatshirt and paced for an hour wondering what to do next. Should I go back to Toronto? Did he leave without talking to me for a reason? Did he want me out the way or just out of his business?

I checked my phone. It was charged and had good signal.

After sunup, Angel and I made our way down the path to the dock. The boat was secure, bobbing gently on the still morning water of the lake. I didn't know why I had gone down to the water, or what I was looking for. Aimlessly, I limped back up the hill and sat down on a rock. Breathless, I gritted my teeth. My bad leg hadn't bothered me much when George was here, but then again, the world felt better when he was near.

I checked my phone for messages. None.

If he doesn't call by noon, I'm calling him.

Thinking I might be leaving at any moment, I unloaded my bike from the trailer and pushed it into the barn in case it rained. Nothing was going to ruin my third paint job. Poor Rusty would have a breakdown. I smiled at the thought of him.

All kinds of scenarios raced through my mind—none of them good. At eleven thirty, I was wired on caffeine and couldn't hold back any longer. I called George's cell phone.

" . . . The party you are calling is not available at this time . . ."

"Shit, George, what the hell is going on? Answer your damn phone."

CHAPTER SIXTY-ONE

GEORGE fumbled under the little sofa pillow for his cell when he felt the vibration. He stepped over his clothes strewn on the living room floor and shuffled into the bathroom as he answered the call. "Jackson?" he whispered.

"Trouble, boss. It's old man Portsmith, Kenny's dad. He got pissed out of his mind and came over here packing and bent on killing you. Says Kenny told him you and him were throwing down and now Kenny's missing. He's swears you killed him."

"Where's he now?"

"Tied up in the kitchen. What should we do with the drunken old prick?"

"Gag him and keep an eye on him until I get down there. Two hours, tops."

George splashed some water on his face and eased past the closed bedroom door. He rubbed at the tightness in his chest, pulled his clothes on and stuffed a .38 down the back of his jeans. Heading out the kitchen door he made sure to close it softly behind him. Fuck, he wished he'd made up with Annie and gone to bed with her proper last night.

Fuck. What should I tell her?

He tiptoed back into the kitchen, scribbled a note on a torn envelope and tossed it on the kitchen table.

Releasing his bike from the trailer was a bitch of a job in the dark. After fighting with it for a bit, he cut two of the ratchet straps with his boot knife and rolled the Eagle backwards onto the path. Gravity pulled the bike down the steep hill and when he rolled onto the paved shoulder of the road, he started the engine.

The pain in his chest was constant, but he wasn't sure if it was from the stress of the situation or because he had to leave Annie. His money was on the latter.

The road was clear, and the air was warm as he roared down the center line. No traffic at that hour, just the odd deer on the side of the road grazing. His single headlight pointed the way to the city and to the promise of a bad night ahead.

WHEN he arrived at his place, the little wartime shack was lit up like a county fair. The boys waited for him, drinking and playing poker. Snake Portsmith was tied to a rickety red chair in the kitchen, his hands bound behind his back and a filthy bandana in his mouth. His eyes widened when he saw George burst through the door. Portsmith was a tall, lean man with black straggly hair, sharp features and rotten teeth. Kenny definitely got his looks from his mother.

"Hello, Snake. I hear you came here to kill me." George leaned down and ripped the gag out of his mouth. "That true?"

"Cops can't find Kenny 'cause you killed him," he slurred, and spat at George.

"Not gonna lie. I wanted to kill the greasy little shit. Fuckin' wish I had," George hollered, wound up and punched Snake in the face. His skull rings tore into the flesh under Snake's right eye. Blood gushed from his nose and ran down into his mouth making him cough until he choked and gagged on his own vomit.

George picked up a sawed-off twelve gauge pump from the floor, ejected the shells and put them in his pocket. "This your gun?"

Snake nodded.

He walked over and stood the gun up in the corner. After lighting up a smoke, he took a big drag and called to the boys in the front room. "Anybody know where this scum lives?"

"Out by the zoo, down Reesor's Road," hollered Rusty.

"Leave him tied up and dump him on his front lawn," George said and snarled.

"Gonna' let this low life piece of shit go, boss?" Jackson asked with raised eyebrows.

George punched his fist through the drywall in the kitchen and grumbled, "Yeah, I'm in a good mood." After he ripped the handle off the fridge, he grabbed two beers and chugged one. "Deal me in."

They played poker until the boys came back from dumping Snake on his home turf.

"Get him home safe?" George asked without looking up from his hand.

"If you call that shack a home, yeah—dog shit all over the grass where we dumped him."

"Somebody do a Tim's run. Get coffee and breakfast. We need to have a meeting . . . and don't forget the fuckin' hash browns," George yelled and pounded his fist on the table.

The boys made a grab for their tipping bottles.

When Jackson and Rusty came back from Tim's', George made it clear that he wasn't pleased with the way things had been handled in his absence over the past few days. The boys swore business would run smoothly for the rest of the month and George said he wanted to believe them. He also made it clear what would happen if it didn't.

When the meeting ended and the boys straggled off, George used his leather jacket to cover the small window in his bedroom at the back of the clubhouse. The early morning sun was creeping into the room and his body craved rest. Since his heart attack, he was incredibly tired and testy, but he didn't want Annie to know how shitty he felt. She was the only thing in his life that was worth having. He fell into a deep sleep, dreaming of her beautiful face.

Three hours later, he woke with a start when he heard his phone vibrate. Annie. Shit. He'd forgotten to call her. He sat on the side of the bed and pressed the button to call her back.

"Annie, it's me."

"Thank God," she said, choking back a sob. "I'm losing my mind here."

"Shit. I'm sorry baby, I should have called sooner." He scrubbed his fingers through his hair and sighed. "I'm also sorry for being a prick last night. I swear I'll make it up to you, but right now I'm trying to straighten out a bunch of shit down here. Can't leave these boys alone for more than a minute."

There was a long silence and George worried that she really was still pissed at him.

"Annie? Are we all right?"

"I'm sorry about last night, too. I was scared when I woke up and you were gone . . . I thought you left because you were mad at me."

George laughed. "You couldn't make me mad enough to leave you, baby girl. I'll sort out these assholes and I should be leaving the city in a couple of hours."

"If you're tired or you have a chest pain, stay at the house and come up tomorrow. Just let me know what your plan is."

After they said their goodbyes, George hung up, lay back on the small cot and closed his eyes. Four hours later, he woke, showered, changed his clothes and began the long ride back to the cabin.

Halfway to Maynooth, he pulled his bike up to the pumps at an Ultramar station and filled up. At the cash, he paid for the gas, bought a Coke and a pack of smokes. When he stepped outside he lit one up and noticed an old blue pickup with rusted out fenders, sitting at the edge of the lot. The engine was running with no one inside. He shrugged, put on his helmet, flicked his butt onto the pavement and took off. Every once in a while he checked his mirror, but the highway was deserted behind him.

CHAPTER SIXTY-TWO

ONE-THIRTY the next morning, Angel growled and bolted from her blanket to the front of the house. I tiptoed through the dark cabin into the living room to take a look, hoping to quiet the dog and not wake George. He'd been exhausted after his long ride home.

I roughed up the scruff of her neck and peered out the window. "What is it, girl? Another bear?" Through the trees and undergrowth, I could see the flicker of headlights on the road at the bottom of the hill but couldn't catch any movement in the trees. Angel's growling exploded into barking and scratching at the door.

"What's wrong with the dog?" George grumbled as he stumbled into the room. "It's only one-thirty. She doesn't need out yet."

"Somebody's out there," I whispered. "Car lights down at the road."

"Where's the shotgun?"

"Under my side of the bed. It's loaded."

"Get your Beretta, Annie. Don't take any chances."

"Probably just some locals out drinking."

"Don't feel like that to me," George whispered his breathing fast and louder than usual. "When some asshole's trying to kill me, I always feel it. Always."

George retrieved the shotgun from under the bed

while I checked the Beretta to make sure it was loaded and had one in the chamber.

"Leave the lights off," George said as he opened the door for Angel. "Go get 'em, girl."

Angel took off barking and running like she was on fire. George watched until she vanished into the bush and then stepped out onto the porch. "Stay in the house, Annie." He pulled the door closed and disappeared into the darkness.

My hands were shaking as I held tight to my Beretta. How could I see to shoot in the pitch dark? Nights up here in the woods were blacker than in the city and there was only a sliver of moon in the sky. I opened the door and silently slipped out onto the front porch. I stood in the shadows and listened. Angel was growling and running through the bush on the west side of the property. Twigs snapped, leaves rustled, and boots thumped on the moss and pine needles. The dampness of the lake and the night air chilled my skin.

George shouldn't be running through the bush after his heart attack.

I limped back to the bedroom, tugged sweats over my thighs, pulled on a sweatshirt and shoved my feet into a pair of sneakers. I crouched down on the porch steps with my gun, waiting and listening. When my eyes grew more accustomed to the dark, I saw a flicker of movement over by the bike trailer. I waited, motionless, kept my breathing even, like George taught me—there was shifting—just a shadow—much too small to be George. I lined up the Beretta and fired.

The shadow groaned and fell down behind the trailer

out of my range of vision. He might be only wounded and yet able to return fire if I tried to move closer in the open. Getting behind him was the better option.

I hurried through the cabin, out the back door, then skirted through the pine trees and down the bank. Big gasps of pine-filled night air filled my lungs as I struggled against the ever-present ache in my leg. Branches clawed and scratched at my arms, slowing my progress up the hill.

My Beretta was zeroed in on the legs of the man when I saw the flash. Dropping flat on my stomach, I fired at the flashpoint and heard him yelp when the bullet found its mark. Crawling on my belly I got close enough to see him lying motionless in the long grass. I didn't recognize him.

Getting to my feet was a challenge on the steep hillside. I put my weight on my good leg and propelled myself forward with a grunt. I approached with caution and quickly pried the Glock out of his hand before returning to the porch.

One down.

Angel hadn't been barking for the last few minutes and I wondered if she had run too far away for me to hear her. Maybe George had caught the other guy. Were there only two? I had no way of knowing for sure and calling out for George was not an option. He wouldn't answer and give away his position. I waited on the porch steps, staring into the darkness and shivering in the increasing dampness.

Sitting stock still for what seemed like an hour, gave me a cramp in my good leg. I stood up and massaged my calf. The sound of a twig snapping froze me to the step, and I peered into the blackness. I heard panting and relaxed when I realized it was Angel coming back home. She ran up on the porch beside me and I stooped down to hug her.

"Good girl. Where's George?" I whispered in her ear.

"Right here, baby girl, shouldn't you be in the cabin?" he said, quietly reprimanding me.

"How many are there?" I asked. "I shot one over there by the trailer."

"Fuck. Annie, I should have known."

"Thought there were two running ahead of me and Angel but could have been three at the start. Couldn't see shit. Even darker in the bush. Angel put a good run on them. They'll be a while circling around and getting back here, but they'll make another try. No doubt about it."

"Who are they?"

"Must be friends of Snake Portsmith—Kenny's old man. He came to kill me at my place in the city, but I thought I convinced him to give it up."

"Guess not," I said. "Are we putting on a pot of coffee while we wait for the second run, or are we moving out?"

"I don't run from a fight, Annie. I'll keep watch with Angel, out here. She could use a drink."

I started the coffee maker, swallowed two of my pain meds, and carried Angel's water bowl out to the front porch. She lapped up half of it and lay down beside George. She would definitely hear anyone approaching through the bush, long before we would. When the coffee was ready, I poured two mugs and sat with George on the front steps.

"Won't be light for hours yet."

"Wish I had my night vision scope up here," George said. "It would give me an advantage."

"Did you look at that guy over there? I don't know where I got him."

"Yeah, I looked while you were inside. He's done, Annie. You finished another one."

"I was aiming for his legs when he shot at my head, so I bore down on him."

"His fuckin mistake," he whispered.

A low growl came from Angel's throat and we both stopped talking. She bolted off the steps and ran to the left of the cabin into the thick underbrush.

"*Ughh*," someone cried out.

George ran after Angel and a few seconds later a shot echoed in the night.

"*Fuck.*"

George. Running on my sore leg was awkward and painful, but that had been George swearing. I'd know his cursing anywhere. Another shot rang off directly in front of me. I tripped and fell. What the—

George pulled back his outstretched leg and I scrambled to my knees. He was sitting up against a tree holding on to his right leg, his gun in his hand.

"Are you okay?" My voice cracked. "Where are you hit?"

"No big deal, Annie, through and through," he gasped, "I think I got him. Be careful." His breathing was rapid, and I needed this excitement to end.

As I moved forward, a low menacing growl rumbled from Angel. About three feet away I could make out a figure lying partly covered in a bed of ferns. Angel had his throat. He wasn't moving. I scooped his rifle out of his hand, called Angel off and groped my way back to where I had left George.

He was gone.

Scrambling back through the dense undergrowth towards the cabin, another shot went off. Angel took off and I was right on her heels. My breath was coming in short gasps as I pulled myself up over the hill. Blood was oozing from the cuts in my arms and felt molten hot against my ice cold skin. Angel was barking rabidly about twenty feet in front of me.

Another shot rang out as I stepped into the clearing around the cabin. A tall skinny man was standing over George with a rifle pointed at his head. It hadn't started to get light yet, but his outline was clear against the stainless steel of the bike trailer across the driveway behind him.

The *click* of his gun being cocked was followed by the guy shouting in a high pitched whine. "I'm gonna' kill you for what you did to Kenny. You think breaking my nose would slow me down? Then you don't know Snake Portsmith. You don't know who you're fuckin' dealing with. You killed my boy, and now I'm gonna kill you."

"I killed him," I shouted, and when Snake cranked his head to the right to look at me I fired. He dropped like a stone and fell on top of George.

Angel growled and grabbed him by the neck. "It's

okay, girl. I think we're done for tonight," I said. I used my foot to roll the body off George, then helped him sit up. "What about your leg?"

"It's nothing. We can clean it up ourselves, baby girl." He leaned back against the steps and blew out a big breath. "You're some sidekick, Annie. You're fuckin' amazing."

He held out his arms and I kissed him and held him for a few minutes. "Let's get you inside and look at your leg."

"First, Annie, go down and drive that truck up here. Those assholes left it running thinking they would hit me quick and be out of here. I'll call the boys and tell them we need a cleanup."

"I'll be right back." I limped down the driveway to the pickup. My leg was seriously protesting the abuse I'd put it through in the bush. The motor was still idling, and the lights were on. I steered the old clunker up the hill, parked it beside the bike trailer and shut it off.

George put one arm around my neck, we leaned on each other, and he was able to hobble up the steps and into the cabin. I unzipped his blood soaked jeans and pulled them down while he leaned on the doorframe. Then I helped him to a kitchen chair and propped his leg up on another while I applied pressure to stop the bleeding.

After twenty minutes the blood had slowed to a trickle. I filled a basin with warm water and dish soap, cleaned the wound and bandaged it. He downed four of my pain killers with a fresh cup of coffee and called Jackson.

"Had a bit of trouble up here, Jackson. That fucker, Snake, followed me all the way up here with two other guys and took another run at me. Annie took two of 'em out and left one for me. I was lucky she even gave me one," he laughed and winked at me. "Okay, see you in three."

"Let's get you into bed and you can sleep until the boys come," I said.

George lay on the bed covered with a quilt and I crawled in beside him in my clothes. My leg was throbbing. Angel plopped down on her blanket and heaved a big sigh. "Hard night, girl?" I patted her on the head with my eyes already closed.

ANGEL barked, and bolted out of the bedroom when the knock came at the door. I threw the quilt back, realized I was still dressed and went to let Jackson and the boys in.

"Any trouble finding the cabin? I didn't hear George give you directions." I tried to smooth my hair down with my hand, but there was no helping it.

"No trouble, Portia," said Jackson. "Always have a GPS on the boss. How is he anyway? Didn't say shit on the phone, so I knew he was hurt."

"You boys know him well. You can talk to him in here." I showed them into the bedroom where George was sitting up in bed in his boxers and a t-shirt, with his bandaged leg on top of the quilt.

"Is it bad, boss?" Rusty asked, frowning down at the bandage.

"Fuck. No. Wasn't for Annie, I'd be lying out there dead like the rest of 'em. Should've seen her knocking 'em off in the pitch fuckin' dark," he said and chuckled.

"We should've been here, boss. Didn't think that asshole had the balls for a second try."

"Me neither. Or I would've killed him the first time. My mistake, being so forgiving n'all."

I laughed to myself and stuck my head into the bedroom. "Can I interest anybody in a hot breakfast?"

"Sure, Portia," Jackson said. "I'm always down for your cooking and they haven't had the pleasure. Fuckin long ride up here."

George straightened and cursed as he shifted his leg. "Boys, while breakfast is cooking, throw those bodies into the back of the pickup and tie a tarp over 'em. Annie will show you where the tarps are in the barn. Then on the way home, drive the whole works to the back of the range and set fire to it."

"Will do, boss," said Jackson heading outside with Rusty and Billy following close behind.

After breakfast, George said, "Annie, show the boys my latest purchase. Maybe they want to come up next weekend and go fishing with me."

I smiled. "Come on, guys. George is super proud of his new toy." I led them down the path to the lake and let them sit in the boat at the end of the dock.

"Holy shit, this is a beauty," Rusty said. "Always wanted a Bass boat. Can we really come up and go fishing on Saturday?"

"George invited you, so yes. George is my family . . . that makes you boys family too."

CHAPTER SIXTY-THREE

THE week up north had passed quickly. George was sitting on the back porch when I made my way from the bedroom into the kitchen. The coffee was ready, and he had taken my mug out of the cupboard for me. The bullet wound in his leg was causing him less distress and had started to heal. I sensed that he was ready to give full-time retirement a try, even though he hadn't put it into words. My leg was healing, and the pain had subsided considerably.

I could tell he was anticipating a good weekend with the boys out on the lake and I was envisioning some heavy duty cooking. The day before, I had gone into town and bought steak, potatoes, hamburgers, coleslaw, several pies and ten cases of beer. I picked up a couple of extra coolers, snacks and everything I guessed men might need for a big fishing weekend. George had been catching minnows and storing them in a bucket at the shore, and I had bought dozens of frogs and worms at the local bait store.

"Did Jackson say what time they would arrive?" I asked, walking out to the porch with my coffee.

"Nope, just said early," George motioned for me to sit on his knee.

"My big butt is going to hurt your leg, mister."

"The day you have a big butt, little girl, is the day I

sell my bike."

I sat down gingerly on his good leg and put my arms around his neck. "This was our best week ever," I said, kissing him.

"No way can I go back now that I've had a taste of life up here with you, Annie. No fuckin' way."

I hugged him tight and buried my face in his neck. "I love you so much, George, it hurts."

Angel jumped up and ran around the side of the cabin when she heard the Harleys rumble up the hill. "We've got company. Sit tight. I'll bring them around here."

George beamed as Jackson, Rusty and Billy rounded the corner of the cabin and sat down on the edge of the porch. "You bastards eat breakfast?"

"Did a drive-through, boss," said Rusty. "We're ready to fish." He lit up a smoke.

"How you gonna' get down that fuckin' hill, boss?" asked Billy.

"I've been practicing with Annie's crutch. I'm good."

While the boys talked over their plans for the day, I packed a lunch for them in the kitchen and loaded it into one of the coolers. The second one, full of ice and beer, was sitting at the ready next to the kitchen door, but I couldn't lift it. "A couple of you strong handsome men want to help me get this beer and food down to the boat?" I called out the door.

"You made us food, Portia?" asked Jackson. "You're the best. Help me carry these coolers, Billy," he yelled. The boys hefted the coolers and headed down the path while I tried to help George get mobile with the one crutch under his arm.

"I'm okay, Annie."

"I want to be beside you going down the hill. And I want Rusty on the other side." I nodded toward Rusty.

"That would be best, boss. Don't want you to roll down the hill and fall in the lake," he snickered.

"You bastards would think that was a fuckin' riot wouldn't you?" George grumbled.

With George using the crutch, and Rusty and I on either side of him, he made it down the steep trail to the dock slowly but with little difficulty.

"We found more rods," I said, "and George has them ready to go. They're standing up against the wall in the boathouse, Billy." I pointed and Billy brought them out and stowed them in the boat. I grabbed the minnows, frogs and worms and handed them to Jackson, "May mother nature smile upon you."

"Thanks, Portia," Jackson said grinning. "I hope the old bitch does just that."

I held George's crutch as he eased himself into the driver's seat of the boat. "I'll leave this here on the dock for you," I said, laying it down.

George nodded.

He doesn't look happy.

"Have fun, guys. Be safe." As they backed away from the dock, I waved then turned my back and trudged up the hill into the woods.

Life was bizarre. One minute I'm living what I thought would be a perfect life but was alone and scared and wondering if I was ever meant to find happiness and the next I'm waving across a sparkling glass lake and looking forward to feeding the most threatening bunch of fishermen I'd ever seen when they made their way back home tonight. Huh.

Angel and I had the day to ourselves in the cabin. By noon, everything was prepped for dinner and in the fridge. We took a long nap then sat on the porch in the late afternoon sun. At sundown, I started the barbeque and began preparing dinner in earnest. With the table set, the steaks marinating and the potatoes and veggies on the grill on low, I wandered down to the dock to see if there was any sign of the fishermen.

The sky was ablaze in shades of orange and pink as the big fiery ball dropped behind the trees on the other side of the lake. I squinted to see if any boats were in my range of vision, but I saw none.

"I hope they make it back to shore before long, Angel. George will have a hard time with the hill in the dark."

After another twenty minutes of staring out at the water, I went back up to the cabin. The potatoes were almost done, so I moved them to the upper rack, shut the lid and waited.

I woke in the same chair on the porch, when I heard shouting down at the dock. My body was uncoordinated jumping up from a deep sleep, and my sore leg buckled under me. I fell on my face into the dirt. I picked myself up and hobbled down the path, my pulse pounding in my ears as I stumbled through the trees. My lunch was burning its' way up my throat, and I hurled at the bottom of the hill.

Darkness had fallen over the water and the scene on

the dock was illuminated only by the sliver of the waxing moon. Rusty, Billy and Jackson were sitting on the dock, drunk and yelling things at each other that didn't make any sense. My eyes were riveted on the empty boat.

"Where's George?" I screamed. "Where is he?"

Jackson looked up, got to his feet and started walking towards me. The utter dissolution in his eyes pegged me square in the heart.

"I'm sorry, Portia, he's gone."

EPILOGUE

Thursday, August 30th.

ACCORDING to Jackson, two months have passed since I lost George at the lake. My memories of that last day at the cabin are hazy at best, and I continue to dread the moment that clarity prevails.

I can't recall returning to the city, or much that came after. Today is the first day I've been dressed in all that time. Jackson hasn't left my side for a second and has been my life line. We are back in the house on Hawthorne Lane for the time being with Jackson housed in the guest room. He told me George had arranged for him to be my bodyguard after the first heart attack. George couldn't bear to think of me alone and vulnerable, if anything happened to him.

Jackson said George suffered a massive heart attack in the boat the day they were fishing and fell overboard before any of them realized what was happening. They searched the water all around the boat, but out in the middle of the lake it was deep, and the water was black and murky.

A memorial service was held for George in the city. Hundreds of bikers attended to pay their respects. Jackson said it was one of the largest gatherings ever in Toronto. He took a video of the bike procession and said he would show it to me some day when I'm ready. Angel hasn't been the same. She misses George terribly.

When George came into my life after Matthew died, I was alone, without direction and frightened of being on my own. Even though things didn't turn out the way I'd hoped, loving George revealed inner strength I never knew I possessed and taught me I could do anything I put my mind to.

Maybe in the fall, Jackson will take Angel and I up to the cabin, but for today my big excursion will be down to the kitchen.

~~ THE END ~~

I sincerely hope you enjoyed reading Lily, the prequel to The Regulator Series. Next in the reading order comes Book # 1, Bad Beat.

If you'd like to know more about my other series, drop by my Facebook page.

Reviews on and Goodreads and Amazon help other readers find books. I appreciate all reviews and look forward to hearing your thoughts.

Regulator Series:

1. Lily
2. Bad Beat
3. Panama Annie
4. Coulter
5. Searching for Billy
6. End of an Era
7. Wingman
8. Triple Homicide
9. The Foundation
10. Hotline
11. Powell
12. The Last Regulator: Donald McKenzie Ferguston

Quantrall Series:

1. Quantrall
2. Ink Minx
3. Ray Jay
4. Blacky
5. The Coven
6. You Forgot to say Goodbye
7. Payback
8. Rags to Rage
9. The Corner Office
10. Race
11. Coma
12. No Defense
13. Full Circle
14. Stick a Needle in Your Eye
15. Crude

The Blackmore Agency Series:

1. Double Down
2. Splitting Aces
3. Dead Man's Hand
4. Drawing Dead
5. Under the Gun
6. Rivered
7. The Turn
8. Final Table
9. Cat
10. Dog
11. Vigilance
12. Mystere
13. Hole in the Heart
14. Dead Eye
15. Backwater
16. Road Kill
17. Street Rat
18. Hoodoo
19. Crowbar
20. Night Vipers
21. Short Fuse
22. Cinnamon
23. Parole
24. Eight Seconds
25. Junkyard Dog
26. Revoked
27. Blackbird
28. Random
29. Stone Cold Revenge
30. Branded

The Regulator, Quantrall, and Blackmore series are best read in series order.

Paradise Park Series:
1. Paradise Park
2. Return to Paradise
3. Paradise Sparks
4. Alone in Paradise
5. Together in Paradise
6. Prisoner in Paradise
7. Escape from Paradise
8. Deliverance

Misty's Magick & Mayhem Series:
1. School for Reluctant Witches
2. School for Saucy Sorceresses
3. School for Unwitting Wiccans
4. Nine Saint Gillian Street
5. The Ghost of Pirate's Alley
6. Jinxing Jackson Square
7. Flame
8. Frost

Broken Spur Series:
1. Picking up the Pieces
2. Comeback Trail
3. Rodeo Ranch.
4. Rodeo Bride

Made in the USA
Middletown, DE
19 June 2021